READY, AIM, UNDER FIRE

LEXI GRAVES MYSTERIES

Camilla Chafer

ISBN-13: 978-1976268137

ISBN: 1976268133

ALSO BY CAMILLA CHAFER

Lexi Graves Mysteries:
Armed and Fabulous
Who Glares Wins
Command Indecision
Shock and Awesome
Weapons of Mass Distraction
Laugh or Death
Kissing in Action
Trigger Snappy
A Few Good Women
Ready, Aim, Under Fire
Rules of Engagement
Very Special Forces

Deadlines Mysteries:
Deadlines
Dead to the World

Stella Mayweather Series (Urban Fantasy):
Illicit Magic
Unruly Magic
Devious Magic
Magic Rising
Arcane Magic
Endless Magic

CHAPTER ONE

"Solved it!" I chirped before tossing the manila file onto the desk. My brother, Garrett, otherwise known as Lieutenant Graves of MPD's homicide division, sat across from me. His face was grim but I suspected that was more because of his youngest son's latest prank than the case he just handed to me. The evidence was there: two black rings around his eyes. I was pretty sure Garrett knew about the rings but neither of us had mentioned them yet. That didn't stop me from darting surreptitious glances at his face and biting the insides of my cheeks so I wouldn't laugh.

"You did not," he said. Folding his arms across his chest, he relaxed into the chair, waiting for me to speak.

"Did too."

He gave me a shallow smile, clearly unsure whether to believe me or not. "Tell me how the crime was committed."

"It wasn't the boyfriend. I remember that night and not just because of the murder splashed across the front page of the *Montgomery Gazette* the next day. After the spate of burglaries, since he'd only been out of prison three weeks—he was inside for burglary, since you didn't ask—and even though he didn't want to give an alibi, he definitely had one. Focusing the investigation on him meant not looking too closely at her brother and his drug habit. He was sleeping on her couch after losing his apartment and owed a lot of money to the wrong people. They came looking for him and shot her instead. It was either meant as a message to him, or they intended to shoot anyone, whomever was with him. Purely good luck for the brother that he wasn't there. It was a horrible, senseless murder. But you knew all that, so why are asking me to solve a case you've already solved?" I sat back and steepled my fingers under my chin, hoping to evoke a professional look. In reality, I was doing that so I could check out the engagement ring that had recently made its home on my finger. It sparkled as the sun caught it and I couldn't help smiling. Only a week ago, Solomon threw us the most beautiful engagement party.

"How did you know all that from the file?"

"I didn't. I remember a bunch of details from when it was headline news nine years ago," I admitted.

Garrett narrowed his eyebrows. "What details? What made that case stick in your head?"

I narrowed my eyebrows right back at him. "I don't want to talk about it." That's because I couldn't. What happened that night could have gotten me and my best friend, now sister-in-law, Lily, arrested. I didn't want

Garrett digging into why I remembered that case specifically. It was just lucky for me that he asked me to solve a case of which I was already familiar with the details. All he had to do was remove a couple of reports from the file before he handed it to me.

"What are you really here for? I know for a fact it's not because of this case," I told him as I released my previously steepled fingers and tapped my forefinger on the file for added effect. "Plus, since when are you in the market for a PI?"

The PI was me, Lexi Graves. Unlike my brother—and a large segment of my family—my background isn't in law enforcement and I just sort of fell into the PI game. By falling, I mean, stumbling over a dead body and landing myself in the middle of a nasty case of fraud and murder—two crimes I helped solve—and also acquiring a very enticing job offer from the man I now planned to marry.

Back then, marriage wasn't at the top of my list of reasons to join the Solomon Detective Agency, in fact, it was nowhere on the list. Solomon observed something in me that motivated him to ask me to join his company. I didn't have to wonder too hard at what he managed to see: he made that clear. I was so perky and cute that no one ever suspected me of investigating anyone about anything. He was right. Fortunately for him, I lived up to his initial assessment most days of the week, including today. This day, however, involved jeans so tight, I shouldn't really have been sitting, and a pink blouse with little, gold buttons and the cutest pair of pink leather pumps. Why conform with my co-workers and wear a drab uniform of jeans, t-shirts, and boots with my weapons securely strapped in conceal-'n'-carry holsters? Especially when I could stand out like a rare beacon of pink joy?

"Okay, you got me. I wanted to know how you'd examine a cold case and if you could see something I missed. So I pulled this one from archives."

"That begs another question. What's the real cold case?"

"That's the issue. It is and isn't a cold case. I'm not even sure what it is."

That grabbed my interest. "Go on."

Garrett reached into his bag and extracted another file, this one thinner and dog-eared, like he'd thumbed through it many times. Perhaps he even kept it on his desk along with other cases that evaded but still troubled him. From my prior knowledge of his office at MPD, the stack was at least a foot high. He placed the file on the table but didn't open it. Instead, he tapped his forefinger on top of it, like it was his turn for finger-tapping amusement.

"This was a case, then it became a cold case, and two weeks ago, it was officially closed. Something about it keeps bothering me. Something's wrong."

"Go on."

"Ten years ago, a missing persons report was filed on Deborah Patterson, or Debby, as everyone knows her. MPD did a cursory check. She hadn't been to her apartment in a couple weeks and didn't show up for work. Nothing alarming was found at either place. No signs of a struggle, nothing obviously stolen or missing. No signs of foul play at all. Following procedure, her family were interviewed but even they weren't worried. They said Debby took off sometimes but she always turned up."

"Wait… her family didn't report her missing?" I asked, sure he must have omitted a key piece of information in his opening assessment.

"No, it was her landlord." Garrett nodded at the look I gave him. "We found that strange too."

"Why would her landlord report her missing and not her family?"

"That's what we asked. The landlord said he only noticed she was missing after she was two weeks past due on her rent. When he discovered she hadn't been home at all, he filed a report."

"That's a conscientious landlord."

"At the time, we thought he might have had a thing for her but it seems he was just a nice guy looking out for his tenants."

"And his rent," I pointed out.

"That too. You can read the interview in the file along with the rest of the report. He couldn't tell if anything was missing but he said skipping rent wasn't her usual behavior. She hadn't been late with a payment in two years."

"Okay, so far, so interesting. How did he know she hadn't been home?"

"Mail had piled up in her box dating back two weeks. There was also a quart of sour milk and some other items in the fridge that were all expired a week prior to his call."

"Could you whittle the disappearance down to an exact date? Sounds like she could have disappeared anytime over a period of several days?"

"We narrowed it down to a window of three days. The last time she was seen at work was on Friday. Then it was the weekend and no one saw her, and there was mail from the previous Thursday but she didn't return to work on Monday.

"That leaves Friday night, Saturday, and Sunday," I mused out loud, making a quick calculation. More than forty-eight hours. Not a huge amount of time, but someone could travel to the other side of the world in less time.

"That was our assessment too."

"What haven't you told me?" I asked, sensing Garrett was holding something back.

"We hit a dead end. Her apartment didn't have any security cameras and there weren't any nearby that covered her apartment so we could never pinpoint when she came in or left home. Her cards were never used. Her face didn't show up anywhere and there were no sightings by anyone. Without any leads, we couldn't proceed with the case. Then something strange happened."

"Go on."

"Two months after Debby disappeared, and after we'd interviewed everyone we could associate with her, her family got a postcard. They brought it into the station."

"Who was it from?"

"It was signed Debby. Came from somewhere overseas, and was in her handwriting. Not much of a message but enough to say she was fine and intended to do some traveling."

"What did you make of that?"

"We tossed around the idea that it could have been fake. We thought maybe the family invented it to keep the case open, or else, someone was messing with them. We told them we'd look into it. I made a couple of calls to the local police where the postcard originated but by then, there was no trace of her. Truthfully, I'm not even sure they looked any further."

"That must have been disappointing."

"A little but it happens a lot. People think they're helping us by giving false information but ultimately, they just cause more hurt. We told the Pattersons to come back if they got anymore correspondence. A month later, they did. Another postcard. Then another."

"Did her parents believe they were from her?"

"Yes, there were a couple of comments that only their daughter could have made. Some reference to an old family trip, I think. Anyway, without a return address or phone number, there was no way for them to contact Debby but still enough questions to call into doubt that she was actually missing."

I frowned. "So she wasn't missing?"

"Officially, she remained a missing person. The occasional email or postcard turning up may have appeased her family but we could never verify if they were really from her and we had to do that in order to close the case. Without anything else to go on, we had to move onto other cases. MPD just didn't have the manpower back then to keep looking for her. We still don't. I always had a funny feeling about this case, so the file remained on my desk for nearly ten years."

"So what changed? Why was the case suddenly closed?"

"Because two weeks ago, she came back."

"That's great!" I watched Garrett's face. "That's not great?"

"It's freaking weird. She and her parents turned up on my day off. I jumped into my car and drove to the station as soon as I got the call that she had returned. I didn't get the chance to speak with her, just her parents briefly, but I saw her leaving the station after the interview and something hit my gut."

"MPD cafeteria food?"

"Ha-ha. No. I can't tell you what it was that got me but I don't think Debby Patterson is really Debby Patterson."

~

"Where are you with your case?" Solomon asked.

The six-person-strong team that made up the PI division of the Solomon agency sat around the long table in the boardroom beside the shared office space. Tony Delgado, Steve Fletcher and Matt Flaherty were all ex-law enforcement of various positions. Both Fletcher and Flaherty had taken bullets while in the line of duty, which, no doubt, played a part in prompting their exits from their prior professions. Lucas, on the other hand, was an ex-criminal whom Solomon had taken under his wing. Solomon was an enigma and I was the most recent addition. I didn't come from the same professional background. My family is comprised of serving and retired police; however my only brush with serving my nation came from an ill-thought-out decision to join the Army. Then I went on to fail boot camp. Solomon hired me for numerous reasons, however, predominantly it was for my appearance. Few suspected the innocent-looking chick of trying to extract information, and whoever investigated anything in pink pants and heels? Me! That's who.

A large box of fresh donuts lay open in front of us. With the thoughts of wedding gowns currently occupying my head, I was trying to resist all temptation. My resolve weakened with every sugary bite my colleague, Fletcher, took along with the amused grin that played on his lips. He popped the last bite into his mouth, chewing it up before licking the grains of sugar off his sweet lips. "Mmm," he murmured, his eyes rolling with unmitigated satisfaction.

"I'd say in the case of who ate the last jelly donut, the culprit is—" Lucas, our resident tech genius, began drumming his fingers against the table then gestured excitedly at Fletcher. "He did it!"

"Guilty as charged," said Fletcher, holding up one hand and bowing his head.

"And back to the world where the grown-ups live," sighed Solomon. "Where are you with your case, Fletch?"

"I wrapped it up. The neighbor did it, just like I said when we first met the client," replied Fletcher. He licked a sugary finger and I narrowed my eyes at him some more. "The report is right here." He pushed a file across the desk and Solomon opened it, quickly scanning the material inside. While Solomon's eyes were averted, he plucked another donut from the box.

"Good work," Solomon said finally. "I have a new case for you. A contact in New York needs some help with a gang thing."

"Oooh!" I perked up. "New York?" That sounded perfect for me. I could even squeeze in the time to see the sights: Bloomingdales, Macy's, Century 21, and Saks Fifth Avenue.

"Can you masquerade as a biker?"

I slumped in my chair. *Perky* got me into a lot of places but unfortunately, not everywhere. "I'll get back to you after I grow a goatee."

"Guess I'll take it," said Fletcher. He finished his donut before leaning in and peering at the remaining donut.

"Flaherty, you're going too," said Solomon, turning to the former cop. "You'll need to work as a tag team."

"I am so disappointed," I said to no one in particular.

"You could be a biker chick if you like," said Flaherty.

"No," said Solomon before I opened my mouth.

"I hope you have something interesting for me because I've always harbored a secret ambition to be a biker chick involved in crime."

"Really?" asked Lucas.

I ignored him, thinking about the time that Lily and I suggestively danced on the tables of a biker bar on the outskirts of our home town of Montgomery. It was enormous fun until the bar fight broke out around us and we had to crawl out on our hands and knees to avoid all the glass bottles and fists flying above us. I was pretty sure Solomon didn't want to hear about that. Anyway, those days were long gone. Lily was a married mom now and I was a professional PI who absolutely did not dance on table tops in bars on any day between Sunday and Thursday.

"I have a special case for you to investigate," said Solomon.

"Sounds thrilling but can we talk about the missing person case that Garrett brought to me."

"Are they also invisible?" asked Lucas, "because I didn't see Garrett come in with anyone."

"Ha!" I snorted. "The missing person might not be a missing person."

"Fastest case ever solved," said Fletcher. "Well done!"

My jaw dropped open and I pointed behind him, fear flooding my face. When he looked around to see what had suddenly terrified me, I grabbed the last donut. He turned back, looked into the box, then at me, his face full of disappointment. I smiled and bit into the donut. "No, I mean, Garrett brought a cold case that just got closed except he thinks something strange happened. The person who came back isn't the person who went away. I think I should look into it."

"Is MPD springing for this?" Solomon inquired.

"Actually, I thought we could take it pro bono."

"Why?"

I had my answer ready. "Because it would be nice for MPD to owe us one." I briefly considered adding that my brother rarely asked for help of any kind, other than babysitting, so if the case had him bamboozled, it was definitely something that should interest us; but I figured Solomon probably already knew that. Plus, MPD owing us a favor was the most important bit. We should have been eager to help them; there were plenty of times when they helped us in the past. It was a win-win situation.

Solomon nodded slowly. "Point taken. Do you have the file?"

I handed it to him and he perused the first couple of pages. "Interesting. Take it but don't spend too much time on it. If there's nothing in it, tell Garrett we can't help them but we'll investigate anything else he needs us to look at. If this person is truly an impostor, like Garrett suspects, then find out who the hell she is and what she wants."

"On it, boss."

CHAPTER TWO

"I could eat your cute, little toes! I could eat them. Eat them all up!" Lily leaned over Baby Poppy and kissed each teeny, weeny toe while Poppy squeaked and burbled indecipherable baby noises.

"I'll make you a snack," I said. "Please don't eat her up. I want her to graduate from every life stage with all her extremities intact."

"I can't help it. I want to put her between two slices of bread, throw in some chicken slices and Poppy can be the ickle-pickle on top. Then I'm gonna eat her. Yes, I am," said Lily, not looking at me once. "Aren't babies amazing? They look so deliciously edible."

I glanced at Poppy who wore a pink top and a brighter pink tutu that fluffed around her middle with pink, footed leggings. She definitely looked like a baby and not a sandwich. "Maybe you need to get out more often."

Lily looked up and yawned. "I get out plenty. I went to… um…" Wrinkling her nose, she pulled a face, apparently not recalling anywhere she'd been lately. "Actually, you're right, I do. I haven't left the house in three weeks. Or have I? I'm too tired to remember."

"Too busy snacking on Poppy?"

Lily giggled. "Too busy trying to get ready and by the time that happens, I'm too tired to go out. I'm disorganized, untidy, badly dressed, and my house is a mess. Plus, I think I lost a diaper somewhere. I can smell it but I can't find it. Unless…" She looked hard at Poppy. "You did another one, didn't you?" Poppy giggled, her tiny mouth plumping and making little popping noises.

"Poppy looks cute," I said, finding a positive.

"Isn't she? It's amazing what four outfit changes per day can do for a month-old baby." Lily sat back and looked up at me. "Whose idea was it to have a baby?"

I held my hands up. "Not mine!"

"How am I supposed to live my life when I can't even get dressed anymore? How am I going to get to the market? Or go out for coffee? How am I supposed to run my bar? Or help you solve cases? Babies are so time-consuming! I'm not sure I've even used my brain since she was born."

"You can help me solve a case right now."

"You have a case? That's awesome! Tell me before my brain turns to mush and I'm no use to you at all."

"Believe me, this will test your brain," I said. I launched into Garrett's story about the impostor while Lily listened patiently. When I finished, she raised her eyebrows.

"So is she or isn't she Debby Patterson?"

"I don't know. Garrett doesn't think so but there's no reason I can see to believe she isn't. It's weird."

"Is Garrett officially hiring you?"

"Not exactly. It's more of a favor."

"For MPD?"

"For Garrett. MPD closed the case."

"What did Solomon say?"

"He said MPD would owe us one and that can't be a bad thing."

"Is he happy about Garrett's case?"

"I have no idea. He doesn't seem unhappy, so long as I don't take too much time on it. Plus, I did remind him that having an MPD favor is a nice thing."

"So, what's the first step? Do we confront her? Do we break in and steal her DNA to match to some old evidence? Do we need to surveil her?"

"Actually, I thought I would go home and read the file."

"Do you want to cuddle Poppy before you go?"

I pretended to gasp. "Really? You'll let someone else touch her?"

"Did Jord complain again that I'm a baby hog? I do not hog the baby!"

I laughed. "No, he didn't but I really want to cuddle her. Please!"

Lily scooped Poppy off the padded play mat and placed her in my arms. I forgot all about reading the file as I gazed into Poppy's big eyes. Her warm, tiny body wriggled in my arms and she rested her head against my chest, staring up at me. All my nieces and nephews were pretty babies; and Poppy had clearly inherited the

Graves' pretty baby gene. Combined with Lily's DNA, which gave her a smattering of blonde hair, she was perfect. Lily however, looked less than perfect. Her usually bouncy blonde curls were flattened and I was pretty sure I could see a Cheerio stuck on one strand on her left side. Her eyes looked tired and she wore baggy pajamas. I was fairly certain the top half belonged to Jord, Lily's husband, and the youngest of my three brothers. This wasn't the usual Lily and I had to concede she looked like she was having a hard time.

"Go take a shower," I told her. "Get dressed in something for daywear and take your time. Poppy and I will clean up the kitchen and do the laundry."

"This is the last time you'll ever see me like this," said Lily. She stepped gingerly around Poppy as if she couldn't quite pry herself away.

"You're a new mom. Don't worry."

"I'm not exactly an Instagram mom. I'm a failure. I'm not even wearing makeup! I tried to put concealer under my eyes before you came but I picked up a lip liner instead. The only reason I washed my face today was because I drew on it in bright red lip liner!"

I pinched my cheeks to hold back a laugh. "You're sleep-deprived."

"Tomorrow, I start over. Today is the last day in this… this… What the hell am I wearing, Lexi?"

"Jord's shirt, yesterday's leggings." I waved a finger towards the door, being careful not to jolt Poppy. "Take a shower."

The moment I heard the water running, I shuffled to my feet and cuddled Poppy's tiny, warm body against me, regretfully placing her in her buggy so I could wheel her to the laundry room. I stuffed the laundry into the machine, set it to wash and wheeled Poppy to the kitchen. I unloaded the dishwasher, put everything away, and re-stacked the dirty dishes, all the time singing silly songs to the baby. I tidied the counters and checked the refrigerator, throwing out a couple of items past the expiration date. Remembering the dryer, I stepped back into the laundry room and emptied the dry laundry into the large wash basket, which I brought into the kitchen. A spot check confirmed Poppy was fast asleep in the buggy.

Smiling, I folded the numerous tiny onesies, miniature pants and t-shirts. Her socks could have been made for a doll. Somehow, laundry was a lot more fun when the clothes didn't look like they were designed for a real human.

I left the laundry in the kitchen and wheeled Poppy to the den, parking her in the corner of the room while I grabbed a magazine from the coffee table and sat down to read it. Being a mom didn't seem so hard but then again, I felt sure I really had no idea. I got plenty of sleep, had a peaceful shower this morning, and my boobs were neither sore nor a constant food source for a tiny tyrant. On the other hand, Poppy was still asleep, I did all the laundry that wasn't even my own, and was officially winning at being a grown-up.

By the time Lily returned, she looked like her old self. "Now that I'm me again, how do we catch the criminals?" She eagerly wanted to know more as she took a seat on the couch opposite and leaned her head back to rest against the pillows. "Do you want to good cop, bad cop them?"

"Neither," I told her. "First, I want to make a plan. If I went missing, who would you... Lily?"

Lily's eyes were closed, and her face looked soft with sleep.

"I'll ask someone else," I whispered. After tucking a blanket over Lily, I then tested Poppy's restraints. Both were fast asleep and I hoped they stayed that way for a while. Gathering my things together, I tiptoed out of the house.

~

Back home at Solomon-Graves Towers, I fixed a snack of raw vegetables and hummus, adding a bottle of water before I took out my notepad, pondering the question I started to ask Lily. "Who would report me missing?" I wondered, my pen poised. I didn't need to note my personal answer. That was more a case of who would report me first.

Of course, Solomon would most definitely find me, probably before I even knew I was missing. I was close to both of my parents who would also definitely notice if I disappeared. My brothers would probably report me missing before my sister did, although I wasn't sure if that is because they were all police officers or because they care more about me than my sister does. My sisters-in-law would all notice, and most especially, Lily, since she is also my best friend. My other very close friend, and former boyfriend, Adam Maddox, would definitely know if I went missing. He had the full force of the FBI behind him, along with his own law enforcement contacts.

Apparently, there was no shortage of people who would not fail to report me, a thought which warmed me.

So why was it left to Debby Patterson's landlord to report she was missing but only when the rent check failed to arrive on time?

Where were her parents? Her family? Her friends? Did no one care enough or worry about her? Had she alienated her closest people so much that they no longer cared? Did she make a habit of disappearing so her behavior wasn't viewed as anything abnormal? Or had something else happened?

My hand began to cramp as I quickly wrote down my questions.

I reached for Garrett's file and double-checked the missing person report. There was little to add to what Garrett had already told me but I noted that Debby's parents didn't corroborate her missing person status for another two weeks after the landlord filed his report. By that time, Debby hadn't been seen for a whole month.

After a month, my family would have set up a brand new alert system across the nation, broadcasting my face to millions of people. No way would they wait a whole month to simply agree I was missing.

That told me two important things. One, I had the best family ever. And two, I needed to speak with Debby's family. I had to find out why her unscheduled disappearance didn't worry them enough to be seriously upset.

I flicked through the file as I formulated my plan. Her parents lived in Chilton, one of the nicer parts of Montgomery and not far from me, now that I lived with Solomon in his big townhouse. Since MPD had officially closed the case, I needed a good reason to see them and ask questions about it. I added a big question mark next to the word "parents" and moved onto the small section about Debby's professional life.

Ten years ago, Debby worked as a junior graphic designer at a small boutique firm in downtown Montgomery after graduating from a private college. There was an unfamiliar address listed so I used Google Maps on my phone to check its location. It was only a block from The Coffee Bean, a popular coffee shop where I'd drunk more coffees than I could count, and only about a block from the busy shopping on the street.

At the same time, she rented an apartment within walking distance from her workplace but there wasn't any record of a roommate in the file so I surmised that she probably lived alone. It must have been small, especially given the location, which had increased in cost over the past decade, currently making it a sought-after, pricey area. The information in the file said Debby had signed the lease around the time the downtown area was just starting to become trendy. If she were smart, she would have found somewhere under rent control, but I guess that point was moot since she hadn't stuck around long enough for housing prices to become an issue.

I quickly made a plan. My investigation could start at the apartment with the landlord if he were in residence. Then I would walk the route Debby probably took to work, just to get a feel of what her daily commute was like. Afterwards, I would visit her parents in my semi-official capacity of consulting for the Montgomery Police Department.

I cleared my plate, tossed the now empty bottle in the recycling can, and grabbed my purse, fumbling for the car keys that I knew lay inside somewhere.

At The Coffee Bean, I hung a right, drove a block, and shoehorned my black VW into the last parking space on the street, almost opposite Debby's former apartment. I got out, crossed the street, and peered at the eight entry buzzers on the brass plate fixed to the brickwork. I picked the one marked "supervisor" and pushed.

"Yes?" came the voice.

"Hi, I'm looking for the supervisor."

"You got him. Are you a resident? Did you lose your keys?" replied the gravelly voice.

"No, I'm a visitor. I wanted to ask you a couple of questions about a resident."

"You can't press their buzzer?"

"No, they don't live here anymore."

"Then why are you here? Shouldn't you be asking them at their new place?"

"Well…"

"If you want a reference for the girl who lived in apartment 2B, don't rent to her. She's a pain in the ass."

"Good to know. Could I come inside and speak with you? I promise I won't take up much of your time." I glanced up at the sky, grimacing when the rain that was threatening to fall all day began to spatter. Having a conversation through the intercom in the rain would be tiresome and I didn't want to wait around for the hours it could take before I could slip through the doors behind another resident.

"Were you here about renting 2B?" he wondered.

I seized on that. "Yes. I really want to see it. Please!"

"I'll be with you in a minute." The intercom went dead. Seconds later, a man approached from the corridor and opened the door. I expected an elderly man from the sound of his voice but the supervisor couldn't have been older than forty. When he spoke again, his voice was just as gravelly. "I'm Dan. So you want to see 2B?"

"Absolutely!" I beamed.

"I'm sure you are probably aware already but, just in case, you gotta know, the open house was yesterday and I already took four applications from viable candidates. If you want the apartment, you've got plenty of competition."

"Thank you, I'll bear that in mind. Have you worked here long?" I asked, edging forwards before going inside as he took the hint and stepped back.

"Three years."

"Oh. What happened to the guy before you? I thought the building was owned by the supervisor," I said as the man headed for the stairs, leaving me to hurry after him. Thankfully I'd changed to sneakers and I didn't have to teeter after him in heels.

"It was, but my brother took off three years ago to travel the world and hasn't seen enough of it yet. I'm managing it in his absence."

"That sounds exciting," I said, thinking of all the places I'd never seen. "Didn't he like being a supervisor?"

"Not as much as he likes Bora Bora."

Images of azure ocean, pure blue sky, and sandy beaches washed into my mind. "I can understand that."

The man shot a smile over his shoulder. "Me too."

"So, who else lives here?"

"We've got fifteen apartments here, mostly singles or couples. All professionals. We have a strict vetting policy for the benefit of all residents. Only small pets. Absolutely no snakes. Are you a professional?"

"Of course," I said, hoping he didn't ask what I did professionally. PIs weren't all that popular. At a guess, more popular than snakes, but probably not by much. People seemed to think it was because PIs had a higher propensity for getting shot at, stabbed, or tracked down by psychotic lunatics. Unfortunately, in my case, they were right.

"Single or couple?"

"Couple."

"Your husband will need to be your co-applicant on the lease. Is he a professional?"

I thought of all the things Solomon was very professional at, but with all modesty, I said, "Most definitely."

"We don't accept smokers, parties, or pets, especially not crocodiles."

"Crocodiles?"

"It doesn't matter how little they are, they grow bigger and they make the other residents uncomfortable. Here's 2B." He pushed his key into the door and opened it up to a small apartment. "I hope you don't mind me saying, but this is a little undersized for a couple. It's one of our smaller units."

"I appreciate that," I said. I didn't need to step much further to know that he was telling the truth. The apartment was a large studio with some clever storage across one wall and the tiniest kitchen I'd ever seen: no more than a hot plate and a sink, which filled the entire

23

counter surface. On the plus side, it had lovely, wide-planked flooring and high ceilings. Light flooded through the tall windows taking up one side. I crossed over, looking out at the street below. "I think you're right about it being too small for us. I wanted to see the building because an old friend used to live here. Debby Patterson? It was about ten years ago."

"That's a long time to sit on a recommendation."

I laughed. "She just got back to town and mentioned how much she enjoyed living here," I lied, crossing back to Dan. It took me a whole ten seconds to walk the entire studio. "Do you remember her?"

His eyebrows pinched. "Something about the name sounds familiar."

"I wanted to organize a little get-together for her. Maybe some of the other residents knew her? It would be nice for some old faces to be there."

"No one has lived here that long. Not for ten years. We're not that kind of building. People tend to outgrow these apartments. We're more of a starter home for people. First place they rent out of college. You know, to escape their parents. You see?"

"I do. You know what would be great? Perhaps I could get your brother's number and see if he's available? Debby always said the nicest things about him," I lied.

"I can't give out his number. Plus, I don't think he has great reception while he's traveling."

"Could I give you mine? If you tell him it's about Debby Patterson, I'm sure he'll find a way to call back." I handed him my card. He took it and scanned it. I could tell the moment he read "Private Investigator" by the way his eyebrows rose. Crocodiles and snakes had my eyebrows arched a lot higher.

"I'll let him know next time I speak with him," he said. "So do you want to fill out an application, or what?"

"Like you said, I think it's too small for us, but I appreciate your time," I told him, reaching to shake his hand. "Thanks for the tour."

"Anytime."

I showed myself out as he excused himself to attend to a resident's plumbing issue. My initial foray into Debby's life failed to glean any extra information but hopefully, my number would reach the landlord so I could ask him directly. It was a shame no other residents were left from a decade ago but I knew it was a long shot.

I could imagine Debby living there, her first apartment out of college, feeling like a young professional and surrounded by others in the same position just starting to make their way in the world. So why would she disappear? Or, as she claimed now, according to the letter Garrett included in the file, suddenly take off and leave? What could have happened to make her skip out on her rent and jump on a plane to enter an uncertain future? Few people entered into such a drastic life decision without either a great deal of planning and anticipation, or because something horrible happened that changed the way they looked at everything. For me, the horrible event was an impulse sign up for the army but fortunately that only lasted a few weeks before they'd not-so-polity suggested me and the army would never be happy together. Debby's life change had last ten years

With the door shut behind me and my car safely parked, I consulted my Maps app and took off on foot for the graphic design studio where she was last employed.

The fifteen-minute walk was pleasant and I enjoyed the back streets of Montgomery, noting things I'd never noticed before. The app took me along a pedestrian-only zone, flanked on either side with juice bars staffed by young men wearing enormously bushy beards, cafes with pretty teacups lining the walls, and boutiques selling the latest fashions and gifts. Hip apartments nestled among the vibrant office buildings, their architecture restored to pre-war grandeur. Apparently, I had wandered into trendy Montgomery without even trying.

"You have reached your destination," said my phone. I switched off the app and looked up. The building was a squat, three-story but had been prettied up by two bay trees flanking the glass doors. I stepped inside and marched over to the reception desk.

"Hi, I'm looking for Litmus Design," I told the red-lipped receptionist.

"We don't have any business by that name," she replied, consulting a list with one dangerously pointed fingernail. "We have a vlogger studio, a production office, a digital consultancy and a food publisher."

"I think they were here ten years ago. Maybe they moved on? I'm trying to find someone who worked with Debby Patterson."

The receptionist glanced up. Or, I thought she did. With eyelashes more than an inch long, I had no idea what was going on under those eyelids. "I have no idea."

"Do you know anyone who would have an idea?"

"Um…" She pondered that and tipped her chin to the ceiling before her eyes rolled back, leaving only the whites visible. A look that had once, undoubtedly, terrified her parents and teachers. "So, no," she said after a long look into her own brain.

"Do you know if anyone else worked here ten years ago?"

"Ten years ago, I was in elementary school. That was, like, fifty years ago."

I blinked. "I'm pretty sure it was ten. What's a vlogger?" I asked, immediately regretting it.

"Oh, babe," pouted the receptionist. "A vlogger is *now*."

"Okay," I said, deciding I would find out later. "Do you know where Litmus Design might have moved to?"

"Have you tried the Internet? It has, like, everything. Like, your generation's *Yellow Pages*."

"Thank you so much," I faux-smiled and turned to leave before, I, *like*, exploded!

Outside the sputtering rain had begun in earnest, fat drops hitting the sidewalk. I reached for the hood of my purple jacket and pulled it over my head, wondering if I needed to turn the app on again to find my way back to the car. I was already rehearsing what to say to Debby's parents about their magically reappearing daughter before my foot hit the sidewalk.

CHAPTER THREE

Debby Patterson's parents lived in the same house they'd lived in when their daughter first went missing. For me, that was excellent news! If I drew a third strike on Debby's past, after my failed attempts to look into her landlord and previous employer, I would have had to renew my search efforts back at the office. For me, it meant a lot of Internet and database searching, not to mention, a little begging to Lucas.

Property records showed the Pattersons still lived on Lincoln Street, a lovely avenue comprised of large homes and small, pristine lawns. With matching doors and windows at each house, it was the epitome of cookie cutter conformity. I wondered if the residents got a discount for bulk-buying minivans, although the Pattersons had a nice Mercedes parked in their driveway.

I knocked on the door and stepped back, waiting for someone to answer.

The woman who appeared had the loveliest wavy, red hair and big, green eyes. She wore a pantsuit that suggested she was a professional in some capacity although I wasn't sure what. "We don't buy at the door," she said, glancing over at me with visible disinterest.

I held my hands up. "Not selling anything," I assured her. "Actually, I'm here on a follow-up call from the Montgomery Police Department. My name is Lexi Graves. May I speak with you, Mrs. Patterson?" There was no need to tell her it wasn't strictly official business but fortunately, she didn't ask to see a badge. If she had, I was prepared with a little speech about consulting for MPD and only hoped that Garrett would back it up.

She frowned. "Is this about Debby? We already went down to the station. I thought everything was all cleared up?"

"Just dotting our i's and crossing our t's, ma'am." I held up the clipboard I'd armed myself with partly as a prop, and partly so I could actually take notes.

She stepped back and opened the door wider. "Come in. I just got home and was going to get changed for my tennis lesson."

"I promise I will be as quick as I can."

"Well, okay then."

I followed Mrs. Patterson into the living room, observing the large, beige couches and framed watercolors of flowers. On the mantel was a large, silver framed photo of a man between two women. The woman on the right was clearly Mrs. Patterson. The other was younger with pale brown hair. She didn't look a lot like the portrait photo of Debby that Garrett kept in his file but she must have only been in her teens when this photo was taken.

"I just need to check over a few things for the paperwork," I told her, trying to sound as nonchalant as I could. "I noted in the file that the landlord originally filed the missing person report but there was no reason stating why neither one of you didn't."

Mrs. Patterson took a deep breath. "I know it sounds bad but my husband and I didn't think we had to."

"You weren't worried?"

"No, not at all. Debby has always been terrible about calling so it wasn't unusual for us not to hear from her. She was forgetful too. Plus, she warned us that she was throwing herself into her new job so we figured she'd drop by when she was good and ready."

"Did she often do things like that?"

"Frequently." Mrs. Patterson shrugged but if she were disappointed, she didn't show it.

I pretended to check a box on my clipboard. "When did you first realize she was missing?"

"When her work called and said she hadn't shown up in a few days. That's when we started to get worried."

"Aha." I nodded, making a note. "Everything okay at work?"

"Debby said she was tired but she wanted to put in the extra hours. It was her first real job out of college and she was trying to stay focused."

"Any problems with colleagues?"

"I don't think so. She never mentioned any."

"What about with her landlord?"

"No. She always said he was nice."

"I was trying to locate a list of her friends. Did you provide that to MPD?"

"She didn't have many friends. She didn't keep in touch with any of the kids from high school or college. She mostly kept to herself except for a couple of friends. Anna Colby and Marley McFadden. I already told the detective about them."

"Do you know where they are now?"

"No, I'm afraid I don't. I think Anna might have gotten married a few years ago."

"And Marley?"

"I think she moved away after high school. I think they still kept in touch although I'm not sure where she is now."

"I see from the notes that you wanted to close the case shortly after it was opened." I paused, waiting for Mrs. Patterson to fill in the blanks even though I already knew about the postcards.

"That's right. Two months later, Debby sent us a postcard. It was a huge relief to her father and me."

"I'm sure it was. Did you keep a copy of it?"

"I did and I gave a copy to the detective."

"It must be in the file at the station," I lied smoothly. "That was the only communication?"

"No, there were more. Every few weeks. We started getting emails too. Debby decided she wanted to travel. She realized work wasn't going in the direction she liked and she wanted to try something new. So, you see, she wasn't missing after all! It was simply a big misunderstanding."

"Did that sound normal to you? People don't normally take off without telling their families first."

"I did find it puzzling initially, so I asked her. She said she had a bit of a crisis and just decided one day to go away to work out what she wanted to do with her life. She didn't want to be talked out of it so she didn't tell anyone."

"But…"

"It was typical Debby," Mrs. Patterson cut in. "She would get an idea into her head and just run with it."

"So she'd taken off before?"

"She switched colleges at the last minute. She walked out of her summer job. She was supposed to visit my sister but instead, she got on a plane to LA and didn't even tell anyone until my sister called when the plane she was supposed to be flying on touched down. We didn't hear from Debby for two weeks! She said she forgot!"

"So going abroad so suddenly seemed like something she would do," I surmised. It would have been something that could have gotten me into a whole lot of trouble with my family. I couldn't imagine taking off and forgetting to tell them. I could never start planning a huge change in my life without their input. It appeared that Debby wasn't as concerned as I was with other people's feelings. Given the nonchalant manner in which Mrs. Patterson told me what happened, perhaps they had become resigned to it.

"Unfortunately. Listen, Officer…"

"Graves," I supplied, hoping that I wouldn't get into trouble later. It wasn't like I could help what Mrs. Patterson assumed.

"Officer Graves," she started again, "I don't know what else I can tell you that I didn't tell I-don't-know-how-many detectives ten years ago and fairly recently, too. We're just so happy Debby decided to return home."

"Did she tell you she was coming home?"

Mrs. Patterson laughed. "Would you be surprised if I said no? She just said she missed us and was coming home."

"There's just one more thing. Do you have any photos of Debby? I have a really old photo but I can't find another one." I pretended to flip the pages, then looked up, plastering an apologetic look on my face. "It's for the people upstairs. They're always worried about litigation." I hoped Mrs. Patterson wouldn't ask what on earth that meant. I was in luck when she nodded.

"There's a few around the house but we're not big camera people. There's a family shot on the mantel," she said, pointing. "And I think Debby has some others in her old bedroom."

"Her bedroom is still intact?"

"I never really had the heart to change it. We don't need the space plus she's my only child."

"My mom feels the same," I said, although it couldn't be further from the truth. My parents had five children with a wide range of ages and I was the youngest. As my older brothers and sister gradually left home, I ended up with my own room. I was pretty sure my old bedroom was now a guestroom for my nieces and nephews. Almost everything was changed, from the painted walls to the furniture.

"Do you have children?"

"No."

"Having a child is a strange thing. You think you have all the time in the world, then one day, they're eighteen years old, and all they want to do is escape from you without explaining themselves to anyone."

I opened my mouth, ready to confide in Mrs. Patterson that I'd been escaping on a regular basis since my mid-teens. I closed my mouth again, pretty sure now wasn't the best time. Instead, I asked, "May I see her room?"

Mrs. Patterson checked her watch. "My friend will be here soon."

"It's all I need to see," I told her. "Then I can finish my report."

"Come this way." Instead of going upstairs, Mrs. Patterson led me toward the back of the house and opened a door. "This is Debby's room."

"Is she staying with you now that she's back in town?" I asked.

"No. She has a hotel room. She likes her space. I guess after traveling so long, one gets used to it."

"I guess," I agreed.

"The photos are over here on the bookcase," she said, crossing the room. She picked up a couple of photos and handed them to me. I saw the same framed photo as the one on the mantel but a smaller version. In the other one were three teens and I recognized Debby on the left. "This is Marley and Anna. Marley had this framed for Debby for a birthday present."

"That's a thoughtful gift," I murmured, looking closer. The girl called Marley had the same haircut as Debby and seemed the same height. The other girl was a few inches taller and black.

"Debby thought so too. She never bothered with photos. She always asked what was the point? She could be looking at stuff for real, not looking through a lens at real stuff."

The doorbell chimed and Mrs. Patterson glanced over. "That must be Fiona. I'll be right back." The moment she left the room, I took out my phone and snapped pictures of the photos, making a mental note to find both Marley and Anna later on. I had to get their take on all the events. I wondered if they thought Debby's disappearing act was regular behavior for their friend too.

While alone, I looked around the room carefully. Double bed in the middle, plain blue duvet with pink trim. Blue and white rug underneath. A desk that didn't hold much although I could imagine it covered with high school texts. Now there were just a few notepads and a yearbook along with a couple of paperbacks stacked on top of each other. I picked up the novels. Both were trashy, teenage romance novels. I returned them to their place.

A big, white mirror hung on the wall above and I wondered if Debby used the desk as a dressing table too. I opened the drawers and found each of them empty. The closet held a few clothes on hangers. Nothing remarkable. No prom dress, I noted. I wondered if the forgetful, self-absorbed Debby even attended the prom.

Perhaps she found something better to do at the last minute. I wondered if she stood up her prom date and emailed him two weeks later to tell him she bailed.

Taking another look, I noticed the lack of college paraphernalia. No college mug or sweatshirt, no varsity pennant hanging anywhere. No photos from that whole era of her life.

"My friend is here," said Mrs. Patterson, her footsteps sounding soft on the carpet. "Was there anything else?"

"No, thank you." I smiled at her as I crossed the room to where she waited in the doorway. "Thanks for all your time."

"Does this mean it's over?" she inquired as we walked to the door. A woman waited there, dressed in tennis whites, her sweatshirt tied casually around her shoulders. She smiled as we walked over.

"I just file the reports, ma'am." I held up my hands as if to say *not my job*.

"Are you here about Debby?" asked the woman.

"Yes, she is," said Mrs. Patterson, answering before I could.

The woman's eyes darkened. "Did she take off again?"

"No, Fiona. Debby is here to stay now."

"Hmmph," said Fiona, glancing from Mrs. Patterson to me.

"Thanks again for your time," I said, shaking Mrs. Patterson's hand after realizing an introduction to her friend wasn't forthcoming. I stepped through the open door and walked to my car, thinking about what I learned. It wasn't much but at least I knew why Debby's parents weren't worried initially. Her mother seemed to think taking off without any word or contact was normal; so people who didn't know Debby as well naturally sounded the alarm first. I had to concede my understanding of Mrs. Patterson's inaction. Debby had already set a precedent for that sort of thing and they hadn't gotten to the worrying stage yet. I wondered if the Pattersons ever once worried about Debby or were always so blasé about their daughter's penchant for acting on whims.

Just as I was about to get into my car, I felt a hand on my arm and almost jumped. I whipped around, finding the woman in tennis whites barely a step behind me.

"Sorry. I didn't mean to startle you."

"Fiona?"

"Yes, that's right. Fiona Queller. I'm a friend of Margaret's. You came here about Debby?"

"Yes."

"From the police?"

"Yes." Kind of.

"Ah."

I frowned, waiting for Fiona to say something. When she didn't, I prompted, "Is there something you wanted to tell me about…?"

Fiona cut in before I could finish. "I don't believe it."

"Don't believe what?"

"I don't know. I just… It's not normal, is it? To suddenly take off and not tell anyone where you are for months?"

I held my palms upright and raised my eyebrows. "Her mother seemed to think it was okay."

"Margaret has always indulged her daughter and her insistence on silliness. Debby has been away for ten years and she just pops up out of nowhere with no warning. That is not normal."

"It's not abnormal either," I pointed out, even though I personally agreed with her.

"I don't know what you people are doing. Ten years ago, you all practically gave up the moment an email turned up."

"I wasn't around ten years…"

Fiona spoke over me. "One interview for ten minutes and the case is closed? That's odd, very odd."

"We can't keep a missing person case open when the missing person finally shows up."

"That's just the problem! Debby is still missing! I don't know who showed up but it's definitely not Debby. I don't care what her mom says, she's not Debby." She folded her arms across her chest and stared at me, almost daring me to defy her.

"Have you met Debby since she came back?" I asked.

Fiona seemed surprised by my question. "I've met someone calling herself Debby. My friends threw a little welcome home surprise party for Debby and of course, I was there. I know that anyone would have changed over ten years, not only in their personalities but also their hairstyles and appearances, but they don't become *different people*. I'm telling you exactly what I told that girl, whoever she is. She's not Debby!"

"You told her that at the party?"

"Not in front of everyone. I didn't want to embarrass Margaret or Rod so I took the girl to one side and I told her I was damn sure she was a fake. Then I demanded to know what her game was. She said she didn't know what I was talking about."

"Did you tell the Pattersons?"

Fiona sighed. "I tried to but they didn't want to hear any of it. I don't know what you're doing here, since I heard the case was closed but I hope you can look deeper into it."

I didn't want to give Fiona any false hope but I knew this was the kind of break Garrett was looking for. I had to speak to Fiona. As a long-time family friend, she would undoubtedly have knowledge that others didn't, not to mention her own suspicions. Something must have sparked her memory besides Debby's appearance. "I'm just helping to tie up a few loose ends but I…"

"Fiona?" Mrs. Patterson appeared in the doorway. Her pantsuit was replaced by tennis whites similar to Fiona's.

"I must go now but perhaps you and I can talk later at my home?" Fiona pressed a card into my hand. I turned it over, reading her name, address and phone number. "I want to know what the girl wants from my good friends. If she's planning on scamming them, I want to make sure it stops. Come and see me at my house later after our game. Around eight? Promise me?"

"I promise," I said and she quickly walked back to the house where Mrs. Patterson waited, a quizzical look on her face. The door was shut on me a moment later.

I got into the car, wondering what just happened and uncertain of what to do next. I had a mother who welcomed her daughter home, and a family friend who was heavily suspicious. I didn't want to risk Mrs. Patterson getting annoyed with me, or overstay my welcome, so with Fiona unavailable until later, I turned the car around and headed back to the office.

Only Solomon was there when I arrived. "Hi," I said, sticking my head around the door of his enclosed cubicle. It was situated away from the shared office space the PIs used. Why he didn't move upstairs into one of the more spacious offices I didn't know but I suspected it had something to do with staying in close proximity to me. Or maybe he just didn't need so much space. "What are you up to?"

"Thinking up plans for world peace." A smile played on his lips.

"Good for you. Are you hungry?"

"Very. Where have you been all day?"

"Chasing ghosts, maybe. I don't know."

"Garrett's cold case?"

"Mmm."

"Any merit?"

"Something's not quite right. I'll know more when I've tracked down some people from her life ten years ago."

"Did you try her employer?"

"They moved on from their previous address so not yet. Do you know what vlogging is?" I asked, recalling my earlier conversation with the unhelpful receptionist.

"Flogging?"

"No. Vlogging."

"No idea."

"It's a mystery to me too. Are you busy?"

"No, just finishing some paperwork. I'm all yours."

"Then let's get something to eat and you can help me work out what to do next."

"Help you?" Solomon raised his eyebrows in a rare flash of surprise. "You don't ask for help very often."

"Just humoring my boss," I said and he laughed. He pushed back his chair, stood up and rounded the table. He placed his hands on my arms, rubbing them slightly and I couldn't help pressing my head against his chest and wrapping my arms around him. He was warm and firm and very comforting. Plus, he smelled great.

"Why don't I take your mind off things?" he whispered in my ear.

A smile sprang up and my heart thudded. "Here? In the office?" I replied in mock shock.

"What better place to discuss the case I'm not paying you to solve," he whispered back.

I pushed off him, laughing. "Very funny! I thought you were being..." I searched for a word, something more professional than *horny* and gave up.

"Plenty of time for that," Solomon cut in. "I'll order dinner and we can eat in the boardroom so long as you don't mind slumming it? I've had meetings all day and I'm beat."

"No problem. I have a meeting with Fiona Queller at eight anyway, and if I go home, I won't want to go out again." With that, I yawned and my stomach rumbled.

"Chinese food?"

"Order the entire menu," I told him.

~

I pushed back the plate and patted my stomach. We'd spent the past half hour discussing my steps today and I recounted my conversation with Fiona and Mrs. Patterson several times.

"I can tell you what I would do," said Solomon, "but I'd rather hear what you would do."

"Hmm." I thought for a moment. "Tomorrow, I'll get started on some background checks into Debby Patterson and try and track down her landlord, her former employer and the two friends she appeared so close to. What would you do?"

"The same. I'd also get my hands on the emails and postcards that were sent and find something older than ten years ago to match them to."

"To see if the handwriting is the same? Smart! I saw some notepads in Debby's old bedroom. They might have her handwriting in them." I stopped and thought about the look on Mrs. Patterson's face when she saw Fiona speaking to me. "I'm not sure Mrs. Patterson will let me inside again. I implied that the case would be wrapped up right after we spoke."

"Tell her you made a mistake or something else came up. Or ask the friend."

"Fiona?" I glanced at my watch. "She should be home soon. I can ask her."

"Do you have your car?"

"In the lot downstairs. I parked next to you."

"I'll follow you."

We drove in tandem, and I went first in my VW while Solomon followed in his black SUV. I wasn't familiar with Fiona's address, but when I turned a corner, I realized I was on a road I knew. Harbridge was a nice neighborhood, a pleasant mix of couples and families of all ages, and this road was no exception. Its crime rate was low except for the recent epidemic of burglaries, something which made my stomach drop when I saw several police cars parked at odd angles, their lights flashing. Worse still, there was an ambulance parked at the curb.

I pulled over and got out, looking around for a house number or at least, someone I knew. Behind me, I heard Solomon slamming his car door shut and the subsequent footsteps told me he was approaching me fast.

"I see Garrett," I told him, standing on my tiptoes for a better view. Garrett was beside his motor pool vehicle, talking to a uniformed officer. "I'm going to find out what's going on."

"What number is Fiona's house?" asked Solomon.

"Three hundred twelve."

"That's not good," said Solomon, raising his hand to point. I followed the direction of his finger, my stomach dropping even further when I saw the numbers to the side of the door where a policeman stood. I looked around for Garrett and found him, and this time, I caught his eye. He waved us over.

"What happened?" I asked him once he finished instructing the officer to tape off the area.

"You just driving through?" he wanted to know.

"No, I'm interviewing the woman who lives there." I pointed to the house. "What happened?"

"Looks like a home invasion gone bad."

"That's awful. Is Fiona okay?" I craned my head towards the ambulance, wondering if she walked right into the ongoing burglary. She must have been terrified.

"I'm not sure who is inside but if Fiona is the homeowner, then no, she's not okay. She's been murdered."Debby Patterson's parents lived in the same house they'd lived in when their daughter first went missing. For me, that was excellent news! If I drew a third strike on Debby's past, after my failed attempts to look into her landlord and previous employer, I would have had to renew my search efforts back at the office. For me, it meant a lot of Internet and database searching, not to mention, a little begging to Lucas.

Property records showed the Pattersons still lived on Lincoln Street, a lovely avenue comprised of large homes and small, pristine lawns. With matching doors and windows at each house, it was the epitome of cookie cutter conformity. I wondered if the residents got a discount for bulk-buying minivans, although the Pattersons had a nice Mercedes parked in their driveway.

I knocked on the door and stepped back, waiting for someone to answer.

The woman who appeared had the loveliest wavy, red hair and big, green eyes. She wore a pantsuit that suggested she was a professional in some capacity although I wasn't sure what. "We don't buy at the door," she said, glancing over at me with visible disinterest.

I held my hands up. "Not selling anything," I assured her. "Actually, I'm here on a follow-up call from the Montgomery Police Department. My name is Lexi Graves. May I speak with you, Mrs. Patterson?" There was no need to tell her it wasn't strictly official business but fortunately, she didn't ask to see a badge. If she had, I was prepared with a little speech about consulting for MPD and only hoped that Garrett would back it up.

She frowned. "Is this about Debby? We already went down to the station. I thought everything was all cleared up?"

"Just dotting our i's and crossing our t's, ma'am." I held up the clipboard I'd armed myself with partly as a prop, and partly so I could actually take notes.

She stepped back and opened the door wider. "Come in. I just got home and was going to get changed for my tennis lesson."

"I promise I will be as quick as I can."

"Well, okay then."

I followed Mrs. Patterson into the living room, observing the large, beige couches and framed watercolors of flowers. On the mantel was a large, silver framed photo of a man between two women. The woman on the right was clearly Mrs. Patterson. The other was younger with pale brown hair. She didn't look a lot like the portrait photo of Debby that Garrett kept in his file but she must have only been in her teens when this photo was taken.

"I just need to check over a few things for the paperwork," I told her, trying to sound as nonchalant as I could. "I noted in the file that the landlord originally filed the missing person report but there was no reason stating why neither one of you didn't."

Mrs. Patterson took a deep breath. "I know it sounds bad but my husband and I didn't think we had to."

"You weren't worried?"

"No, not at all. Debby has always been terrible about calling so it wasn't unusual for us not to hear from her. She was forgetful too. Plus, she warned us that she was throwing herself into her new job so we figured she'd drop by when she was good and ready."

"Did she often do things like that?"

"Frequently." Mrs. Patterson shrugged but if she were disappointed, she didn't show it.

I pretended to check a box on my clipboard. "When did you first realize she was missing?"

"When her work called and said she hadn't shown up in a few days. That's when we started to get worried."

"Aha." I nodded, making a note. "Everything okay at work?"

"Debby said she was tired but she wanted to put in the extra hours. It was her first real job out of college and she was trying to stay focused."

"Any problems with colleagues?"

"I don't think so. She never mentioned any."

"What about with her landlord?"

"No. She always said he was nice."

"I was trying to locate a list of her friends. Did you provide that to MPD?"

"She didn't have many friends. She didn't keep in touch with any of the kids from high school or college. She mostly kept to herself except for a couple of friends. Anna Colby and Marley McFadden. I already told the detective about them."

"Do you know where they are now?"

"No, I'm afraid I don't. I think Anna might have gotten married a few years ago."

"And Marley?"

"I think she moved away after high school. I think they still kept in touch although I'm not sure where she is now."

"I see from the notes that you wanted to close the case shortly after it was opened." I paused, waiting for Mrs. Patterson to fill in the blanks even though I already knew about the postcards.

"That's right. Two months later, Debby sent us a postcard. It was a huge relief to her father and me."

"I'm sure it was. Did you keep a copy of it?"

"I did and I gave a copy to the detective."

"It must be in the file at the station," I lied smoothly. "That was the only communication?"

"No, there were more. Every few weeks. We started getting emails too. Debby decided she wanted to travel. She realized work wasn't going in the direction she liked and she wanted to try something new. So, you see, she wasn't missing after all! It was simply a big misunderstanding."

"Did that sound normal to you? People don't normally take off without telling their families first."

"I did find it puzzling initially, so I asked her. She said she had a bit of a crisis and just decided one day to go away to work out what she wanted to do with her life. She didn't want to be talked out of it so she didn't tell anyone."

"But…"

"It was typical Debby," Mrs. Patterson cut in. "She would get an idea into her head and just run with it."

"So she'd taken off before?"

"She switched colleges at the last minute. She walked out of her summer job. She was supposed to visit my sister but instead, she got on a plane to LA and didn't even tell anyone until my sister called when the plane she was supposed to be flying on touched down. We didn't hear from Debby for two weeks! She said she forgot!"

"So going abroad so suddenly seemed like something she would do," I surmised. It would have been something that could have gotten me into a whole lot of trouble with my family. I couldn't imagine taking off and forgetting to tell them. I could never start planning a huge change in my life without their input. It appeared that Debby wasn't as concerned as I was with other people's feelings. Given the nonchalant manner in which Mrs. Patterson told me what happened, perhaps they had become resigned to it.

"Unfortunately. Listen, Officer…"

"Graves," I supplied, hoping that I wouldn't get into trouble later. It wasn't like I could help what Mrs. Patterson assumed.

"Officer Graves," she started again, "I don't know what else I can tell you that I didn't tell I-don't-know-how-many detectives ten years ago and fairly recently, too. We're just so happy Debby decided to return home."

"Did she tell you she was coming home?"

Mrs. Patterson laughed. "Would you be surprised if I said no? She just said she missed us and was coming home."

"There's just one more thing. Do you have any photos of Debby? I have a really old photo but I can't find another one." I pretended to flip the pages, then looked up, plastering an apologetic look on my face. "It's for the people upstairs. They're always worried about litigation." I hoped Mrs. Patterson wouldn't ask what on earth that meant. I was in luck when she nodded.

"There's a few around the house but we're not big camera people. There's a family shot on the mantel," she said, pointing. "And I think Debby has some others in her old bedroom."

"Her bedroom is still intact?"

"I never really had the heart to change it. We don't need the space plus she's my only child."

"My mom feels the same," I said, although it couldn't be further from the truth. My parents had five children with a wide range of ages and I was the youngest. As my older brothers and sister gradually left home, I ended up with my own room. I was pretty sure my old bedroom was now a guestroom for my nieces and nephews. Almost everything was changed, from the painted walls to the furniture.

"Do you have children?"

"No."

"Having a child is a strange thing. You think you have all the time in the world, then one day, they're eighteen years old, and all they want to do is escape from you without explaining themselves to anyone."

I opened my mouth, ready to confide in Mrs. Patterson that I'd been escaping on a regular basis since my mid-teens. I closed my mouth again, pretty sure now wasn't the best time. Instead, I asked, "May I see her room?"

Mrs. Patterson checked her watch. "My friend will be here soon."

"It's all I need to see," I told her. "Then I can finish my report."

"Come this way." Instead of going upstairs, Mrs. Patterson led me toward the back of the house and opened a door. "This is Debby's room."

"Is she staying with you now that she's back in town?" I asked.

"No. She has a hotel room. She likes her space. I guess after traveling so long, one gets used to it."

"I guess," I agreed.

"The photos are over here on the bookcase," she said, crossing the room. She picked up a couple of photos and handed them to me. I saw the same framed photo as the one on the mantel but a smaller version. In the other one were three teens and I recognized Debby on the left. "This is Marley and Anna. Marley had this framed for Debby for a birthday present."

"That's a thoughtful gift," I murmured, looking closer. The girl called Marley had the same haircut as Debby and seemed the same height. The other girl was a few inches taller and black.

"Debby thought so too. She never bothered with photos. She always asked what was the point? She could be looking at stuff for real, not looking through a lens at real stuff."

The doorbell chimed and Mrs. Patterson glanced over. "That must be Fiona. I'll be right back." The moment she left the room, I took out my phone and snapped pictures of the photos, making a mental note to find both Marley and Anna later on. I had to get their take on all the events. I wondered if they thought Debby's disappearing act was regular behavior for their friend too.

While alone, I looked around the room carefully. Double bed in the middle, plain blue duvet with pink trim. Blue and white rug underneath. A desk that didn't hold much although I could imagine it covered with high school texts. Now there were just a few notepads and a yearbook along with a couple of paperbacks stacked on top of each other. I picked up the novels. Both were trashy, teenage romance novels. I returned them to their place.

A big, white mirror hung on the wall above and I wondered if Debby used the desk as a dressing table too. I opened the drawers and found each of them empty. The closet held a few clothes on hangers. Nothing remarkable. No prom dress, I noted. I wondered if the forgetful, self-absorbed Debby even attended the prom. Perhaps she found something better to do at the last minute. I wondered if she stood up her prom date and emailed him two weeks later to tell him she bailed.

Taking another look, I noticed the lack of college paraphernalia. No college mug or sweatshirt, no varsity pennant hanging anywhere. No photos from that whole era of her life.

"My friend is here," said Mrs. Patterson, her footsteps sounding soft on the carpet. "Was there anything else?"

"No, thank you." I smiled at her as I crossed the room to where she waited in the doorway. "Thanks for all your time."

"Does this mean it's over?" she inquired as we walked to the door. A woman waited there, dressed in tennis whites, her sweatshirt tied casually around her shoulders. She smiled as we walked over.

"I just file the reports, ma'am." I held up my hands as if to say not my job.

"Are you here about Debby?" asked the woman.

"Yes, she is," said Mrs. Patterson, answering before I could.

The woman's eyes darkened. "Did she take off again?"

"No, Fiona. Debby is here to stay now."

"Hmmph," said Fiona, glancing from Mrs. Patterson to me.

"Thanks again for your time," I said, shaking Mrs. Patterson's hand after realizing an introduction to her friend wasn't forthcoming. I stepped through the open door and walked to my car, thinking about what I learned. It wasn't much but at least I knew why Debby's parents weren't worried initially. Her mother seemed to think taking off without any word or contact was normal; so people who didn't know Debby as well naturally sounded the alarm first. I had to concede my understanding of Mrs. Patterson's inaction. Debby had already set a precedent for that sort of thing and they hadn't gotten to the worrying stage yet. I wondered if the

Pattersons ever once worried about Debby or were always so blasé about their daughter's penchant for acting on whims.

Just as I was about to get into my car, I felt a hand on my arm and almost jumped. I whipped around, finding the woman in tennis whites barely a step behind me.

"Sorry. I didn't mean to startle you."

"Fiona?"

"Yes, that's right. Fiona Queller. I'm a friend of Margaret's. You came here about Debby?"

"Yes."

"From the police?"

"Yes." Kind of.

"Ah."

I frowned, waiting for Fiona to say something. When she didn't, I prompted, "Is there something you wanted to tell me about…?"

Fiona cut in before I could finish. "I don't believe it."

"Don't believe what?"

"I don't know. I just… It's not normal, is it? To suddenly take off and not tell anyone where you are for months?"

I held my palms upright and raised my eyebrows. "Her mother seemed to think it was okay."

"Margaret has always indulged her daughter and her insistence on silliness. Debby has been away for ten years and she just pops up out of nowhere with no warning. That is not normal."

"It's not abnormal either," I pointed out, even though I personally agreed with her.

"I don't know what you people are doing. Ten years ago, you all practically gave up the moment an email turned up."

"I wasn't around ten years…"

Fiona spoke over me. "One interview for ten minutes and the case is closed? That's odd, very odd."

"We can't keep a missing person case open when the missing person finally shows up."

"That's just the problem! Debby is still missing! I don't know who showed up but it's definitely not Debby. I don't care what her mom says, she's not Debby." She folded her arms across her chest and stared at me, almost daring me to defy her.

"Have you met Debby since she came back?" I asked.

Fiona seemed surprised by my question. "I've met someone calling herself Debby. My friends threw a little welcome home surprise party for Debby and of course, I was there. I know that anyone would have changed over ten years, not only in their personalities but also their hairstyles and appearances, but they don't become different people. I'm telling you exactly what I told that girl, whoever she is. She's not Debby!"

"You told her that at the party?"

"Not in front of everyone. I didn't want to embarrass Margaret or Rod so I took the girl to one side and I told her I was damn sure she was a fake. Then I demanded to know what her game was. She said she didn't know what I was talking about."

"Did you tell the Pattersons?"

Fiona sighed. "I tried to but they didn't want to hear any of it. I don't know what you're doing here, since I heard the case was closed but I hope you can look deeper into it."

I didn't want to give Fiona any false hope but I knew this was the kind of break Garrett was looking for. I had to speak to Fiona. As a long-time family friend, she would undoubtedly have knowledge that others didn't, not to mention her own suspicions. Something must have sparked her memory besides Debby's appearance. "I'm just helping to tie up a few loose ends but I…"

"Fiona?" Mrs. Patterson appeared in the doorway. Her pantsuit was replaced by tennis whites similar to Fiona's.

"I must go now but perhaps you and I can talk later at my home?" Fiona pressed a card into my hand. I turned it over, reading her name, address and phone number. "I want to know what the girl wants from my good friends. If she's planning on scamming them, I want to make sure it stops. Come and see me at my house later after our game. Around eight? Promise me?"

"I promise," I said and she quickly walked back to the house where Mrs. Patterson waited, a quizzical look on her face. The door was shut on me a moment later.

I got into the car, wondering what just happened and uncertain of what to do next. I had a mother who welcomed her daughter home, and a family friend who was heavily suspicious. I didn't want to risk Mrs. Patterson getting annoyed with me, or overstay my welcome, so with Fiona unavailable until later, I turned the car around and headed back to the office.

Only Solomon was there when I arrived. "Hi," I said, sticking my head around the door of his enclosed cubicle. It was situated away from the shared office space the PIs used. Why he didn't move upstairs into one of the more spacious offices I didn't know but I suspected it had something to do with staying in close proximity to me. Or maybe he just didn't need so much space. "What are you up to?"

"Thinking up plans for world peace." A smile played on his lips.

"Good for you. Are you hungry?"

"Very. Where have you been all day?"

"Chasing ghosts, maybe. I don't know."

"Garrett's cold case?"

"Mmm."

"Any merit?"

"Something's not quite right. I'll know more when I've tracked down some people from her life ten years ago."

"Did you try her employer?"

"They moved on from their previous address so not yet. Do you know what vlogging is?" I asked, recalling my earlier conversation with the unhelpful receptionist.

"Flogging?"

"No. Vlogging."

"No idea."

"It's a mystery to me too. Are you busy?"

"No, just finishing some paperwork. I'm all yours."

"Then let's get something to eat and you can help me work out what to do next."

"Help you?" Solomon raised his eyebrows in a rare flash of surprise. "You don't ask for help very often."

"Just humoring my boss," I said and he laughed. He pushed back his chair, stood up and rounded the table. He placed his hands on my arms, rubbing them slightly and I couldn't help pressing my head against his chest and wrapping my arms around him. He was warm and firm and very comforting. Plus, he smelled great.

"Why don't I take your mind off things?" he whispered in my ear.

A smile sprang up and my heart thudded. "Here? In the office?" I replied in mock shock.

"What better place to discuss the case I'm not paying you to solve," he whispered back.

I pushed off him, laughing. "Very funny! I thought you were being..." I searched for a word, something more professional than horny and gave up.

"Plenty of time for that," Solomon cut in. "I'll order dinner and we can eat in the boardroom so long as you don't mind slumming it? I've had meetings all day and I'm beat."

"No problem. I have a meeting with Fiona Queller at eight anyway, and if I go home, I won't want to go out again." With that, I yawned and my stomach rumbled.

"Chinese food?"

"Order the entire menu," I told him.

~

I pushed back the plate and patted my stomach. We'd spent the past half hour discussing my steps today and I recounted my conversation with Fiona and Mrs. Patterson several times.

"I can tell you what I would do," said Solomon, "but I'd rather hear what you would do."

"Hmm." I thought for a moment. "Tomorrow, I'll get started on some background checks into Debby Patterson and try and track down her landlord, her former employer and the two friends she appeared so close to. What would you do?"

"The same. I'd also get my hands on the emails and postcards that were sent and find something older than ten years ago to match them to."

"To see if the handwriting is the same? Smart! I saw some notepads in Debby's old bedroom. They might have her handwriting in them." I stopped and thought about the look on Mrs. Patterson's face when she saw Fiona speaking to me. "I'm not sure Mrs. Patterson will let me inside again. I implied that the case would be wrapped up right after we spoke."

"Tell her you made a mistake or something else came up. Or ask the friend."

"Fiona?" I glanced at my watch. "She should be home soon. I can ask her."

"Do you have your car?"

"In the lot downstairs. I parked next to you."

"I'll follow you."

We drove in tandem, and I went first in my VW while Solomon followed in his black SUV. I wasn't familiar with Fiona's address, but when I turned a corner, I realized I was on a road I knew. Harbridge was a nice neighborhood, a pleasant mix of couples and families of all ages, and this road was no exception. Its crime rate was low except for the recent epidemic of burglaries, something which made my stomach drop when I saw several police cars parked at odd angles, their lights flashing. Worse still, there was an ambulance parked at the curb.

I pulled over and got out, looking around for a house number or at least, someone I knew. Behind me, I heard Solomon slamming his car door shut and the subsequent footsteps told me he was approaching me fast.

"I see Garrett," I told him, standing on my tiptoes for a better view. Garrett was beside his motor pool vehicle, talking to a uniformed officer. "I'm going to find out what's going on."

"What number is Fiona's house?" asked Solomon.

"Three hundred twelve."

"That's not good," said Solomon, raising his hand to point. I followed the direction of his finger, my stomach dropping even further when I saw the numbers to the side of the door where a policeman stood. I looked around for Garrett and found him, and this time, I caught his eye. He waved us over.

"What happened?" I asked him once he finished instructing the officer to tape off the area.

"You just driving through?" he wanted to know.

"No, I'm interviewing the woman who lives there." I pointed to the house. "What happened?"

"Looks like a home invasion gone bad."

"That's awful. Is Fiona okay?" I craned my head towards the ambulance, wondering if she walked right into the ongoing burglary. She must have been terrified.

"I'm not sure who is inside but if Fiona is the homeowner, then no, she's not okay. She's been murdered."

CHAPTER FOUR

"Yes, that's Fiona," I said, sighing as I looked at the photo of the woman I'd met only a few hours before. I may not have known her well but her face was very fresh in my memory, not least because I was expecting to see her again so soon. I never imagined I'd see her dead face on Garrett's phone screen. Garrett tucked his phone into his pocket and I tried to blink away the sight of the dead woman. Apparently, without her husband on scene, I was their best candidate for providing a positive identification. I didn't need to ask for proof of death. The hole in her head, a literal *head shot*, was testament to that.

"We still need to get an official identification from a close relative," said Garrett. "I sent uniforms to pick up the husband at his office."

"Yes, naturally. I barely knew her," I told him as Solomon's hand tightened around mine. His reassurance was welcome. "I only met her a few hours ago."

"While investigating a case?" Garrett glanced toward Solomon, a mix of suspicion and annoyance on his face. "What are you involved in this time?"

"Actually, yes, it was in regards to a case but it's your cold case," I told him.

Garrett frowned and blinked. "I don't follow."

"I went to visit Mrs. Patterson and Fiona was there. They were playing tennis together. Fiona and I only spoke for a few minutes but she said she wanted to meet here later. I think she might have had some information about Debby Patterson. She was adamant that the Debby who returned is not the same Debby that went away."

"Shit." Garrett ran a hand through his hair and gulped. "I thought we were dealing with a burglary gone wrong but this could change everything."

Someone shouted his name and he excused himself, crossing over to the uniformed officer now exiting the house. They conferred for a few minutes before Garrett walked back. "It's got the hallmarks of a robbery. A few things got trashed, and pictures were moved like the perp was looking for a safe. We're not sure yet if money or credit cards are missing. The victim's purse was open."

"This could be a horrible coincidence," I pointed out.

"Or someone was trying to cover their tracks," said Solomon. He glanced at the house before looking back at Garrett. "Are you going to check on this Debby woman's alibi?"

"Definitely," said Garrett. "Plus, I'll find out if there are any obvious signs she's been in the neighborhood recently. I'll get a trace on those credit cards as soon as I know if they're missing."

"What about any other evidence?" I wondered. "Fingerprints? DNA?"

"Our forensic guys are already on that but I won't know for a while. I appreciate the heads-up about the Debby Patterson connection but you might as well take off. There's nothing you can do here."

"Do you want me to stay on the case?" I asked.

Garrett hesitated, then nodded. "Be careful," he warned. "This could all be about nothing but until we know for certain, stick with Debby. There's a strong chance that it's unrelated, owing to the large number of burglaries in the area recently but the connection still has me worried. Keep me in the loop."

I assured my brother I would and Solomon and I headed back to our cars. As we drove away, I pondered the strange coincidence of Fiona's death just as I had arranged to meet her. Of course, it could have been something so simple as a home invasion, interrupted by Fiona at an inopportune moment, causing the thief to panic and shoot her. Even as I thought about it, it didn't sit right in my gut. What kind of thief takes a gun if they were only going to steal cash and cards? Unless there was something far more valuable they wanted? Something that hadn't been discovered as missing yet? Garrett mentioned the pictures had been moved so a thief could have been looking for a safe. What could Fiona have had that was so valuable to a thief they were willing to take her life for it?

What if there was nothing and the burglary were simply staged? It had happened before. That meant somebody must have had it in for Fiona and killed her for a specific reason, perhaps they even lay in wait for her to return from her tennis game. If they knew it was a regular appointment, they would know exactly when the house was empty and when to expect her return. I turned up the heat to push away the bone-chilling shiver that my last thought gave me.

Veering my thoughts away from a home invader to Debby, I had to agree with Garrett that the connection was worrisome. Fiona intended to share her suspicions with me but what could have been so terrible about what she would say that she had to be silenced? Surely the worst thing was what Fiona already told me. Debby wasn't Debby, according to her, and she suspected whomever the woman was, she might have been trying to scam the Pattersons in some nefarious way. Assuming that were true, did the impostor need Fiona out of the way so her scam could be completed? Yet, if Fiona were faced with a gun, wouldn't she say that someone else knew? It would be a reasonable assumption that if the killer knew she had already told someone, the connection would immediately be made between the cases, rendering her murder pointless and unnecessary.

Something didn't seem right about that either. It was very public and shocking, not just a way to silence a person, although the home invasion aspect could explain the murder as nothing more than a freak tragedy. Could that be what it truly was? A freaky, horrible coincidence?

By the time we reached home, I was starting to expand the plan Solomon and I discussed. With Fiona unable to help me with whatever she thought she knew, I needed to find out a lot more about Debby. I had to know everything about her life from ten years ago. I had to learn what her former colleagues and friends had to say about her and what they thought of her strange disappearance. I wanted to track down her old boyfriends, not that the Pattersons mentioned any, although I didn't ask. All the people that could tell me about Debby before her disappearance would certainly add to the conflicting information Mrs. Patterson and Fiona had already told me. It would be a lot of work to track them all down but now I was intrigued. How could a mother claim her daughter as her own while a close family friend insisted that wasn't the case? Out of the two people who knew her, both assumed opposite sides in the case.

That led to other important considerations: where could I find Debby now? And how could I get her to talk to me?

I found a parking space just one house down from ours and slid right in. Solomon drove past me and parked at the end of the street, jogging back to meet me on the steps to the house.

"I miss my driveway," I told him.

"Do you miss the crazy dog from next door?"

I smiled, thinking about my neighbor's hearing dog. It had an amazing ability to break into my house despite its delightful countenance. It was hard to be angry at anything so adorable. "Kind of," I said, making a note to drop by Aiden's house and visit them both. Plus, it would give me a chance to walk through my house. It had an alarm and all, but without anyone living there, I was relying on Aiden's offer to keep an eye on it for me until I decided what to do with the place. That decision was taking some time for me to determine. I didn't want to sell it. The pretty, yellow bungalow was my dream house but practically, real estate was such a good investment. I wasn't sure I wanted to rent it out either. I had to make a decision soon, since Solomon and I agreed to live in his larger and better equipped home for now.

Solomon was studying me. "Do you want a dog?"

"I'm a PI. Shouldn't I get a cat?"

"No, you're not single."

"Good point." I slipped my hand into his and we took the steps up. Solomon let us into the house. After sliding off my shoes, I followed him into the kitchen, hoisting myself onto a tall kitchen stool. He reached inside one of the sleek cabinets and extracted two wine glasses. The refrigerator, hidden behind another faceless panel, contained a bottle of white wine. Solomon extracted the cork and poured us both a glass. I clinked mine against his in a quiet toast and swallowed. "This is nice."

"It is."

"Do you want to talk about work?" I asked, my mind flitting back to Fiona and Debby.

"Nope. I think we should take our minds *off* work."

"What do you want to do?" I asked.

Solomon smiled. "Why don't I show you?" Then he did exactly that.

~

The next morning found me sitting outside the morgue, my absolutely least favorite place, but it was necessary. Garrett called me first thing with information about the autopsy and ballistics reports. I was eager to know more so long as it didn't include any show-and-tell with the body. Fortunately, he told me to wait in the lobby.

"Hey, you're here already," said Garrett. I stood up from the plastic chair and smiled although I was sure it didn't reach my eyes. Garrett looked exhausted, even minus the black-ringed eyes, and I wondered if he worked through the night. I'd had a much more comfortable night in bed with a very warm Solomon but didn't get a lot a lot sleep for all the wrong reasons. The image of Fiona, her gunshot wound glaringly obvious, kept appearing behind my eyelids.

"Bright and perky," I replied, plastering on a sunny countenance for cover.

"I hate you."

That confirmed it; Garrett did work all night. The fresh shirt and tie probably came from his locker, where he kept his spare clothing. "I brought you a bacon roll," I told him, holding up the paper bag that was warming my hands.

"I love you," he said as he grabbed it, tearing into the roll. "Did I ever tell you you're my favorite sibling?"

"Probably, but you can say it again."

"You're my favorite."

"Say it in front of Serena!"

Garrett paused in the middle of his chewing. "No. I'm grateful, not suicidal."

"Okay, sure, but we all know it's true and that's what counts."

Garrett snorted but didn't correct me. Instead, he said, "The preliminary report on Fiona Queller is in," flapping the file in his hand pointlessly. I'd already noticed it the moment he walked in and was waiting for him to mention it. He tossed the paper bag into the trashcan and dropped into the plastic chair adjacent to mine before opening the folder and flipping through the photos quickly. I sat next to him, trying to peek. "There isn't much to add yet beyond what I surmised yesterday. Fiona was shot in the head and died instantly. The bullet is a 9mm. Very common, unfortunately. On the brighter side, we found the bullet at the scene and there's a mark that makes it very easy to match the gun when we eventually find it."

"When? Not if?"

"A professional hit man would never have left a casing so I'm ruling that out. A smart killer, even if he were just an opportunist, would get rid of this gun pretty damn quickly, especially if they know about the unique striations on the bullet. I expect it will turn up during the search of the immediate area."

"I don't suppose fingerprints are too much to ask for?"

"Let's not hold our breaths." Garrett turned the page, running his finger down it. "We'll check the bullet of course, just in case the perp didn't wear gloves when he loaded the gun but it's a longshot. Says here, there were *no defensive wounds and no DNA under the victim's fingernails* so she didn't fight him off before he shot her. That's not corroborated with the scene at the victim's house. Lamps were smashed, pictures were torn off the wall and they all indicate a fight could have taken place."

"The staged robbery could have been done afterwards," I said.

"True. Or the victim could have been incapacitated in some way—" Garrett broke off as he continued to read ahead. "No, scrap that. There's no evidence she was restrained or drugged; plus, we can be reasonably sure she hadn't been home long. A neighbor was walking their dog and saw her park on the driveway around thirty minutes before we got the call."

"Did the neighbor hear anything?"

"I sent a uniform to knock on all the doors and so far, no one heard a thing until the gunshot was called in."

"What about entry? Was it forced?" Nothing suggested that on the front of the house, but someone could have jimmied the back door or a window at the rear of the property without being noticed. They could have been waiting in the house for Fiona to return.

"Nothing. We think she probably let her killer in."

"So she opened the door to someone she knew or trusted. That keeps Debby Patterson on the suspect list. She knew her but I doubt she trusted her, not after what she said to me."

"Did she say anything to you about why she suspected Debby?"

I shook my head. "No, just that she was sure it wasn't her and she thought it might be a scam of some sort. She couldn't say much because Mrs. Patterson was waiting for her and I doubt she wanted to upset her. Is Debby a suspect?"

"She's not a suspect until there's reason to believe she is. She would need a motive."

"Fiona didn't think she was Debby and she knew it. She told her at the Pattersons' welcome home party. That's plenty of motive."

"It's a pretty big leap and we both know it."

"Got anything better than a leap?"

Garrett shook his head. "Nope."

"What else is in the report?" I asked. Garrett and I could talk on end about Debby but there wouldn't be much to say until one of us knew more. For the time being, we had to focus on the information we had.

"Not much. Victim appeared to have showered recently—"

"She was playing tennis with Mrs. Patterson shortly before. I'm sure you can verify that."

"Thanks, I spoke to a manager at her club and he confirmed she had a game with Mrs. Patterson. Stomach contents consisted of peanuts and a small amount of alcohol. A glass of champagne. Both were consumed an hour before death. No issues with the time of death, thanks to the 911 call and the dog-walking neighbor."

"The champagne and peanuts sound like club snacks to me. Perhaps Mrs. Patterson and Fiona stopped at the bar before going home?"

"I'm lucky if I can get a fresh donut," grumbled Garrett.

"I brought you a bacon roll!"

"So you did." He hesitated and I saw the suggestion in his eyes before he could verbalize it. "Yes, I will bring you a donut too, next time," I told him before moving on to my subsequent question. "Did Fiona have any enemies?"

"Not from our initial interview with the husband but he was too cut up to talk properly yesterday. I'll know more when we expand the investigation. Listen, Lexi, if I hadn't handed you the Patterson file yesterday, and you hadn't met Fiona, I wouldn't have thought this was anything more than a bungled burglary. Now? I don't know what to think of it. Have I got a pre-meditated murder or just a home invasion gone wrong?"

I didn't get the impression he wanted to hear an answer. "I'll leave it to you to work that out."

"Really?" Garrett regarded me with visible suspicion. "You're not going to butt into my murder investigation?"

"No!" I smiled as an idea flashed in my head. I knew exactly how I could get close to Debby and conduct my investigation without raising her alarm. "I'm going to use it to get to Debby Patterson."

CHAPTER FIVE

I found Debby at her hotel. The Montgomery Hotel and Conference Center was a mid-priced resort, better than a cheap motel but not as fancy as The Belmont. I'd gone undercover at this hotel once. Either there was a complete staff turnover since then or I arrived during the wrong shift to put any faces to the names. I didn't recognize anyone when I took a seat at the bar and that was probably a good thing since I was aiming for anonymity.

Without any prior surveillance to work from, I didn't know Debby's routine. I figured if she only recently returned to town, she probably didn't have a job yet so she didn't have any fixed hours to keep. I also assumed that no one liked to stay in a hotel room all day. Just as soon as she appeared, I planned to make my move.

"What can I get you?" asked the bartender.

"Coffee, thanks," I told him. With a brief nod, he moved to the other end of the bar and the large coffee machine. I watched him for a moment as he reached for a cup from the stack, then glanced toward the lobby. My position at the bar gave me a good view of the lobby but I still had to be careful not to miss Debby. She could easily slip out in a crowd although something told me she probably wouldn't. Garrett assured me no one from MPD had approached her. She had no reason to be on alert.

When Garrett gave me the case, I wasn't sure how to approach Debby in order to ascertain the truth about her identity, but now I had the perfect ruse. Regardless of what Fiona Queller said to her that night, social etiquette required that Debby not refuse to answer a few questions about her parents' close friend, especially given her violent death.

I didn't have to wait long. I'd already relocated from the bar to one of the small tables where I sat in a chair directly facing the lobby. Debby appeared as soon as I finished my first cup of coffee. She stepped out of the elevator and crossed over to the reception desk. With a quick glance at the description supplied by Garrett, I confirmed it was she. The pale brown hair was shorter and the cut much nicer, and the high school-era sweatshirt was replaced with a smart sweater in the palest blue and a pair of skinny jeans tucked into long, leather boots. Her slim trench coat ended mid-thigh and the tan leather purse looked well-made but inexpensive. She had a polished, stylish look of which I approved. She said something to the concierge and waited for a reply before nodding and heading toward the entrance doors. I grabbed my purse and followed her out to the parking lot. When she took her keys out of her pocket, I saw my chance.

"Excuse me," I said, jogging after her, not too steadily in my heels but fast enough to catch her own quick pace. "Excuse me? Debby? Debby Patterson?"

She turned, stopping onto the sidewalk, smiling broadly and expectantly. "Yes? Do I know you?" She peered at me, her eyebrows pinching together as if trying to place me somewhere and failing.

"I'm Lexi." I stuck out my hand and she shook it politely. *That was mostly,* I thought, *because she didn't have the option to do anything else without seeming rude.* "I'm looking into Fiona Queller's homicide case."

"Fiona?" Her eyebrows knitted more tightly together.

"You heard about what happened last night?"

"Yes, yes, I did." She nodded and gulped. "My parents called and told me. I didn't know Fiona very well but my mom is devastated. You said you're looking into it? Are you a detective?" Her eyes lowered, taking in my clothes and I regretted passing up the opportunity to throw on something a little plainer and more professional than my cream floral blouse and baby-blue jeans. At least, I wore a jacket since it was a cool day. I'd gotten used to, and was very happy with, my daily perk of wearing joyous colors and prints rather than the drab, corporate colors of my former temping career. My dress sense, according to Solomon, was one of the reasons why no one ever suspected me of being an investigator. I wasn't entirely sure if that meant no one took me seriously, or they just never suspected me. I was determined I would never resemble a single one of my hard male colleagues.

Opting to be straight with Debby since the murder was my cover story to get close to her, I took her assertion that she wasn't close to Fiona as a blessing. It made it easier for me. If she thought I was investigating one thing, she wouldn't look too closely at the questions that might expose her. "Not exactly. I'm a PI. I'm assisting MPD with the case."

"I don't understand."

"Their resources are stretched," I said with a shrug as if it were a common occurrence and I didn't care if she believed me or not. However, since I didn't want her calling MPD or risking the chance of her speaking to someone who would blow my cover, I added, "Actually, I'm working on behalf of Fiona's family. They want to be sure to get all the information."

"Oh. They must be... I can't imagine, actually. It's so awful for them. I don't know how I can help you."

"I'd like to ask you a few questions; that is, if you're not in a hurry?"

Debby moved the keys in her fingers. "I have to see an apartment but I can give you ten minutes. I can't be late because they're going to show it to some other people."

"That would be great. Can I get you a coffee?" I waved a hand towards the hotel from which we just exited.

"No, thanks. What did you want to ask me? Like I said, I didn't know Fiona very well."

"We're talking to everyone even remotely connected to her. When did you last see Fiona?"

"About six days ago. She came to a dinner party my parents were having. We didn't talk much."

"Was that your welcome home dinner?"

Debby blinked in surprise but recovered quickly. "Yes. I've been living abroad. I recently came home and my parents threw a surprise dinner party for me to welcome me back."

"How sweet!"

"Mmm," said Debby but the smile didn't reach her eyes. "Fiona and I exchanged a few polite remarks but I don't remember saying much else."

"She's been friends with your mom for a long time?" I prompted.

"Oh, wow. Yes! Years. Since I was a teenager."

"So you probably knew her better than you think?"

Debby pulled a face. "Not really. She is, she *was*, my mom's friend, not mine, although I've seen her plenty of times. I wouldn't say we shared any heart-to-hearts. I couldn't tell you her favorite color but I can tell you she and my mom liked to go to the theater together and they've been playing tennis for years."

"Would you know if anyone threatened her?"

"Maybe. My mom would have told me if there was something she was worried about, but she hasn't said anything like that. Do you think someone hurt Fiona deliberately?"

I resisted asking the question of what she thought a bullet hole in the head meant. Instead I said, "We're trying to cover all the bases."

"I thought there was a burglary? Mom said Fiona's house was torn apart."

"Yes, that's our most plausible theory."

"It's so terrible," she said with a shake of her head that sent her hair flying around her shoulders. "I was so shocked when Mom told me. I could never imagine something like that happening to Fiona. She was always so nice and to think she died so horribly—" Debby broke down, sniffling. She grabbed a tissue from her pocket and dabbed her eyes. When she spoke again, her voice was calmer. "I've traveled all over the world and I always thought Montgomery was the most boring, but safe place."

I once thought the same thing, but recent years revealed that Montgomery might look nice on the surface—and a lot of Montgomery really was—but it had an underbelly that contaminated it. I'd had my fair share of tackling criminals who wanted to drag my city down, or simply didn't care about my hometown. I couldn't describe it as boring anymore, nor could I describe it as safe. But I also had to concede I was no longer an average citizen. I didn't stand in the path of crime; no, I fell headfirst into uncovering it. Sometimes, it seemed to follow me around.

"Can you tell me where you were yesterday between seven and eight PM?" I asked, whipping out my notepad and pen, ready to take notes.

"Is that when she died? Why are you asking me?" Debby's voice rose suspiciously.

"It's purely to ensure everyone I speak to is eliminated from further inquiries as fast as possible," I assured her. "Don't think anything of it."

"Okay, I, um, I picked up takeout from Dan's Deli at six-thirty and ate it in the park because it was a nice day. I left around seven and drove back here to the hotel. I think I returned here around seven-fifteen."

"Were you with anyone?"

"No, but I spoke to the server at the the deli and I called my dad from the park. I think I said hi to the concierge when I got back here. Oh, I came downstairs to get some more coffee for the room but I don't remember what time that was. Maybe seven-thirty?"

"That's great, thank you." I noted her answer and looked up. "So... traveling sounds amazing. Where did you go?" I adopted a more conversational tone designed to put Debby at ease as well as distracting her from the alibi she'd just given me. It wouldn't be too hard to corroborate her story and I planned to do just that later.

"First, I went to Canada. From there, I flew to Australia. I stayed there for six months, mostly in Sydney and then went to Hong Kong, Dubai, and from there, Europe. I took the train all over Europe. Portugal, Spain, France, England, France again, then Belgium, Germany, the Netherlands, Denmark. I visited Russia too. Eventually, I went to Italy, and finally Greece."

I was thunderstruck for a moment, thinking of all the places I had never seen except in books or on TV. "Did you work?"

"Yes, sometimes I did waitressing but I tried to work as an English tutor whenever I could. It wasn't great pay but I managed to get by. I always had plenty of students."

"What made you come back?"

"I just got homesick one day. I was sitting in a cafe, eating lunch, and I just started thinking of home and suddenly realized how long I'd been away. I booked a flight home as soon as I could."

"It must have been difficult moving your things each time?"

"Oh, no, not really. I always pack light. I don't really need too many things. I'm sorry," she said, checking her watch. "You were asking me about Fiona and I got sidetracked with my travel story. I don't think I've been very helpful. I wish I could have told you more." She looked away, her car keys jangling, and I could see she wanted to go. She was right; she really hadn't been very helpful when it came to Fiona. It was almost as if Fiona were little more than a stranger to her.

"I appreciate your time," I told her politely as I produced my card. "Would you call me if you think of anything more? Anything at all, even if it seems insignificant."

Debby looked at the card and tucked it into her coat pocket. "Sure will," she agreed. "Nice to meet you…"

"Lexi," I supplied.

I retreated to my own car as Debby took off for hers, which was parked only two rows over. I debated whether or not to follow her but decided against it. There was no reason to follow her just yet. Plus, she'd given me information I needed to verify back at the agency. I waited a few minutes for her car to clear the lot, then took the exit, my thoughts fixed on her travels abroad.

The last thing Debby told me was that she got homesick and I had to wonder how a person could travel for ten years, barely staying in contact with her family, and only get homesick a decade later. She either didn't suffer from it or just resisted the feeling. Had something terrible happened that drove her away from home? Something so awful that it made her determined to put thousands of miles between Montgomery and her? Perhaps a falling out with her family or possibly becoming the victim of a crime? Or did she meet a man that she'd gone to join abroad, a secret relationship that fell apart, making her too embarrassed or ashamed to return? Was it a doomed relationship that would never have been approved of by her family? I pushed aside that romantic notion and thought about it in reverse. Had something terrible happened abroad that caused Debby to hurriedly book a flight and return to safety?

By the time I walked into the office, dozens of thoughts about human traffickers, jilted lovers, witness protection plans, and international crime crossed my mind. Even I had to admit my imagination was well into overdrive with all the possibilities. One thing I was certain of, Debby reeled off the list of countries she visited in a way that sounded rehearsed, like she knew she would be questioned about it and needed a ready answer. It was so neat. Maybe too tidy. I dropped into my chair, another thought forming in my mind. Had Debby even left America? It would be easy to just say she went somewhere when she could have spent the past decade as nearby as the next town.

I frowned, trying to remember something Garrett told me. Ah, that was it! She sent postcards as well as emails. A postmark would be much harder to fake than an email. Unfortunately, I didn't see any postcards on display at the Pattersons' house, nor had Mrs. Patterson volunteered to show me. I had to ask Garrett if he had any copies. I wasn't sure how hospitable Mrs. Patterson would be to me again, especially now that she had the trauma of her friend's death to deal with.

Like most of my cases at the beginning, I had more questions than answers.

I waved hello to Delgado as I sat behind my desk. He was currently listening intently on the phone but he nodded in my direction. I extracted a legal pad from my drawer and quickly added my questions before I forgot them. Next, I called Garrett.

"Any updates?" I asked him.

"If you mean the Queller case, I'm looking at the initial reports of the crime scene," he said. "Jury's still out on the home invasion scenario. The husband said some credit cards were missing so I put a trace on those but nothing yet. Nothing else has been taken and there were a few items in view that could have easily been transported and sold. A digital camera was in the den where we found her, along with a couple of tablets and a laptop in the study."

"Were they marked in anyway?"

"No, the husband said they had an alarm system so they weren't worried about marking the electronics. It's a nice neighborhood. Low burglary rates too, until recently. Low crime in general. The alarm wasn't active because Fiona was home."

"Perhaps the thief knew those items would be too hot to fence?" I suggested.

"If that's the case, I don't think the cards will be used."

"Fiona could have startled the thief before he had a chance to take them."

"I thought about that too, but why not just grab them on the way out?"

I didn't have an answer for that. "How much cash was in the house?"

"The husband says a couple hundred dollars was lifted from the desk in the study. It's not enough to kill for."

"Drugs?" I wondered. "An addict might see it as plenty."

"Addicts aren't concerned with concealing fingerprints or DNA. I'm going to check in with Jord since he's working burglary and see if any of their cases have similarities to this one but I'm not holding out hope. Plus, the gun doesn't look like it was used in any previous crime. I ran the ballistics report and there are no matches. Despite trashing the house, I'm leaning towards pre-meditated murder."

"Any ideas who Fiona could have made an enemy of?" I asked.

"Not yet."

I switched topics since Garrett didn't have much to tell me. "I made contact with Debby Patterson this morning after I saw you," I said.

"Yeah?"

"I told her I was assisting on Fiona's case. I might have implied I was working with her family." I winced, waiting for the admonishment but none came.

"She open up to you?"

"Some. She had nice things to say about Fiona but nothing substantial. She said Fiona was her mom's friend, not hers, so she couldn't tell me much. She also told me a little bit about her travels. It might be nothing, but she reeled off the countries she visited like it was well-rehearsed or practiced."

"What do you mean?"

"Her answer was a little too perfect. I thought, what if she didn't leave the country at all and it's just some big lie? Then I remembered you said she sent postcards. I'd like to get a look at them."

"You want to know if they're real?" Garrett guessed. "I might have photocopies of a couple. I don't remember the dates or locations. It was too long ago."

"Okay, sounds good."

"What did Debby say about the murder?"

"Usual shock that something like that could have happened but she wasn't surprised since her mom had already told her. She mentioned burglary as a motive and said it was what she had been told."

"I'm going to interview her later. Wanna see if we can rattle her cage?"

"Sure do."

"I'll call you with the details. Keep looking for dirt on Debby."

"On it."

I knew Garrett had probably run all the usual searches on Debby when the case was initially filed, but he hadn't mentioned doing any recently. Of course, technology had changed significantly in the past ten years. Regardless of whether his information was ten years old, recent, or both, it didn't hurt to review them all again while I built my own file.

I started with the basics, gathering financial records and sending all the files to the printer. Phone records were difficult since I didn't have Debby's current number but I managed to retrieve a decade-old file for the number she used back then. Social media didn't turn up anything either. No Facebook, Twitter or Instagram.

Her high school and college didn't mention her name online but since other students of her graduating years were noted for their achievements, it seemed Debby didn't do anything remarkable. No sports, music, or academic awards.

An image search combining her name and the countries she visited or lived in turned up nothing, which I thought was odd. If I were traveling the world, seeing *La Sagrada Familia* in Barcelona one week and the Colosseum in Rome the next, I would certainly share my photos. Perhaps, I decided as I leaned back in my chair, I was suffering from an overenthusiastic urge to share like so many other people of my generation with access to a smartphone. But no record anywhere? Not even a crappy website that she could direct potential students to for her English lessons? It seemed Debby had successfully lived as far off the grid as possible.

I gathered the paperwork from the printer and stacked it on my desk, returning my attention to the databases on screen. I added another search, this time, looking for Debby's current records. While the searches were in progress, I took a cursory scan through the pages and pages of information I did amass.

Phone records showed that, ten years ago, Debby didn't make lots of phone calls. There were calls to her parents—with their home and cell numbers present and which were still the same, according to Garrett's file— her former employer's office, and several others that I couldn't identify. I highlighted the numbers and started calling them. Five were disconnected so I crossed through them, adding a question mark next to them. The final number picked up, and a man's voice answered, "Hello?"

"Hi, this is Lexi Graves from the Solomon Detective Agency. We're trying to track down an acquaintance of Debby Patterson."

"Debby? Wow. That's a name I haven't heard in a long time! Didn't she go missing?"

"That's right. Is this—" I scrambled for a name, picking one at random "—John?"

"No. This is Art Litt. Debby used to be one of my employees at Litmus Design."

I punched the air, grinning at my good luck. "Art. Yes, I'm so sorry I had the wrong name next to your number. Do you have a moment to talk? I'm looking into Debby's case as part of a cold case review and I'd like to ask you a few questions about her."

"Sure, I guess. What do you want to know?"

"How long did you employ Debby?"

"Around eighteen months. We hired her right out of college."

"What was your impression of her?"

"Quiet. Introverted. She kept her head down and worked hard. She was good, didn't cause much trouble. Not hugely talented but I think she could have improved in time."

I fixed on the words *much trouble*. Surely a good employee would have been no trouble? "Did she ever have any issues at work?"

"Not that I recall. Like I said, she was pretty quiet. Friendly but wouldn't say boo to a goose."

"Did she socialize much with anyone from work?"

"No, except a couple of Christmas parties and the very occasional drinks after work."

"Would you know if she made any enemies?"

"Yes, but I'm sure she didn't. We were a small firm, open plan office. Everyone could hear everything else. If there were any kind of bullying, I would have known about it and so would everyone else."

"So she didn't seem afraid or cautious of anyone?"

"No. You know, I wasn't really close with Debby but you could ask Kara. They sat together. She might remember a lot more than I can. Memory like a… what's the opposite of a fish?"

"Like an elephant?" I suggested and he laughed.

"Yeah, that's right."

"Do you know where I might find her?"

"Sure. I married her! She's not here now but if you're in Montgomery, you could come by or call and speak to her when she's home."

"I'm in Montgomery," I told him, "and that would be great."

CHAPTER SIX

Eating lunch by myself in the car, I kept reminiscing about the old working days and more pleasant ways of spending my lunch hours. Then I remembered my former career in temping, and all the passive-aggressive notes in the office refrigerator. I decided no, eating by myself in the car was just fine.

I finished the sandwich, wadded up the paper bag and tucked it inside my door pocket, intending to dispose of it later. After checking my teeth for any stray morsels of food, I started up the car and drove around the corner, heading to the address Art Litt gave me an hour before. He said both he and his wife would be home and I hoped between the two of them, they could recall more information about Debby. I knew it was a longshot to find people that remembered any details from so far back. What things would most people remember from ten years ago? For me, only the most significant events and not the minutiae of everyday life, or even former colleagues. However, a person's disappearance was significant and hopefully, that was enough to fix Debby somewhere in their heads. To some people, she would always be the girl that simply vanished. They might not remember the person who sat opposite her at work but perhaps someone might remember some other little details about her.

"You're the PI?" said the man who opened the door. He had short, gray hair, a week-old beard, and a developing paunch, but his smile was warm and welcoming. His t-shirt bore reference to a comedy show I liked and the jeans he had on were well-worn. He was the kind of person most people probably warmed to instantly.

"That's me," I said, producing my license and a business card.

"I thought you'd be older. More grizzled and seasoned."

"I get that a lot."

"I bet. Come in. We were both working in our home office. We freelance, you know."

"You don't own the firm anymore?" I asked.

"No. I started it because I thought I should. Although we made good money, my heart wasn't in managing a company. It's always been more about the work. Now my wife and I work together, so we can be more hands on; plus, I get to see the kids more often." He pointed to the photos of two grinning boys, around six or seven years old, framed on the wall.

"Twins?" I asked.

"No. Born a year apart but they'll like knowing that you asked that question. This is Kara," he said, guiding me into a room that housed two large workstations and a wall of cubed bookshelves. They were laden with paperwork, books and Transformers. A sofa was parked under the window next to a potted palm that had clearly outgrown its container. I didn't need to ask about the Transformers; I was sure they belonged to Art and not his sons.

"Hi," I said, lifting one hand in a half wave.

"Hi." Kara got up from her chair and walked over, reaching me in a couple of strides. She shook my hand, smiling. "We've been talking of nothing else except Debby since you called Art and he told me," she gushed. "Did you find out what happened to her? It was so awful when she disappeared. I hate thinking that her family never got any closure."

"Actually, we did. Debby is alive and well; claimed she suddenly got the itch to go traveling. She returned to town just last week."

"Really?" Kara looked more appalled than pleased. "I thought for sure someone had killed that poor girl. Take a seat," she offered, moving a large stack of magazines from the two-seater sofa. I perched uncomfortably on it while they resumed sitting in their padded office chairs, both swiveling around to face me.

"Fortunately, that doesn't seem to be the case."

"Seem?" asked Art and I realized I picked the wrong word.

"It's been a bizarre case," I told them, ignoring my slip-up. "Debby remained a cold case despite her parents receiving numerous emails and postcards over the years. Since her return, I've been hired to finally close the case."

"Okay. I'm not sure how I can help, but Kara…?" Art glanced toward his wife, slightly raising his eyebrows.

"Art said he told you I sat next to Debby while she was at the firm? I did for the whole time she was with us, but I'm not sure I can tell you anything about her. It was a long time ago." Kara glanced between us, suddenly appearing uncertain of what she would say next.

I gave her a warm smile. "What *can* you tell me?"

"Well, let's see." Kara leaned forward, her brows knitting together as she thought for a moment. "She was pretty shy and quiet. I got the impression she didn't have lots of friends but she was cordial enough. Always on time, and never had any problem staying late. She didn't complain about much either. I thought there might be some family trouble though."

"Such as?"

"It's probably nothing. I remember it because I thought it was sad and if I ever had kids, I wouldn't want to be like her parents. She said they weren't very interested in her. That is, they weren't interested in what she wanted, only what *they* wanted. They thought she should have become a doctor like her dad, or maybe a teacher like her mom, but she was more creative and not solely interested in academics. They were never very impressed with her achievements, only the things they could brag to their friends about. She said her parents' friends had very successful kids in all kinds of professions. I don't think it was all bad though. They were very generous at birthdays and Christmas but their work schedules kept them from attending her class performances or recitals back in elementary school and it never got much better."

"Sounds like you remember more than you thought you did."

"Yeah, I guess so. I remember that stuff because I thought it wasn't right. Parents should never pressure their kids to be something they're not. It's got to be a balance. In order to be productive, you need to be happy."

"Our boys are acing the happy part, but not so much the productive," added Art and they both laughed.

"Did Debby ever talk about traveling?"

"I think she mentioned wanting to go to Europe one day. Her parents took her there when she was younger, in her teens I think, and she wanted to go back one day and see more countries. I think she even mentioned taking a year off and traveling the world when she could afford to do it. Oh, that's it!" Kara's eyes widened. "I asked her if she could borrow money from her folks and she said she didn't want to. She wanted to save her own money for her own adventure. I liked the way she called it an *adventure*."

"Did she ever mention her desire to move there? Or any other country?"

"I don't think so but I can't say for certain."

"You said she'd been found?" said Art. "Why are you asking all these questions if she's okay? She is okay, isn't she?"

"She appears to be fine. We're just checking up on some background information before we close the case," I told him. Addressing Kara, I asked, "Was she friendly with anyone else at the firm?"

"She wasn't unfriendly, just a little shy. She talked to everyone else but we sat together so I guess we were friendliest."

"There was that time…" Art began.

"Oh, I know what you mean. That thing with the other girl who got hired before Debby?"

"What happened?" I asked.

"One of our original employees left and there was a good position to fill. Debby applied for it and so did the other girl. What was her name?"

"Tanya," supplied Kara.

"Yeah, Tanya. Tanya got the job and Debby was so pissed. She trash-talked Tanya in front of the whole office. I had to take her aside and tell her that wasn't cool."

"What kind of trash talk?"

"That Tanya wasn't a good employee and didn't deserve the promotion. Neither statement was true. Debby was talented but Tanya was just a better fit. Plus, she had worked for us almost a year longer than Debby and quite frankly, had earned it."

"What happened afterward?"

"Nothing. Debby promised it wouldn't happen again and I don't think anyone ever mentioned it after that."

"Do you know where I could find Tanya?"

"Sure. She married an English guy and moved to London three years ago. She's having a baby next month."

I eliminated Tanya from my suspect list. There was no way she was flying anywhere. "Aside from that, did you have any other problems with her?"

"I had to give her a warning once when she took off for a long weekend without telling anyone. I told her she had to put a leave request in. It wasn't a big deal though. I don't think I ever refused anyone leave," said Art.

"Art was always too soft to run a company," said Kara.

"True. Anyway, she said she just forgot and shrugged it off."

"What did the other employees think of her?"

"We all got on pretty well but I think there were the occasional comments about Debby getting a little too big for her boots, especially after the Tanya incident. They would get pissed when she got a coffee from the kitchen and didn't offer anyone else a cup," Art replied. "She was inconsiderate like that."

"It's so sad what happened," said Kara. She wrinkled her nose, her confusion etched on her face. "Actually, it was sad when we thought she disappeared, but I guess that's not the case anymore. I was starting a new job the week after she disappeared. She was supposed to come to my goodbye dinner the following week but she never showed up for work Monday morning."

"She mentioned she'd been getting headaches more often, so we thought she was sick and simply hadn't called in. Nobody worried about her for a couple of days," added Art.

"Was it unlike her not to call in?"

"We weren't exactly strict when it came to company policy, but she knew she was supposed to. I left her a message Monday afternoon and when she didn't call back by Wednesday, I called again, then again on Thursday and Friday. Like Kara said, she didn't show up for her party on Friday. We never saw her again. I just figured she'd taken off."

"We didn't even know she was officially missing for another couple of weeks," said Kara.

"By that time, I'd already fired her," said Art. "I felt so bad about that when the police came by and said she was a missing person. And now, you said she's okay, I don't know… I think I'm kinda pissed. We were worried sick about her for months and she just took off to go traveling?" He stopped and shook his head angrily, setting his jaw in a stiff line. Kara reached over and placed her hand over his.

"Did she miss any other planned meetings? Or contact anyone else to explain her absence?" I asked.

"We were supposed to meet for cocktails after work when I started my new job but after she didn't show for my dinner and wasn't answering any of my calls or texts, I didn't go. I don't know if she made it there or not. Art and I had just started dating too, so he told me what happened when the police came to speak to him."

"Did you leave the firm because you were dating?" I wondered.

Kara glanced at Art and smiled. "Ultimately, yes. We flirted for a long time until it became a case of: are we going to do this? I didn't want to work for my boyfriend because if it went wrong, it would be terribly awkward, so I found another job. In the end, I figured I couldn't find another Art."

"Did you speak to the police too?"

"Yes, but I couldn't tell them anymore than I'm telling you now."

"I really appreciate your time," I said, standing up and holding out my business card. "If you think of anything else that might be relevant, will you call me?"

"Sure. We're relieved to hear Debby is okay," said Kara as they showed me out. "I'm glad nothing terrible happened to her although I feel a little insulted that she cut me out of her life completely. I guess something serious was going on with her that none of us knew about if she felt she had to take off so abruptly without any word."

"I wonder why she didn't stay gone," added Art. "She didn't care enough about anyone here to let us know she was fine."

I apologized for not being able to comment on an ongoing case and left the warmth of their home behind. I would add them to the list of people still puzzled by Debby's sudden disappearance. I could also add them to another list: the one with people she hadn't contacted since her unannounced return. Perhaps it was embarrassment that held her back or maybe it was exactly what Garrett thought; if Debby were a different person, and an impostor, the fewer people from her old life she encountered, the better. But it still didn't explain why her parents were so adamant their daughter had truly returned.

Climbing into my car, I pondered what the Pattersons' motivation could be. Why would they accept an impostor? I felt more than sure that my parents wouldn't accept a fake me. They might briefly consider it, but I couldn't see that lasting more than ten seconds. "If you're not Debby, why would your parents want you?" I asked. I tapped my fingers on the steering wheel, wracking my mind for the possibilities. "One, they want something from you. Two, you're blackmailing them in some way. Three, they know what happened to the real Debby and you're helping them, willingly or unwillingly, to cover it up. Four, they're jerks. Five... I don't have five options!"

What I needed to do was wait for Garrett to confirm his interview. Perhaps then, I could extract some information from Debby before I approached her parents again. Surely, if they were complicit in the ruse, they would eventually slip up somewhere? I turned on the engine, firing the car to life. "What if they just don't know?" I asked the empty car as I drove to the next intersection and put the blinker on for a left turn. "Could they be short-sighted, hard of hearing, or just not very bright? Scratch that. Mr. Patterson is actually Dr. Patterson. His wife is a teacher. Neither of them are stupid but it has been ten years."

Ten years changes a person. Sometimes drastically. I remembered an old classmate of mine. High school Cindy Hathaway was quite overweight with frizzy hair and a terrible sense of style. Now she was running the Hot to Trot Travel Agency, and looked damn good in every way except for her appalling taste in sweaters. She was the perfect example of how someone could become unrecognizable in just a decade. Personally, I didn't think I changed too much except for a fun interlude as a blonde and my current aversion to the gym. Aside from that, the only thing that had really changed about me was a couple of wrinkles creeping around my eyes and a few small scars acquired through my PI work.

There was only one way to ask a mother's perspective: to throw myself straight into the fire pit. So instead of heading back to the agency, I pointed the car in the direction of my parents' house.

~

"Lexi, I wasn't expecting you." Mom said, looking furtively over her shoulder as I stepped into the house.

"What are you up to?" I asked, my suspicion immediately rising at her odd behavior. "Is it dangerous?"

Mom gave a shrill laugh. "What a strange question!"

I sniffed the air. Something acrid wafted nearby. "Is something burning?"

"No!"

"It is, isn't it? What are you doing?" I stepped past her, following the faint scent of smoke into the kitchen. The garden door was wide open and I heard voices outside. I stepped out and my mother immediately followed me into a circle of women sitting cross-legged on the ground. In the middle of them was a bucket. Inside it, something burned, the flames barely licking the rim of the bucket.

"We're performing a ritual," said Mom. "You remember Janel, Mary Jo, Ruthie, and Dee?"

"Absolutely," I said, wondering who was whom. I was fairly sure I'd met them all before and at multiple events but my parents had a lot of friends, not to mention, our huge family. Sometimes it was hard to remember everyone's names correctly. "Great to see you all again."

"Are you the one getting married the first time or the second?" asked a small woman with spiky, gray hair and pink tips.

"First time," I told her. Apparently, I wasn't the only one who couldn't work out who was whom. It was rare, however, that anyone mixed me up with my sister, Serena. For many years, Serena ruled as the golden child. Until I came along, she was the only girl in the family. Top grades, accomplishments in everything achievable, a scholarship to Harvard, and a terrific job. Her great job ended around the same time as her first marriage but she managed to pull through that difficult event and start her own business. She is also a fantastic single parent to her little girl, Victoria. I, however, chose a very different route in life.

The small woman turned to my mom. "Maybe she shouldn't be here."

"What *are* you doing?" I asked again. "What kind of ritual?"

The larger woman picked a photo off a stack of ephemera and trinkets in her lap and dropped it into the bucket. "A getting divorced ritual. I'm cleansing my life of all the toxicity infused by my ex-husband."

"Janel's husband is a total bastard," said the woman to her left. "He ran off with a twinkie called Loulah. She's a Hula-Hoop performer."

"What? That's a job?" I asked.

"That's what I said!" answered my mom. "Janel, I knew it wasn't a job."

"She Hula-Hooped Ed's wedding ring right off his damn finger," said the woman referred to as Janel. "And now they're hooping it up together. Good riddance!" She dropped a folded piece of paper into the bucket. The flames quickly consumed it.

"Not all married life is like that," said the small woman.

"Sometimes it's worse, Mary Jo," replied the other lady. "Sometimes they stay just to bore you to death."

"Your Carl bored himself to death," said Mary Jo, receiving a chorus of agreement from my mother and the other ladies.

"Solomon isn't boring," said Mom. "Lexi will never be bored."

"Thanks, Mom, for the vote of confidence."

"He's the one I told you about," she said to her friends.

Mary Jo's eyes widened. "The detective turned FBI agent with twinkling eyes and the sexy...?" she asked breathlessly.

Mom shook her head. "No, he's the one that got away. Solomon is the mysterious one."

"I like a man with one name," said Janel. She picked a small box from her pile of things and toyed with it. "Like Bono."

"He's nothing like Bono," I told her.

"Sting? Eminem? Prince?" she continued.

"No, no, and no."

"Seal?" All the ladies fanned themselves.

"No!"

"Liberace?" asked Mary Jo.

I pulled a face. "No! He has another name. John. John Solomon." I rolled my eyes at my mother, wondering what kind of hormonal hotbed of retired ladies I had mistakenly walked into. I didn't dare wonder what they'd been saying about Maddox.

There were some disapproving noises until I realized what Janel held in her hand. It looked suspiciously like a deodorant can. She took the cap off and sniffed it. "I can never smell this again," she proclaimed as she tossed it into the bucket.

I yelled, "No!"

They all looked at me like I had two heads. At first, nothing happened; then the flames caught hold of the pressurized canister and launched into the air with a boom! We all dived for cover.

Scrambling to my feet, I opened my mouth to admonish Janel for the explosion but Mary Jo beat me to it, saying, "Maybe you should only throw photos and letters into the fire?" They all mumbled their agreement and Janel dug into her pile before extracting two bottles of aftershave. She stacked them on one side as I breathed a long sigh of relief. With my fingers, I checked both my eyebrows to make sure they were still where they were supposed to be and relaxed.

"Can I borrow you for a moment, Mom?" I asked.

"Sure," said Mom without moving, her eyes still transfixed on the burning bucket. "Do you think I should get a bigger bucket?" she asked, glancing towards Janel before she dropped another photo into the fire.

"I think you should consider putting out the fire altogether," I said.

"No!" shouted Janel, stuffing several more items into the bucket. A plume of black smoke trailed upwards. "I must burn it all! Do you think I can fit his sweaters in here?"

"Why don't you return his sweaters to him?" I suggested, shrinking back as all the women's disapproving eyes fastened on me. "Mom?" I tugged her sleeve.

"Mmm-hmm?" replied my transfixed mom.

"If I disappeared for ten years, would you recognize me when I came back?"

This time, she looked at me with narrowed eyes. "Where are you going? And why? What are you involved in now?"

"Nowhere, I promise, but you would know me, wouldn't you?"

"Sure. I would know you anywhere."

"Even after ten years?"

"Absolutely. I knew it wasn't you when you were an hour old and the hospital gave me a different baby to nurse."

"What?" I squealed.

"Don't worry. I made sure they knew they gave me the wrong baby."

"How long did it take you to convince them?"

"Not long."

"But... but... how do I know you didn't take the wrong baby home?" My heart began to race, making my palms hot and sweaty as my breath quickened. What if I wasn't really me? What if the real Lexi Graves was out there leading a whole other life? We would have to meet each other. I would have different parents. What if Garrett, Daniel, Jord, and Serena weren't my true siblings? Would there be a TV drama? Most importantly, who would play me?

"Calm down," said Mom. "I knew you were born a girl and they gave me a boy. It was an easy mistake."

"That doesn't sound so easy. It sounds stupid and very worrying." But my heart rate did begin to slow.

"It was stupid but a mother knows her own baby and I would always know you."

"What if I disappeared for ten years and someone came back, pretending to be me?"

"Is she nice?" asked Mom.

"Um... probably."

"Smart, presentable, hard-working, helpful to her parents?"

I thought about Debby. She was stylish and had worked her way around the world. "Probably."

Mom cocked her head. "I might keep her."

"Mom!"

"Oh, fine." Mom rolled her eyes. "I would know if she weren't you. Why are you asking me weird questions?"

"Just curious. Would you tell anyone that I wasn't me?"

"I would tell the whole damn world if my daughter disappeared and someone was pretending to be her. Is that what you wanted to know?"

"That's exactly what I wanted to know." I stopped as a loud banging sounded from the front door. "I'll get it," I told her. "You make sure nothing else dangerous goes into that bucket. Maybe move the aftershave over, just in case?"

"Got it. What about the trunk?"

"What trunk?"

Mom pointed to a large case, bursting at the zippers. I couldn't fathom what was in it but felt reasonably sure it wouldn't fit into the bucket on the patio. I shook my head and she sighed. "I'll tell Janel," she said. "You get the door. If it's Ed, we aren't here."

I walked through the house, and the banging grew increasingly louder the closer I got to the front door. I pulled it open and the space instantly filled with several large firemen.

"We got reports of an explosion and fire burning," said the one at the front.

"In the garden," I said, pointing to the back of the house without further explanation. Oh boy, those ladies were about to get the thrill of their lives.

CHAPTER SEVEN

Garrett texted me that the meeting was arranged before I made it back to the office so I drove over to the station, parking on the street nearby. As I walked over, I sent him a text telling him I was on my way in. By the time I stepped through the doors in the lobby, he was waiting for me.

"I didn't think you would be here so fast," he said, crossing over to greet me. "Let's walk."

"Where are we going?"

"Interview room."

"Is Debby under arrest?"

"No. She's not here yet. She's coming by in ten minutes as a courtesy. Plus, I can't arrest her. I have nothing to charge her with. I'm not even sure she's involved except that her unexplained reappearance after a decade is damn strange and the dead woman is close to her parents. It could be just a coincidence."

"Fiona was adamant that Debby wasn't the real Debby." I clung to the theory but I knew that if there were a better motive, Garrett would jump on it. I didn't need to ask if he were rummaging through Fiona's life, trying to uncover any grudges or motives for killing her; I just knew he was searching.

"Which is why Debby has been invited here but I'm not approaching her from that angle." Garrett led us into a small room furnished with a table and three chairs. A large mirror almost covered one wall and we took the chairs that let us sit with our backs to it. I wondered if he planned on having anyone watching the interview via the two-way mirrored glass, and if so, who might it be?

"Are you planning on rattling her cage a bit?"

He gave me a tight smile. "Hope so."

"Why am I here?"

"I want you to be on her team."

"I don't follow."

"I'm going to be an ass and you need to stick up for her. She's going to see you as trustworthy and consider you an ally. Plus, we're establishing your cover as investigating Fiona's murder, not whatever Debby is up to. Or the faux Debby, if you will."

"So…" I smiled. "Good cop, bad cop?"

"You got it!" Garrett's phone beeped and he glanced at the screen. "She's here. Hold tight. I'll be back in a minute." He left the room and the door wide open. While I waited, I looked around, noticing the camera in the corner. I turned and stared at my reflection, wondering if someone was already standing in the room beyond, watching my back. Resisting the urge to stick out my tongue, I turned around just in time to see Garrett re-entering the room and Debby immediately behind him.

"This is Debby Patterson," he said, as if I didn't know. I half stood up and stuck out my hand.

"We met earlier," I told him, then I said to Debby, "It's nice to see you again."

"You're the PI Fiona's family hired," she said, shaking my hand but looking confused. "Why are you here?"

"Ms. Graves is assisting us with the case," Garrett told her.

"Isn't your name Graves too?" Debby asked, looking from me to my brother.

"Purely coincidence," said Garrett quickly.

"Oh, okay. What can I help you with?" Debby asked, apparently mollified by his quick statement. With the large age gap, it wasn't a stretch to assume we were not siblings; yet the difference was too small for us to be parent and child. Most people thought all my uncles and aunts had a roomy generation gap too. She took the seat Garrett held out for her before he came over to my side of the table.

"I understand your family is close to Fiona Queller's?"

"That's right."

"Can you tell me where you were between seven and eight PM yesterday?"

Debby glanced at me. "I already told Lexi. I picked up takeout and went to the park to eat it and then I went back to my hotel room."

"Can anyone verify your story?"

"Sure. The server at the restaurant and I called my dad. I'm sure the hotel employees will vouch for me too."

"You think your dad is a good alibi?" Garrett inquired dryly.

Debby frowned and opened her mouth to speak but I cut her off, ready to act the Good Cop. "Sounds like a solid alibi to me. Debby told me exactly the same earlier and I'm sure I can verify it."

"Hmph," grunted Garrett. He looked down at his pad and I almost missed the small, thankful smile she shot me. *Score one for Good Cop*, I thought as Garrett continued.

"You two get along?"

"Who?" asked Debby.

"You and the deceased?"

"Yes. She was a long-time friend of the family and I always found her pleasant."

"Never any arguments? Or bad words?"

"No."

I studied Debby's face, waiting for her to embellish the lie but it didn't come. With only Fiona to confirm their less-than-pleasant words, she probably felt capable of glossing over anything Fiona accused her of. If I didn't already know about their altercation, I wouldn't have suspected anything about Debby's answer.

"Seen her a lot over the years? Family functions, that sort of thing?" continued Garrett.

"Actually no. I've been working and traveling abroad just like I told your colleagues already. I came in for the interview last week to close that ludicrous missing persons case you opened for no reason."

"Fiona visit you often?"

"Why are you asking me that?"

Garrett slapped his hand on the table. "I'm asking the questions here!"

"Don't worry about him," I said to Debby. "He hasn't had enough coffee today."

Garrett shot me a dirty look. "You're here primarily as a courtesy to the family," he snapped, then addressing Debby, he said, "Answer the question please."

"No, she never visited me."

"Fiona keep in touch with you? Fill you in on what's happening at home? Tell you the neighborhood gossip? That sort of thing?"

"Actually, no. My mom mentioned her occasionally but until I saw Fiona last week, I hadn't laid eyes on her in a decade."

"What about her husband?"

"Jerry? No."

"You sure about that?"

"Yes, I'm sure."

"You've known him for a long time?"

"As long as my parents knew Fiona."

"He ever hit on you?"

"What?" shouted Debby at the same time as I frowned at Garrett. I wasn't sure where this conversation was going but I wished Garrett had filled me in prior to now. "No, he's never hit on me! Jerry was practically an uncle."

"Like an uncle who's about to come into a big inheritance and widowhood, with a young twinkie that caught his eye?"

"Did you just call me a twinkie?" gasped Debby.

"That bother you more than the idea your 'uncle'—" Garrett added air quotes while looking appalled "—bumped off his wife?"

"You're an ass," said Debby. "Jerry would never hurt Fiona and we definitely weren't having an affair or planning to run away together. I haven't seen him either in the past ten years."

I spotted my opportunity and jumped in. "Lieutenant Graves, you have no basis for this line of questioning."

"I gotta cover all the bases."

"You got it wrong," I told him sternly, "and I think you should apologize." Garrett glanced at Debby but said nothing so I continued, "I'm sorry, Debby. You came down here to help and now you have to put up with this. It's wrong, I know, but it's best we get it over with."

Debby sighed and shrugged. "I don't know what else I can tell you. Like I said, until last week, I hadn't seen either Fiona or Jerry in ten years. I can't imagine who would want to hurt Fiona but I'm sure her husband wouldn't have harmed a hair on her head."

"What makes you think that?"

"He held her hand."

Garrett knitted his brows together and I felt as confused as he did. "Huh?" he said.

"Last week," explained Debby. "They held hands when they left my parents' house. You don't do that after twenty years of marriage unless you really love someone. At least, that's what I think. So no, I don't think Jerry killed Fiona and I can't think of anyone else who would."

"What did your parents tell you about the Quellers while you were living abroad?" asked Garrett.

"Not much. I think Mom mentioned some dinner they were going to; and there was one time she said they were taking an anniversary trip to Rome. I remember that because I'd just finished working there before I left for Athens. Let me see, I think my mom might have told me they went to New York together to see some Broadway show and could have stayed the weekend."

"This over the phone?"

"No, by email. Time difference," Debby explained with a shrug.

"You still have those emails?"

"I don't think so. I changed the provider and lost some emails. I'm not good with modern technology."

"You never Skyped? Or used FaceTime?"

"What are they?"

"Seriously?" asked Garrett.

Debby's nostrils flared. "Yes, seriously."

"Video chats?"

"Oh, no! I haven't even mastered emails."

"So you said."

"What does any of this have to do with Fiona's murder?"

"We're interviewing everyone close to the family, building a picture of the deceased and her most intimate relationships," said Garrett, evading the answer. "You know their kids?"

"I did. I used to babysit the youngest but I guess she's in college now."

"All okay between her and her mom?"

Debby shrugged. "I wouldn't know."

Garrett flipped the sheet he was looking at and appeared to scan the next page. If he were genuinely reading from it, I didn't know. It might have been all for show, just like his lewd insinuations. "What did you talk about at that dinner last week?" he asked, circling around to the dinner again.

"It was a welcome home dinner, right?" I interjected and Debby nodded.

"My parents got a few friends together to welcome me home," she started. "It was a surprise."

"Who else attended?"

"My mom and dad, Fiona and Jerry. Our old neighbors, Sam and Elsa, and my grandma."

"No school friends of yours? Colleagues?"

"No, I'm sad to say I've lost touch."

"Must have been nice to see Grandma," said Garrett.

"It was. I just wish she still knew me. She has dementia, you know, and is losing her eyesight. She lives in Walnut View Retirement Home now that she needs full-time care."

"Expensive place," whistled Garret.

"My grandparents were well off and Grandma can afford it. Not that she knows it, I guess," said Debby. "My parents take care of all that."

"Can you remember any conversations with Fiona?" I asked, steering the discussion back to the main topic.

"Not really. She sat at the opposite end of the table. I wanted to sit beside my grandma."

"So Fiona didn't say anything out of the ordinary?" Garrett asked.

Once again, I studied Debby for any signs of a lie but there wasn't a single one when she replied, "Not that I recall."

"She mention anyone watching her house? Feeling like she was being followed?"

"No."

"Did she seem happy? Sad? Worried about anything?" he asked, and I knew he was trying to lure her into a candid response.

"Not worried. Happy, I guess. She made plans with my mom to play tennis. I think that was the same day she got killed."

He tapped his finger on the file. "That ties in with what it says here in the report."

"Listen, Lieutenant Graves, I want to help. I really do, but I've been away a long time and I just didn't know Fiona maybe as well as I should have. I don't know what else I can tell you. She was a nice person."

"She's right," I agreed. "It was really great of you to take the time to come here and help."

Garrett looked at her for a long minute but Debby didn't squirm at all. Instead, she simply stared back, barely blinking. "Thank you for your time," he said. "I'll walk you back to the lobby."

"Thanks for helping us," I added, shaking her hand again as we all stood. "I'm sorry for your loss."

"Thank you."

Garrett guided Debby out, one hand hovering over her shoulders, not friendly but definitely authoritative. He was back in under a minute. "What do you make of that?" he asked.

"Which part?"

"The lying part."

"Yeah, I wondered about that. Why didn't she bother to mention that Fiona told her she didn't believe she was Debby and wanted to know what kind of scam she was pulling?"

"I was thinking about the bit where she didn't know what Skype and FaceTime were? Even my kids know how to use them!"

"Grandma O'Shaughnessy uses Skype all the time," I added. We both shivered at the sound of her name.

"And she conveniently lost all her emails?" Garrett added, looking down at me. "Unless she deleted her account, I don't buy it. I wish there were some way someone could take a look at her emails but unfortunately, there is no way I can get a warrant." He gave me another very pointed look.

"Gotcha," I said, making a mental note to ask Lucas to hack Debby's email.

Garrett shrugged. "I don't know what you're talking about."

"Do you think Debby killed Fiona?"

"If she did, it must be to hide one helluva secret. Shame I'll never be able to read her emails to find out what it could be."

"Shame," I agreed.

"No, it's a *big* shame that…"

"Okay, I get the hint! I thought we were being smooth about this?"

"Don't know what you're talking about. Want to come with me to the Pattersons? Check out this alibi with her dad?"

"Definitely. Can I ride in your car and turn on the siren?" I asked hopefully.

"What are you? Five years old?"

I blinked back my disappointment. "So… no?"

"You can follow me."

"Fine. Where are we headed? Their house?"

"No. Rod Patterson has a clinic not far from here. Let's go hit him up."

I expected Dr. Patterson to be a general physician, but when we walked into the lobby of the tall building his surgery occupied, I could tell he wasn't just any old doctor. After riding the elevator to the sixth floor, we stepped out into a plush waiting room, and I realized Dr. Patterson was a specialist with an expensive set of patients. The wall behind the reception desk held large framed photos of him and two colleagues, men in white coats who were smiling.

"We need to speak with Dr. Patterson," said Garrett.

"He's with a client now, but I can schedule you an appointment for…" the receptionist scrolled her computer screen with a wireless mouse. "Eight months' time?" she asked with a joyous chirp.

"How about a much quicker appointment?" said Garrett. This time, he flashed his badge.

"Well, what do you know?" said the receptionist without hesitation. "An appointment just opened up in five minutes."

"Back there?" asked Garrett, stepping towards the glass doors separating the waiting area from the rear corridor.

"That's right but I really must ask you to wait until he's finished with his patient."

"Why?"

"Because Dr. Patterson is an IVF practitioner and I can't caution you about what you might walk in on," she said, still smiling. I bit back my laughter and curiously looked around. The adjacent wall was covered with photographs of smiling babies. Below that was a table scattered with thank you cards.

"Are all these babies the results of this practice?" I asked, nodding towards the wall.

The receptionist nodded. "Every one and plenty more. We just ran out of space."

"Dr. Patterson must be very successful."

"He's the best." A beep sounded from behind the desk and she glanced down. "He's free now. I'll walk you through."

"Thanks."

We followed the receptionist down the corridor and entered the furthest door on the left, stepping into a large, bright corner office. The walls were stuffed with medical journals and photos of more babies. Dr. Patterson sat behind a very old-looking desk, squinting through thin-rimmed glasses at his computer.

"Dr. Patterson, this is…" the receptionist started, then stopped, looking at us to fill in the blanks.

"Lieutenant Graves and my colleague, Lexi Graves," Garrett introduced us.

"Well, aren't you a fine-looking couple? This your first try?" he asked us.

"Pardon?" replied Garrett. Behind us, the door clicked shut.

"Your first attempt at IVF? I don't make promises, of course, but I can tell you I will do everything possible to get you pregnant," he said smiling from Garrett to me.

"No, that's okay," I said. "I don't think I want to be pregnant right now."

"She's my sister!" said Garrett, his voice rising.

"Okay, well, that's not recommended..." Dr. Patterson started, blinking as he took off his glasses.

"We're not here to have a baby! We're here on official business regarding the murder of Fiona Queller." Garrett flashed his badge again. Given Garrett's red face, I was pretty sure he wished he began with that.

"Oh, that makes sense. This would have been the first time in my career I would have found it necessary to give a certain talk."

"No need," said Garrett, cutting him off. "Absolutely no need at all."

"Please take a seat and excuse my error. You have great bone structure," he said to me as I sat down where he indicated.

"Thank you."

"Excellent hips."

"Thanks ag—"

"Fiona Queller," Garrett said loudly before Dr. Patterson contemplated anything else. I figured he saw all people through their baby-making potential so I didn't take any offense. Plus, he did say I had great bone structure.

"Yes, yes, Fiona. It's such a tragedy. My wife is terribly distraught. They were very close. How can I help?"

"We'd like to know where you were between seven and eight PM yesterday?"

"Where I was? Why? Am I under suspicion?" Dr. Patterson's eyes widened and he sat up a little straighter.

"Should you be?" asked Garrett.

"No! I was here at the office. Wading through a pile of paperwork that I had to get through."

"Can anyone verify that?"

"Probably the receptionist, Rhea, who let you in. She's taking the late shift this week. I saw some patients, too. The nurses, definitely, and I had a practice meeting at eight-thirty with the other two doctors who work here. Oh, and my daughter called too. We spoke on the phone."

"What time was that?"

"Around seven, I think. No, a little earlier. Six forty-five perhaps? I'm not sure how to check a call on my office phone but you're welcome to. Is that enough to establish an alibi?" Dr. Patterson asked.

"Yes, that's enough," agreed Garrett. "When was the last time you saw Fiona?"

"Around a week ago. She and her husband, Jerry, came over for dinner at my house. My wife saw her only yesterday, not long before she was killed. It's terrible, isn't it? I feel awful that I'm so relieved my wife came home instead of going to Fiona's house like she sometimes does. I don't know whether to feel responsible for saving my wife's life or terrible for leaving Fiona all on her own."

"Was there a reason for the change of plans?" I asked.

Dr. Patterson nodded. "I called my wife and asked her if she'd seen my keys to the clinic. I was supposed to be the last one in the office that night so I had to lock up and I couldn't find them anywhere. I called her after her tennis lesson and asked her to go home and see if I left them there. She and Fiona must have said goodbye at the club."

"Did your wife and Fiona often go to Fiona's house after a lesson?"

"Occasionally, or Fiona would come to ours."

"Is that common knowledge?"

"I don't know. It's certainly no secret."

"Who else could have known?"

"Aside from me? Jerry. Maybe their kids. Maybe a few friends at the club or someone who worked there. Like I said, it wasn't a big secret that Margaret and Fiona were close friends."

"So anyone close to Fiona could have reasonably thought she would have company that afternoon?" Garrett glanced at me and I gave him a thoughtful nod. If someone close to Fiona knew she would be having company, it was possible they wouldn't pick that night to attack. Overpowering one woman, especially one as active and fit as Fiona, would have been difficult. Overpowering two, significantly harder. Someone targeting Fiona, who knew her routine would wait for another time. That left the theory of a home invasion open again and I knew Garrett couldn't be happy about that.

"Yes."

"You mentioned your daughter called?" I asked.

"That's right."

"What did you speak about?"

"Not much. She called to say hi and that she picked up dinner and was talking a walk in the park. I asked her how her day went and she said it was fine. She mentioned looking at apartments."

"Did the conversation last long?"

"A couple of minutes. Why?"

"Do you often speak to your daughter on the phone?"

"No, not very often. Debby's like me. Not much for modern technology. No, actually she's even worse than me." Dr. Patterson laughed at that. "I can Skype if someone sets it up for me."

"Is she a doctor too?" asked Garrett, even though we both knew she wasn't.

"No, she didn't have the interest or the grades." Dr. Patterson shrugged. "She does a little teaching now."

"Nearby?"

"No, she's been teaching English abroad. She only returned home recently. Oh, you knew that, didn't you? I thought you looked familiar. You dropped by when Debby was making a statement down at the police station last week."

Garrett suddenly snapped his fingers, making me jump. "That's right," he said smoothly. "I thought I remembered your name from somewhere. Debby Patterson went missing a few years ago. *She's* your daughter?"

Dr. Patterson shifted uncomfortably in his seat. "It was all a big misunderstanding. Someone reported her missing when she actually went traveling and forgot to cancel the lease on her apartment. Nothing more to it than that."

"I heard she only just got back after being away for ten years. That's a long time to go without seeing your daughter."

"We're busy people and Debby was off the beaten track, finding herself. Some *Eat, Pray, Love* kinda thing. I don't know what gets into the heads of today's young people."

"You must be happy she's back," I said.

Dr. Patterson turned his gaze on me. "Very happy. The nose job was a surprise though."

"Nose job?"

"Debby had the cutest, little kink in her nose after she broke it when she was six," he said. He picked up a framed photo from his desk and passed it to me. I turned it over, looking at a studio shot of Dr. and Mrs. Patterson side by side, and a little girl in the middle. I could just make out a slight bump on Debby's nose. "I didn't realize she was so self-conscious about it. She said she had it done a few years ago," he explained. "Now that I think about it, Fiona mentioned it too but I asked her not to say anything to Debby. I didn't want her to feel embarrassed. There's nothing wrong with plastic surgery."

"Didn't Debby tell you about the surgery at the time?" asked Garrett.

"Too busy with her travels, she said. She didn't want to dwell on it." Dr. Patterson paused. "I don't know why her case wasn't closed years ago. Debby was never actually missing. She was just a bit lax about staying in contact. It was typical Debby though. Nothing more to it."

"Did you visit her while she was abroad?" Garrett asked.

"No, I'm not much of a flier. I get airsickness easily and my wife didn't want to go alone. Besides, Debby moved around a lot. It was hard to keep track of her, especially when we've got so much going on here." Dr. Patterson pointed to the bookshelf behind him. I'd already noted the numerous photos and newspaper cut-outs of awards and gala dinners. The Pattersons looked like very busy people. "I know the whole thing with Debby got blown out of proportion but we don't like to re-hash it. My wife and I are just thrilled to have our daughter home."

"I'm glad to hear that," said Garrett. "Back to the case at hand, can you think of anyone who might have wanted to harm Fiona? Perhaps she mentioned something at your dinner?"

Dr. Patterson shook his head firmly. "All I remember from her is pleasant small talk."

"No one had cross words with her?"

"No. There were only a few of us there. I would have heard if there had been any kind of disturbance."

"Was she pleased to see Debby too?"

"Yes, of course she was. She did tell us she thought Debby had stayed away too long and I remember her wondering why she returned now."

"Did Debby tell you why?"

"She said she was homesick."

"I see. Can you think of anyone at all who might have wanted to hurt Fiona? A disgruntled colleague? Someone she might have bothered in her personal life? Perhaps someone who was jealous of her?"

"Fiona was one of the the nicest people I knew. She was kind and generous. I can't think of a single person who might have hurt her. The sad truth is, someone broke into her house and murdered her. Given all the burglaries they've had in that area, I guess all the other victims are lucky they didn't walk into it like Fiona did. The sooner you catch that thief, the safer we'll all feel."

CHAPTER EIGHT

"I have a job for you." I stepped back and tried not to laugh as Lucas jumped in his chair and spun around.

"You scared the shit outta me!" he gasped. Running a hand over his tangled, blonde, surfer hair, he sucked in a breath. "Where did you come from? And why the hell did you sneak up on me?"

Holding back a smile at his obvious distress, I answered honestly, "To see if I could."

"I will so get you back for this!"

"Can you exact your revenge after you've done the job I need you to do?"

"Need? Or want?"

"Need," I pleaded. "You're the best, Lucas. No one else can do this job except you."

He perked up. "Really? Lay it on me."

"I need you to hack some emails."

His face fell. "Anyone can do that."

"Yeah? Not me."

"Give me the information and I'll get you what you need. Does it require cracking multiple layers of encryption?"

"I doubt it. It's for someone purporting to be technologically backward so it'll probably be easy." I wrote Debby's full name on a slip of paper along with the email address I gleaned from Garrett's file and passed it to Lucas.

"What are you looking for?"

"No idea yet."

"I will call you when I have something."

"You're truly the best."

"Say it again."

"You're the best."

"I know. I love hearing it."

"Where's the boss?"

Lucas gulped, pale terror passing across his face. "You don't know?"

"No. Do you?" My heart thumped. What hadn't Solomon told me?

"Nope," said Lucas, his eyes widening with guilt. He spun around. I gripped the back of his chair and spun him back. "Yes, you do," I told him. "What's going on?"

"Gotcha! He was in his office last I saw." Lucas laughed at my panic-stricken expression and stuck out his tongue. Apparently, I didn't have to wait long for him to exact his revenge.

"Very funny!" I cuffed him gently on the back of his head as I left his desk and took the stairs down, walking into my own shared office space. Solomon, just as Lucas said, was in his office but he wasn't alone. I managed to glimpse another figure so I guessed he might have been meeting a client.

Sitting down at my desk, I reached for the stack of paperwork I left to peruse another time, that time being now.

Debby's old bank records weren't very interesting to read. Ten years ago, she lived a fairly frugal lifestyle, spending her money primarily on her rent, utilities, and food. There was the occasional charge at a book shop, a weekly yoga studio fee and a smattering of small checks for restaurants and bars. I expected to see a student loan payment but there wasn't one, which made me wonder if her parents were covering her college fees.

One thing that puzzled me was the lack of any transfers to a savings account. As I scrolled through the pages, there were none at all. Surely Debby had to have some kind of savings to allow her to pursue her travels until she could work? If she did, I couldn't find it in her bank records. Nor could I find any significant cash withdrawals that suggested she made cash deposits into another account. I turned the pages, looking for a savings account that she had ceased depositing anything into while hoping to find some withdrawals directly from it.

I struck lucky with the last few pages. There was a savings account totaling four thousand dollars and some change but she had stopped paying into it by the time she left college. Judging by the sporadic amounts, which were concentrated around vacation periods, I figured it had to be money from seasonal work. It made sense that once she was in the "real world," she was more focused on paying her bills than on padding her savings. But that didn't explain why she couldn't build up a more significant nest egg before disappearing. A worldwide adventure takes more planning. I scanned to the end of the savings account records, noting the account had remained dormant since the last deposit, eleven years before. It didn't explain why she never used that money either.

Pulling my stapler from the drawer, I attached the bank accounts together before slipping them into the manila file I created for every client.

Next, I turned to the most recent records. In the past month, Debby hadn't opened a new bank account. My search didn't uncover any lay-away purchases or car payments although she was making a payment to a car rental firm, something I already guessed due to the sticker on the back of the car she currently drove. One phone call later confirmed it was a cash payment. There were no investment plans but I didn't expect to see any. I also couldn't see any income. Debby didn't appear to have any income at all, yet she must have been paying for the hotel somehow. I wondered if the money came from her English teaching jobs. What did she plan to do to earn money? How did she intend to support herself after returning to her former life in Montgomery?

Stapling the recent financial searches together, I rocked back in my chair, staring at the rows of numbers. It struck me that Debby didn't seem to be the type who planned anything. She left without a strategy and apparently, returned without one. I wasn't sure how that matched up with my notes of Debby as a diligent college student, a committed employee—despite the two incidents mentioned by the Litts—and a person with an apartment lease! It did, however, match her parents' assertions that Debby took off without warning sometimes, which was why they hadn't worried initially.

Debby was like two different people, two personalities in one body, each of them fighting with and contradicting the other. Was one side of Debby wild and free while the other side sought stability and security? Perhaps she grew tired of her own clashing expectations of herself while simultaneously disappointing her parents over her academic and career choices. I flipped the page on my pad and made two lists, one for each side of Debby, adding all the personality quirks I could recall.

Dropping my pen, I looked at the pad, frowning. I could see why Garrett was so puzzled. I glanced over toward Solomon's office and saw he was still deep in conversation, so I picked up my phone and called Garrett.

"I'm stumped," I told him.

"Mom and Dad always told you to eat more vegetables when you were a kid."

"Not that kind of stumped. On this case. It's like there are two Debbies."

"That's what I've been telling you!"

"No, I mean, it's like she has two sides to her personality. She vanished even though she signed a lease on her apartment. She took off on an adventure but never touched her money. She turned up, even though she was living abroad. I don't get it. Is there a history of mental illness?"

"No, none."

"Oh. Well, scratch that theory."

"We looked into the idea of her having a mental breakdown when she first disappeared but there was no history of depression or psychosis. We subpoenaed the medical and insurance records. She wasn't receiving any kind of treatment and there was no history of mental health issues in the family."

"I don't remember seeing that in the file."

"It's in there somewhere. Or maybe it's in the box I pulled from storage."

"I'll let you know if I don't find it. Where are you with Fiona Queller's case?"

Garrett sighed. "Going nowhere fast. None of the neighbors saw a thing. Nothing unusual in the neighborhood that day or any other day. No suspicious cars hanging around or people. No one heard any threats or saw anyone harassing Fiona. Her husband corroborates that."

"What about the other break-ins in the area?"

"Jord is digging into that but he doesn't recall responding to anything on that street in the last few months."

"What about violent burglaries?" I asked.

"In the area?"

"Anywhere in Montgomery?"

"I heard about a guy getting stabbed to death in Frederickstown but he had a meth lab. There was a fight with a homeowner in West Montgomery but that turned out to be a sleepwalker in the wrong house. I remember one case about a woman whose house was broken into by a maniac who tried to shoot her…"

"Yeah, that was me," I said, cutting him off. And one night I preferred not to remember.

"A lot of violent crime in Mongomery is linked to you. Anyway, if you're asking if anyone else was killed in a burglary-gone-wrong, the answer is no and there haven't been any other violent burglaries in the past six months and only a few months before that."

"Maybe someone's lying low?"

"If I remember correctly, that perp was caught and is now doing seven years upstate."

"An accomplice?"

"Not getting that feeling."

"So we're back to the idea someone murdered her."

"A hit?"

"In Montgomery?" I thought of all the weird things that had happened in town and wondered why he was asking that question.

"Forget I asked," Garrett continued. "She was a homemaker, not a public figure. I'm not sensing any violent acts of passion either. Her husband had to be sedated. I've never seen a guy like that."

"Could he be covering up?"

"It's possible, but I don't think so. I've been looking into their background and they seemed to have a damn good marriage. House nearly paid off, two kids in college, nice cars, and vacation twice a year. Fiona didn't have to work. Her husband was a tax attorney. Country club membership. Regular date night every Wednesday. Neighbors only had nice things to say about them. The kids said their parents loved each other."

"Could they be too perfect?" I wondered.

"I'm not getting that vibe."

I sighed. "It sounds like they had a good thing going."

"Yeah, well, someone didn't like Fiona. I've got a lot of interviews to do while we wait on the forensic reports from the house."

"Any sign of the gun?"

"Nope. I've got no motive, no gun, and nothing to tie anyone to the murder. I don't suppose you called with any good news?"

"Let's see... no."

"Any chance you can babysit soon?" Garrett asked, changing the subject. "I want to take Traci out."

"I think I can."

"Cool. Chloe wants to talk about weddings with you. She's very excited."

"I'll bring all my bridal magazines."

"And be prepared to watch *Say Yes to the Dress*."

"I am prepared."

"Are you also prepared to discuss every single dress?"

After thinking about it, I decided I could use some help. "I might bring Lily too."

"Great, between a new baby cousin and wedding dress overload, Chloe is going to burst! If she mentions boys, you shut that conversation down. Got it?"

"Yep," I said, not entirely sure what I was agreeing to.

"Alternatively, the kids might agree to watch *Star Wars*. Call me when you get something on Debby."

I agreed I would and hung up, wondering if I should be as excited about wedding planning as my niece. I hadn't given a lot of thought to it since our engagement party a couple of weeks ago. My sister, recently engaged too, had given a lot of thought to it but she had the experience of a previous wedding under her belt, as well as a desire to make things perfect for both her future husband and her. I had no doubt she had already selected her venue for both the ceremony and the reception, honed down her list of welcome cocktails, taken audition tapes for DJs and bands, sampled menus, and booked appointments at every single Montgomery bridal salon. All before I'd even discussed with Solomon the options and themes for our wedding.

The door to Solomon's office opened and my mother stepped out. "Hi!" She waved.

I frowned, looking from her to Solomon but I rose and walked over to greet her. "Hi, Mom. What's going on?"

"Can't a mother just drop in to visit her future son-in-law?"

I opened my mouth to say *not without a reason* but decided against it. I'd prefer to know what the reason was first. "That's so nice," I said.

"I know. I brought these," said Mom, handing me three thick, three-ringed binders. My knees almost buckled with the weight. "They're organized into churches, from large to small, depending on numbers. Then reception venues starting with informal to formal. After that are the decor ideas with fifty-two different themes."

"Fifty-two?" I whispered in disbelief.

"Seventeen are romance-oriented," Mom explained. "There're all the categories: food, beverages, florists within a fifteen-mile radius; and I think you'll be very excited about the man who makes sculptures out of balloons!"

"So excited!" I squeaked.

"That's the first binder. The second is very exciting. That covers music selections with all the top choices over the past twenty years, and a review of each one of your relative's weddings, including your siblings and all their suppliers. We didn't include Daniel's first wedding because I like to pretend that didn't happen."

"What about Serena's?" I wondered out loud.

Mom frowned before reaching for the binder. She rifled through it and tore out a page. "Let's pretend that one didn't happen either. Did you see Lexi's bridesmaid dress, John? Didn't she look pretty?"

"Very," said Solomon, firmly eyeing me and not the binder that she dumped into his hands.

"You will love the third binder." Mom took the remaining two binders from me and dropped one on my desk before she opened the other. "There're ten years of bridal gowns divided into ballgown, mermaid, trumpet, strapless... You'll see! I think you'll find it very useful."

I reached for the edge of my desk, gripping hard before my knees gave out and I sank to the ground.

"Your father and I would like to pay for your dress because we're very, *very* relieved that you're getting married. At last! To a man." My mother neatly stacked all three binders and placed them in my hands, wrapping her arms around me in a bear hug. Then she kissed my cheek and waved as she walked past. "Did I mention I'm taking a class in wedding planning at the Adult Ed center? I'm going to be your dream planner!" The door banged shut.

"Did she leave?" I whispered.

"Did you say something? I can't see your face," said Solomon.

"Don't laugh, please don't," I wailed, launching the binders in what I hoped was his direction. "Why me? Why?"

"Your mom means well."

"She just said she was relieved I was marrying a man!"

Solomon raised his eyebrows. "Aren't you?"

I looked at Solomon, adoring his handsome face, deep brown eyes, clean-shaven jaw, and a physique that made me forget his question. "Hubba-hmph, what?" I mumbled.

"When you look at me like that, I want to do unprofessional things with you in the office."

"Okay," I gasped.

"But I won't because I'm a professional. Also, because I don't know how I would explain it to anyone if they walked in and saw you and me draped across your desk."

"You're the boss. Call it a rigorous assessment!"

Solomon smiled broadly. "Good to know you're already thinking of a plausible reason." He paused, then asked, "Rigorous?"

"What were you and my mom talking about?" I asked, distracted by the array of binders. How had my mother amassed so much information?

"Our wedding."

"Do I want to know more?"

"Your mom came by expecting to find you here and since you weren't and I was, I kept her company. She is very excited about the wedding and wants to be involved. I think it would be nice for her to help."

"Does nice mean scary to you?"

Solomon smiled. "Let her be involved."

"I'm not *not* letting her," I pointed out. Solomon deposited the binders on my desk and we both edged away. "*We* haven't even talked about our wedding."

"You want to talk about it now?"

"I want to talk about it sometime. Maybe not *now*. This is the office."

"Who's being a professional now?" asked Solomon, still smiling. "Take a look at the binders. Maybe you'll find some inspiration. I can give you any kind of wedding you choose, you just have to decide what."

"*We* have to decide," I corrected. "I am not turning into a bridezilla! Oh! Did Mom offer to buy me a dress?"

"She did."

I paused, and smiled up at him. "We're really getting married?"

"Yes."

"I'll look through the binders," I told him. "I'll take them home tonight. It'll be a pleasant distraction from this case."

"I have to see a client but I will join you later. We can resume our discussion at home." Solomon leaned in, kissing me lightly. "Take it easy. It might be a rigorous evening."

I was smiling as he left and I returned to my desk. Ten frustrating minutes later, I had to admit my tolerance for Debby's records was gone. Without Debby's emails to peruse, I didn't have a lot left to examine. Now I had some background, but what I needed to know was more about Debby now. What was she doing in Montgomery when she wasn't with her parents? Whom was she seeing? Where did she go?

I tucked my laptop away into my desk drawer, extracting the zoom lens camera I stored there, packing it into my purse. I hoisted the binders into my arms. Carrying my load, I struggled downstairs to the parking lot and tossed the binders onto the floor. It was time to stake out Debby.

Since I hadn't stuck any tracer on Debby or her car, I started with the place I guessed she'd most likely be: her hotel.

After a short cruise around the lot, I found her car and parked next to it. I hopped out, placing the back of my hand on the hood. It was cold, telling me she had been parked there for some time. Unless she got a cab or a ride somewhere else, she still had to be in the hotel. I just wished I knew where.

Hopping back into my car, I tapped the hotel name into my phone's web browser and called up its contact information. I hit the link for the phone number and waited for the call to be picked up. "This is the Montgomery Hotel and Conference Center. How may I help you?" asked the receptionist.

"Hi, this is Blooming Flowers. We have a delivery to go to, uh, let me see—" I paused as if I were reading an order "—yes, here it is. Debby Patterson. I'm just checking we have the correct address for delivery. I have it down for the Montgomery Hotel and the room number is, oh, it's, um, let's see…"

"Room 324?" supplied the receptionist.

"That's right! Room 324. We'll attempt to make delivery tomorrow."

"Just come in the front door," said the receptionist. "Thank you for calling."

"No, thank you," I said as I hung up, smiling.

Previous experience of the overall layout told me room 324 was at the rear of the hotel. I fired up my car and drove around the hotel to the side lot. Parking up in the far corner, I had a good view of the back and almost certain privacy.

I grabbed my camera and zoomed into the third floor, tracking each window until I narrowed it down to one of four. Two rooms were empty, and housekeeping would be pissed at the condition of the second room. The third window showed a lady working at a desk and the fourth was the jackpot. I watched Debby moving across the room, a hand pressed to her ear. No, not a hand: a hand holding a phone. I watched her mouth moving and wished I could read lips. A couple of minutes later, she hung up and tossed the phone on the bed before picking up a magazine and curling up on a big armchair.

I zoomed in a little closer and saw she was reading a travel magazine. Was that where she got her travel bug? Or the true source of her travel stories? As I thought about those possibilities, I wondered how to verify her travel itinerary. With over a decade of information and no sources in the travel industry, I wasn't sure I could. I knew one thing: Debby never even once touched her credit cards or dipped into her savings from any foreign location. There had to be another account somewhere; maybe she set up a new one in another country. I wondered how easy it would be to set up an account abroad.

For more than two hours, I stayed in position, despite the light dimming as I waited for Debby to do something more interesting than reading another magazine, using the bathroom, or making a coffee. A tap at my window made me jump and swallow hard. I glanced at the torso filling my passenger window and scrambled for a cover story that didn't involve explaining why I was surveilling a target. Fearing it was hotel security, I nearly gasped when suddenly the body stooped, and a head came into view. I clasped a hand to my rapidly beating heart.

Then, smiling with relief, I lifted the locks on the car.

"You started locking the car," said Maddox, climbing in. He smiled warmly and leaned over to hug me, a waft of his familiar cologne teasing my senses.

"Hello to you too!"

"Do I want to know what you're doing?" he asked, nodding toward my camera.

"Nope. Not asking you either," I said, waving a finger at his own camera. "I thought you were out of town?"

"I was supposed to be but my plans changed and the assignment I was expecting to tackle was slightly postponed."

"So, here we are. Just two people hanging out in a deserted parking lot for no reason."

Maddox grinned. "You got it!"

"I'm watching room 324," I confessed. "She's presently reading a magazine."

"What happened? Did you pull the short straw in your caseload at work this week?" he wondered.

"Nope. This is a strange one."

"Anything to do with that murder over in Harbridge?"

I didn't have to ask which one he meant; there was only one. "Actually, yes."

He huffed a laugh. "I knew you had to be involved!"

"It might be a coincidence but... Wait! Are you following me?"

"No!" Maddox shifted his feet on the floorboard and picked up one of my mom's binders. He opened it before I could snatch it from his hands and hurl it out of the car. "Nice dresses. Didn't ever imagine you in this," he said, turning the binder so I could see the page he opened it to. A white dress, slashed to the navel, looked like it was glued onto the model's lithe body.

"That's my mom's! See the big 'no' written next to it?"

"Ah, I see." Maddox turned the page, his eyebrows rising. "Is your mom renewing her vows?"

"No, she's trying to plan *my* wedding."

"Interesting choices," he said, tapping his finger over a terrifyingly daring dress apparently constructed from all the lace ever made, and featuring visible shoulder pads.

"I think that's another 'don't pick'," I told him, feeling somewhat hopeful.

"I want to agree with you but there's a question mark next to it. I think it's still in the running. Speaking of running…"

"I'm not becoming a runaway bride!"

Maddox bit back a laugh. "I was not going to suggest that but if your mom tries to make you wear this, I will aid in your getaway."

"Do you promise?"

He made a cross over his body. "Absolutely."

A thought popped into my head. "Could you find out someone's past travel itinerary? Airplanes, trains, hotels, that kind of thing?" I asked.

"I can find out if someone sneezed seven years ago in Bogota," he said.

"Weird. I just need to know if my target was where she says she was. She says she traveled a lot over the past ten years and I need to verify it."

"Do you have her passport information?"

"No." *Not yet.*

"Give me her name and date of birth and I'll look into it."

I reached for my notepad and wrote down the information. "What would I ever do without you?" I asked him as I handed it over.

"Pray you never have to find out."

"Anything I can help you with?" I asked. My curiosity niggled at me and I was dying to know what really brought Maddox *and a camera* to the hotel.

"Too dangerous to divulge," he said.

"Since when did you become the man of mystery?"

"You'll never know," he said as he winked. He leaned over and kissed my cheek, then got out the car without a backward look.

I watched him in the rearview mirror and seconds later, lost him. If he still remained in the parking lot, I couldn't find him. I had no idea if he even watched me when I picked up my camera and checked in on Debby again. I observed her a little longer until she closed the curtains and turned out the light. With dusk falling and the moon already high in the sky, I figured she'd gone to sleep. Feeling disheartened at her lack of criminal activity, I went home, ready and willing to cocoon myself in my own bed.

CHAPTER NINE

I slipped out of the house at dawn, cursing that I had to slide out of my warm bed where a sleepy Solomon was running hot. My plan was to catch Debby as soon as she left the hotel so I could spend the day following her. I needed to find out what she did with her time but first, I wanted to make a few checks into her alibi.

Another thought crossed my mind while I was getting dressed. Though Debby said she only returned because she was homesick, I needed to know if there were another reason. Not only that, but what did she expect to find here? It was hardly as glamorous as the French Riviera, and sadly lacking the history of Italy, or the cuisine of Greece. If she were truly homesick, she could have stopped in for a visit of days or even weeks but with the apartment hunting Debby showed every intention of staying here. Something must have attracted her and I had to know what it could be.

Debby said she picked up takeout from Dan's Deli and took it to Fairmount Park at six-thirty. Armed with the restaurant name, I parked on the same block and hopped out, looking around. No surveillance cameras could be seen on the street but luck was working in my favor today. The restaurant was open for breakfast, but thankfully hadn't any queue yet for coffee, pastries, and other tasty items from the hot counter. I grabbed a sugary raspberry pastry and an apple (just to be healthy), taking both to the counter before ordering a coffee.

Behind the counter, I spotted a small camera mounted above the door to the back room.

"Can I get you anything else?" asked the cheerful clerk as she rang up my items.

"I hope so. A friend of mine came in a few days ago to pick up some food to go and she went to the park but she got the feeling someone was following her; and she's a little freaked out," I lied smoothly. The clerk's jaw dropped, and she seemed slightly appalled. "She mentioned you had a camera and asked me if I could find it in the records? She's been a nervous wreck since it happened," I added, laying it on thick.

"That's awful. The camera doesn't record but maybe I'll remember her. When did your friend come in?"

"Two days ago, around six-thirty," I said, describing Debby.

"I was working that shift and I do remember her. Let me see," she started, wrinkling her nose. "She ordered the chicken special and fries and I think she got a Coke too. She wore a trench coat and had a tan leather purse."

"That's her. Great memory!"

"Thank you. I don't remember anyone else hanging around. We get a lot of workers usually between five-thirty and six and then it gets a little quieter until seven. I think I remember a mom coming in with two kids but that doesn't sound like any stalker."

I agreed it didn't and thanked her kindly for her time. Two parts of Debby's alibi held up. That didn't mean she actually ate in the park, even though her dad said she called him from there. She could have been calling from anywhere.

Taking out my coffee and snacks, I left the shop and walked in the direction of the park, reaching it only minutes later. A couple of years ago, the city added surveillance cameras to the park, perching them atop street lamps. I had no idea where Debby would have been sitting to eat, but I figured if she drove there, she probably wouldn't have strayed too far from her parking space. It made sense that she would have parked near where she picked up the food.

I sent a text to Lucas asking if he could find any sign of Debby being in the park in the region where I now stood. If she were caught on film, there would be almost no way she could have left the park, gotten across town, and murdered Fiona.

Almost immediately, a text pinged back. *Issue with city cameras over last two days. Film not recording.*

"Just great," I said to the air. That might have worked in Debby's favor if she were the true killer but the timing didn't jive. I knew where she was at six-thirty. If the hotel confirmed she returned there at seven-fifteen, then stopping by Harbridge just to turn over a house and murder its owner was too tight a time frame.

Turning away from Fairmount Park, I walked back to my car and headed over to the hotel. I parked and thought hard about how to get the hotel staff to turn over Debby's check-in time. Finally, after finishing my pastry, I hit on an idea.

"Montgomery Hotel and Conference Center," reeled off the bored-sounding receptionist.

"Yes, hello. I have a complaint," I yelled in a nasal-toned voice. "I think one of your guests scraped my car and I'm really mad! My husband is outraged. I'm going to sue her."

"What makes you think it was one of our guests, ma'am?"

"It happened in your parking lot! Her name was Debby something. I know because I saw her name on an envelope inside the car," I yelled. "She drives a rental car and her driving is *bad*. I might sue you too!"

"When did this happen?"

"Let me see," I squawked before answering the day and time. "Unless you can tell me that she wasn't there by some miracle then I demand you give me all of her information for my insurance!"

"We do have a guest with that first name but I can assure you she checked into her room at seven-fifteen and one of my colleagues spoke with her at seven-thirty. She couldn't possibly have been in the parking lot at the time you say."

"My mistake," I yelled. "I should wear my driving glasses." I hung up and tried not to giggle at the atrocious voice I managed to put on. I even felt pity for the poor concierge who had to start his day with an angry woman yelling at him. It was well worth it; Debby's alibi was confirmed every step of the way.

With my coffee cup almost empty and the remaining liquid cold, I checked my watch, wondering who else was likely to be awake at this hour, but not rushing to get to work or take care of kids. I knew one kid that couldn't walk yet. *Are you awake?* I typed before tapping send.

Always, came Lily's immediate reply. *Sleep is for the weak.*

How's Poppy?

She's the only person in the world who gets praised for pooping on me.

I didn't know how to reply to that so I was relieved when Lily sent another text. *Motherhood is boring. I love it but no one says how boring it is. Or how much you miss sleeping. I need to do something for me.*

Meet me later. Bring the baby.

Cool. Who are we stalking?

No one. I'll take a break.

You used to involve me. I feel so left out.

I'm sorry!

Seriously, I will do anything. I can be the mom with a baby no one ever looks at. It's the perfect cover.

Tapping my phone against my chin, I was thinking of something for Lily to do, something that would make her feel involved, but I came up with nothing. It was a shame because Lily was very committed to helping me. She never complained about staking out houses, breaking in when necessary, questioning or running interference with suspects, and was particularly enthusiastic when it came to disguises. Now that I thought about it, I felt her absence more acutely. I knew life changed for all new mothers but I never realized how much it would change my life. It was a selfish thought but I couldn't deny the pang I felt in missing my best friend now she had a new favorite lady in her life.

I will think of something, I typed. Then I decided to pump her ego with *I need your expert skills.*

I waited a long five minutes for an answer. Finally, the phone beeped. *Poppy is sleeping. I will call you after I've had a nap.*

I smiled, grateful for more time to think of how Lily could help me. I was sure I could figure out something for her to do, even if it were something to distract Lily, rather than actually helping me.

By the time Debby appeared a few minutes before nine, passing through the hotel doors and belting her coat around her middle as she pulled the car keys from her pocket, I had already checked my emails, read the weather report, browsed the nation's headlines and scanned the local news report. I also booked a manicure, checked out the menu of a new restaurant and browsed multiple cabin listings on Lake Pierce. In my quiet desperation, I was looking for any way to kill my time. What I needed most was a good breakfast but in my eagerness to get out of the house at an early hour, I forgot to bring any and the morning's pastry had only served to pique my hunger. I could only hope Debby was heading somewhere that I could pick up a quick snack.

I watched her crossing over to her car and getting inside. I switched on my car's ignition and followed her out of the lot, staying at a discreet distance as she turned onto the road heading into town. My radio blared out Taylor Swift and I sang along, blurring several lines of the lyrics and not caring one bit.

Debby drove without stopping until she pulled into a parking space downtown. I continued along the street, finding a space on the next block, and keeping one eye on Debby in my rearview mirror. I hopped out, fed the meter, and hurried after her when she rounded a corner and walked out of view. I slowed down to a walk when I reached the corner and looked around for her. No sign of her anywhere. I strolled ahead, looking into the stores and spotted her inside a florist shop, browsing a book at the counter. Retreating to a bench nearby, I sat down and waited ten minutes for her to point to something in the book before producing a card and sliding it into the pay machine.

As she turned to leave, I bent down and very studiously played with the laces on my boots until she passed me, walking towards the coffee shop. Over my shoulder, I watched her go inside. She smiled at the man who held the door open before taking her place in the queue. I counted the people in front of her. The queue was long and the service slow. Hoping she was desperate for her coffee, I strode over to the florist.

The bell over the door tinkled as I entered and a woman appeared from a rear room, a pair of clippers in her hand. "Hi," she said. "Can I help you?"

"I'm just looking, thank you." I moved my gaze to the array of colorful blooms stacked in buckets on multi-tiered shelving to my right. Although I couldn't name most of them, I did not fail to appreciate the bounty of nature and the heady scents mingling in the air. "Do you have a book I could see?" I asked. "I'm looking for a bouquet."

"Sure do. Birthday, anniversary, or some other special occasion?" she asked.

"Special occasion," I decided. I stepped over to the counter and watched her reach for a pink card file with metal edges from the bookshelf behind the counter. Glancing down, I noticed the order book. Casting another glance over my shoulder across the small plaza, I saw the coffee line shuffle forwards. Debby was now fifth in line.

"Let me know if any of these are what you're looking for," the lady told me. "We can customize any bouquet so long as we have enough prior notice." She laid the book open and moved to the side. I flipped through it quickly, wondering how to get a look at the order book. In its current position, I couldn't read it and the lady would surely notice if I reached for it. "I have some more photos in the back room," she said. "I was just organizing them into a new folder. Would you like to take a look at them too?"

I seized on her offer. "Yes, please!"

The moment she stepped through the door, I reached for the order book and turned it around. Debby's entry was last. One small condolence bouquet for Jerry Queller addressed to the Queller's home and a funeral wreath, however, the funeral home was not listed. I wondered if MPD had released the body yet. Hearing footsteps, I dropped the order book, spinning it back to its previous position. "These are lovely," I said, "but I can't decide. I need to consult my father before I pick one."

"Take a card and drop in whenever you can," she said, pointing to a stack of postcards. "All our information is on the back. We provide flowers for all occasions."

"Thank you." I took the postcard and deposited it in my purse before aiming for the coffee shop. Debby had reached the front of the line and was taking the cardboard cup, smiling at the barista as she turned, making for the exit. With the bench now occupied by two elderly men, I crossed the plaza and ducked to one side of the coffee shop. I casually lounged against the wall, pretending to check my phone.

Debby exited the coffee shop and turned away from me, walking at a steady pace. I pushed off the wall and followed her, never more than forty paces behind. I had to be able to see her without being obvious. She turned into a grocery store and picked up a basket. Following her inside, I did the same.

I was careful not to follow her down every aisle, criss-crossing the sections as she moved slowly through them, her basket gradually filling. I threw a couple of freshly baked muffins into my basket for effect and because I was hungry, then moved to the end of the aisle. I was fully expecting to see Debby as I crossed the next one but she wasn't there. I turned around, looking for her, then moving to the next aisle and the next. There was no sign of her! Had she recognized me? If she had and given me the slip, I would have to seriously reconsider my tracking technique. I turned around and hurried back, checking each aisle again. Turning, utterly confused now, I bumped into someone.

"I am so sorry," said the woman as we caught each other's eye. "Lexi? Hi."

"Hi, Debby," I squeezed out, trying not to wince. Just what I didn't want to have happen: running into my mark. "What are you doing here?"

"Shopping," she said, pointing to her basket.

"Me too! Did you move out of the hotel?" I asked, knowing already that she hadn't.

"No, I'm still waiting to hear about the apartment I applied for. Actually, I'm making dinner for my parents. I miss cooking and thought I would treat them to a *mezze*, just like I used to have when I was in Greece. I got Greek sausage and ingredients for *souvla*. I'm also going to make *tzatziki* and I found these imported olives and the bakery had fresh pita bread that smells amazing. I can't wait!"

"That sounds really nice," I said genuinely as my stomach gurgled and I remembered my longing to pick up a snack. Muffins would have to suffice.

"I just hope they like it. My dad is a meat and potatoes man but I want him to try something new. I miss cooking so badly. I can hardly wait to get my own apartment and start cooking all the time. I tried to pick up a new skill and recipe everywhere I went. In France, it was all about the butter and the bread. In Italy, I learned how to make my own pasta. In Germany, the sausages are insanely good and I learned how to make great cakes."

"Have you always liked cooking?" I asked, glad she was feeling so chatty and not suspicious.

"Nope. When I lived in Montgomery, I existed on the easiest food to make. I always thought I couldn't cook. Turns out all I needed was someone to teach me. But enough about me, have you heard anymore about Fiona? I don't know if you can tell me anything but my mom is so worried and it's so awful."

"It's still pretty early in the case. There isn't much to say."

"Well, I just want you to know that I'm glad someone is helping Jerry. I can't imagine how awful he must feel. I might make him something and take it by his house but I can't help thinking how a stupid casserole is no replacement for a wife."

"No, I don't imagine it is but I'm sure he'll appreciate it all the same. No one wants to think about food at a time like this."

"Then I will make him one! I should have just enough time in between getting to my parents' house and Dad getting home from having drinks with his old hunting buddies."

"Hunting buddies? The gun-toting type?" I zeroed in on this slip of information. Garrett mentioned the gun used to shoot Fiona still hadn't been recovered.

"Yeah, he's hunted ever since I was a kid. He tried to get me interested in shooting but I can't aim worth a damn."

"Can your dad?"

"Yeah, but I don't think he's ever shot anything really. I think he just likes hanging out with his buds."

"Does he keep his guns at home?"

Debby stopped and her eyes narrowed. I realized I might've poked a bit too far, and too obviously. "I have no idea but I can tell you this: I don't have access to any of them," she said, her voice cooling. "You can tell Lieutenant Graves that, too. I better get going. Like I said, I have a lot of things to do today. Bye, Lexi."

"Bye," I said, not daring to follow her in case I spooked her further. Now that she was on alert, I sensed she would find it more than a little suspicious if we ran into each other again. This was one occasion where I wished I could tag-team my target, dropping out when it got too hot for me and letting someone else take over. Instead, I had to be glad to finally get time for a snack. I took my basket and headed for the checkout, making sure I was far away from Debby.

Back in my car, I called Lucas. "I don't have the emails yet," he said.

"Okay. Can you check into gun licenses? Under the name of Rod Patterson?"

"Sure. Am I looking for anything in particular?"

"A 9mm."

"On it."

"Also, see if Debby Patterson has ever possessed a shooting license," I added. Debby might say she couldn't aim, but that didn't mean it was true. Her father was a long-time gun owner, and if she had access to his weapons, she might have had access to the one that killed Fiona. Garrett didn't say that the weapon had been found yet so I had to assume it was still missing. Even if he thought it might have been disposed of, it had to come from somewhere.

"Done."

Next, I called Garrett. "I'm watching Debby," I told him. "Did you know her father shoots?"

"Shoots what?"

"I don't know. Animals, possibly. He's a hunter, or he used to be."

"Oh, yeah, I know. A marksman too."

"Like a sniper?"

"Not exactly. Shoots in competitions. Has one of those high-powered marksman rifles. I saw some certificates at his house."

"So he could have taught Debby how to shoot? Does that connect Debby to Fiona's murder?"

"Not really. Anyone could have killed Fiona with a shot of such close range. Plus, the murder weapon was a handgun not a rifle. Something about Debby make you wonder?"

"No, she just mentioned her dad's old hunting buddies. I ran into her at the grocery store a few minutes ago. She didn't seem like someone who just killed a person. She seemed almost happy."

"Some killers are."

"I know but she was talking about cooking and other stuff and even bought a condolence bouquet for the Quellers."

"Not unusual. Some killers like to attend their victim's funerals. Even help out the victim's families. They get a kick out of being in the middle of things."

"People are so weird."

"Tell me about it. Did you find anything else out about Debby?"

"Just that she likes cooking and seems to be nice to everyone. I guess she blossomed out of that awkward Debby everyone remembers from before she left."

"Like maybe blossoming into a different person?"

"I haven't found anything strange about her and I'm still checking into her story. I think she's a bit pissed at you though. She said to tell you she doesn't have access to her father's guns. Any news on Fiona's case?"

"We found the gun late last night. An officer picked it out of a dumpster three blocks away. Ballistics confirmed it this morning. Before you ask, there was a print but it was too smudged to run through AFIS. However, there is a tiny amount of DNA on the grip, like the shooter nicked him or herself."

"That's great!"

"I wish. You know what a defense lawyer is gonna say? That gun was sitting in a dumpster for almost two days and that trace could have come from anywhere. We're running it anyway but I'm not hopeful of getting a match in the system."

"What if you had something to compare it to?" I asked.

"Like a nationwide database?" asked Garrett.

I ignored his sarcasm. "No. Something closer to home."

"There is nothing to compel anyone to hand over their DNA for comparison tests."

"Could you ask for the purposes of elimination? And if someone close to Fiona refuses to comply, wouldn't that point towards their guilt? If they are innocent, there should be no problem in handing over a cheek swab."

"You're so sweet," said Garrett. "I like how you think it's that easy."

"What if I got some DNA that you could compare it to and then you can find…"

"Inadmissible in court," cut in Garrett. "I can't risk a murder case getting thrown out on a mere technicality. The DA would tear me a new one."

"What if I happened to collect DNA for another case? You might helpfully run that DNA for me and put it in the system. Then, if anything else comes up… yay?" I paused, waiting.

"Might work. It would have to be official police business."

"Cut the agency a consultancy check and that makes it official."

"It will be a very tiny check."

"Tiny doesn't matter as long as it's official."

"Then we have a deal. If you come up with the goods, I'll work out how to get it admissible for your case; and if it happens to benefit mine…"

"It's a win-win!"

"Yeah. Hey, what do you know about the fire department being called out to Mom and Dad's?"

I paused. "Nothing. I will get back to you when I have something," I told him, hanging up and smiling.

I was still smiling as I placed my third call. An idea was forming in my mind and I couldn't do it alone. "How was your nap?" I asked.

"Amazing. Best nap ever."

"Can you get a sitter? I need your help."

Lily squeaked and I knew she was already anticipating the plan I had in mind for her. "I think I can. Let me make a call."

"Do it. I have a job for you."

CHAPTER TEN

"I'm in position," said Lily. She sounded serious so I knew she was eager to begin. Either that, or she was simply too tired to make wisecracks. "Where is the mark?"

"She's inside with her parents," I said, looking around for Lily's car, wondering where she parked. I'd been tailing Debby all the way from downtown, and was not surprised to find out her promise to make a meal for her parents was actually true. I parked almost a block away, neatly shoehorning my VW between two other cars, their roofs sticky with fallen leaves, indicating they hadn't moved for a few days. The cars provided coverage but allowed me enough of a view to monitor Debby's entry or exit from behind my camera. With her rental car parked on the street in front of the Pattersons' garden, I could easily see if she left. So far, I had a good angle of her talking with her mother, catching up I assumed, or, when Debby passed a box of tissues to her mom, perhaps consoling her. Worst case scenario: she was continuing to establish herself as the *real* Debby Patterson. Just as I thought that, I saw Debby stroke her mother's back with a look of genuine concern on her face as her mother wiped her eyes. Dr. Patterson walked into the room with two mugs in hand. He set them down in front of his wife and wrapped an arm around her shoulders. To anyone else, they were simply a family comforting each other. Heck, they looked like that to me.

I hoped that whatever they were talking about, along with the cooking adventure Debby had planned, would take a good, long time; but just in case it didn't, Lily was assigned to spend a thrilling few hours watching closely over Debby, ready to alert me if she left the premises.

"Where is your car?" I asked.

"Ahead of you, near the bend."

I craned my head and spotted it. "I see it. Where are you?" I asked, panning the camera across until I zoomed into Lily's blue Mini. The driver's seat was empty.

"In the tree, right above you."

I was not expecting that. I pushed the car door open, hopped out, and looked up. Perched in the tree was Lily, wearing a black hoody and skinny jeans. A black cap covered her hair and a pair of binoculars hung around her neck. "Holy crap," I muttered. Hanging up, I stared at her in the tree. "What are you doing up there?" I called out.

"I have a great view," she replied, adding two owl hoots for no apparent reason.

"You would have had a great view from your car too!"

"What if she saw me?"

"If anyone sees you hanging out in a tree with a pair of binoculars, they will call the police!"

Lily frowned. "I didn't think of that."

"How did you even get up there?"

"I climbed!"

I looked around for an obvious route to get up or down. There were no low branches and I couldn't see any ladder. "Get down now! Before someone sees you!"

"Okay." Lily didn't move.

"Can you get down?" I asked, suspecting the only flaw in Lily's plan.

"Mmm-hmm," said Lily, but not at all reassuringly. She scanned the air below her. "Turn around."

"Why?"

"Please," she pleaded.

I turned around and leaned against my car. After a rattle of leaves, the sound of a branch breaking, and one heavy thump, Lily appeared next to me. I opened my mouth to ask, but thought better of it and signaled to her to get into the car.

She slid inside and removed her cap, brushing off a few twigs and leaves. "Just how dangerous is this going to get?" she asked. "She could be a criminal in disguise!"

"Or she could be Debby Patterson and not at all dangerous. Like I said, all you need to do is watch the house and if Debby leaves, call me."

"I can't tackle her."

"That's fine," I replied quickly. I did not need to explain *that* to Garrett. I felt pretty sure I would have had to if Debby reported being attacked by a black-clad lunatic.

"No, I mean I can't. I would but my boobs hurt."

"You don't need to tackle her!"

"Good." Lily looked disappointed. "So... just watch her?"

"Yep, and make sure she doesn't see you."

"I hope she does something interesting like engaging in a huge argument with her mom and then yelling her real name. What if she comes over?"

"Make something up. Say you ran out of gas and you're waiting for your husband to bring you a gallon. If she asks anything else, start crying."

"Cool. I can do that. You know what else I'm going to do?"

I winced internally. "What?"

"I have a flask of hot coffee and I'm going to drink it all, in a moment of peace, while it's still hot. Babies don't like you drinking hot beverages or eating hot food. The minute you start to, they know, and then they want to eat too. Only I have to carry Poppy and I don't have enough arms to do everything at once."

I laughed. "Enjoy your peaceful coffee."

"I have a magazine too..." Lily trailed off and glanced up to the roof. "Oh, crap."

"Don't tell me you left them in the tree."

"Okay then. I will be back in a few minutes," said Lily. She climbed out and I took the brief interlude to raise my camera and check on Debby. Both she and her mom were no longer in the living room. I hoped they were in the back of the house where they couldn't see Lily jumping under the tree, holding her hands as far above her head as she could get them. A moment later, she returned with the flask and magazine in hand. "Can you give me a ride to my car?" she asked.

"It's right there!" I said, waving a finger at her car. "How did you get into that tree without me seeing you anyway?"

"Easy! I snuck around the block and approached it from the rear. You were too busy slumping in the seat to notice me."

I made a mental note to be more observant. First, Maddox managed to ace me and now Lily. Was I losing my touch? I glanced down at my jeans, sneakers and sweater. Thanks to the early morning start, I was definitely losing my *fashion* touch. Something urgent had to be done about that, along with deciding what to do about detecting the people who were sneaking up on me unawares. "Go back that same way and I'll watch for you; then I need to go."

"Where are you going anyway? On another case?"

"No, still this one. I just need Debby out of the way so I can..." I stopped, wondering how culpable to make Lily. Whatever she didn't know, she couldn't confess or leak later.

"Oh, man!" she groaned. "You're breaking in somewhere without me. This is so unfair! I could have called Ruby and asked her to watch the mark while I helped you with a little B&E."

"Then how could you drink hot coffee?"

"Good point. Where are you breaking into anyway?"

"My lips are sealed," I told her. "Call me the minute she moves."

"Wear gloves," said Lily as she hopped out. This time, I watched her vanish around the corner. A couple of minutes later, she appeared at the other end of the block and slipped into her car. I waved to her and drove away, hoping the coffee would ensure Lily made it through the next couple of hours.

I circled back to the hotel, driving as quickly as I could without breaking any speed limits. Despite Debby's plans, I knew she could leave the house anytime and I didn't dare get caught. With little traffic, I made good time and parked in a quiet spot, away from the prime parking real estate that was closer to the hotel doors.

While driving, I formulated my plan. There was no way the hotel would willingly let me into someone else's room without their knowledge so I either had to trick them or break in. I could have called on an old contact at the hotel but I didn't want to risk having Debby find out and scaring her away before I had a chance to investigate. Tricking my way in would have been almost impossible, given that housekeeping had most certainly finished their duties by this hour, so breaking in would have to be the only alternative.

I called Lucas. "What's the best way to break into a hotel room?" I asked.

"Did you call me because I'm an ex-con or because I'm the tech expert?"

"Both."

"What system do they use?"

"I don't know. The kind with electronic key cards."

"Hypothetically, the easiest way would be to get a master key from the hotel's key-writing machine. Can you get one?"

I was reasonably sure housekeeping turned in their master keys at the end of their shifts and the concierge desk was always manned by at least one person. However, I didn't know the password for the computer. I once helped the hotel's manager on a prior case but I didn't want to involve him in this. "Unlikely," I sighed.

"Then, the next best option is to get your hands on a key card from the same hotel and rewrite it, using a cool, little gadget I have."

"Okay," I decided. "I'll call you back."

"Before you hang up, I have the emails you asked for," he told me. "Electronic or paper copy?"

"Both, please."

"Done. One more thing, those gun licenses. I got a permit for Rod Patterson but nothing came back for his wife or daughter."

I expected as much but was disappointed to hear there wasn't any evidence to suggest Debby currently owned or had ever owned a gun. "Thanks," I told him.

We hung up and I hopped out of the car. I walked into the hotel, stepping through the double doors, and strode over to the reception desk. I didn't recognize the female concierge, which was probably a good thing. The last time I'd been here in any official capacity was as an undercover investigator. It was an early investigation in my career, and an occasionally humiliating case, although it ended very successfully.

"I'd like to book a room," I told the young woman.

"Tonight?" she asked, stepping in front of her monitor and reaching for the mouse.

"Yes."

"We have a range of options from a standard double to a deluxe suite," she offered.

"I'll take the cheapest. Do you have any rooms on the third floor?"

"There is a room available. How many nights?"

"Just one."

"Will you be staying alone? Or will someone be joining you?"

"Just me."

"Shall I have your luggage taken up?"

"No luggage. Just a spur of the moment thing," I told her. "I unexpectedly need a room for the night."

"Of course." She narrowed her eyes a little bit but didn't say anything. Instead, she produced a key and gave me a brief speech on where to find the elevator and breakfast room before wishing me an enjoyable stay. I took the key card, crossed to the elevator and rode the car to the third floor. My room was at the opposite end from Debby's, annoyingly. Hers was closest to the elevator and stairwell, while mine was at the far end of the corridor. If, for any reason, our paths crossed, it would be very awkward to explain what I was doing in her hotel. Especially when she knew I worked locally and could reasonably have assumed I also lived here and thus had no reason for a hotel reservation.

I swiped my key card through the electronic lock and let myself into a small room where I found a neatly made bed, a desk, flat-screen television, and a small bathroom carved out of nearly a quarter of the room. Sitting on the bed, I called Lucas again. "I have a key card," I told him.

"And I have the gadget. Unfortunately, there's a huge gap between us."

I didn't think of that and time was passing rapidly. I calculated how long it would take me to get to the agency, have Lucas rewrite my key card and then return. "Can you come here?"

"You mean... go outside?"

"Yep."

"Leave the office? See people?"

"Dammit, Lucas, I know you leave the office! I know because I checked the store cupboard and it isn't equipped for the world's smallest apartment. Also, you're engaged and you have to see your fiancée at some point. Get into your car, or whatever it is you drive, and get over here! I don't have much time."

"I ride a bike," said Lucas. "A push bike."

"You're an adult!"

"I know but my apartment is close to the office."

"Can you get a ride?"

"Yes," he replied begrudgingly before hanging up.

A moment later, Solomon's face and name flashed on the phone screen. "Hi," I said, upping my perky tone as I answered.

"Why is one of my employees asking me to drive him over to a hotel to meet you?"

"I rented a room."

There was silence, then, "Why?"

"To get a key card. Can you please bring Lucas over here? Please!"

"We're on our way," said Solomon and he hung up. I looked long and hard at my phone and wondered how my call plan was faring. While I waited for Solomon, Lucas, and the mystery gadget, I reclined on the bed and read the room service menu, wondering if I had time to order a sandwich, or maybe some fries, for an early lunch. I switched on the TV and turned it off again. I read my emails on my phone and played a game, all the while clock-watching. Finally, my saviors arrived.

"Which room are you in?" asked Solomon.

I told him and he hung up instantly. When the knock came at my door, I was ready, and answered it quickly before the two men slipped inside. "Here," I said, handing the key card to Lucas. "Can you turn this into a master key? I need to access another room and get back into this one."

"Sure. Give me a couple of minutes," he said, taking the card and moving over to the desk. He withdrew a laptop from his bag and a small machine and plugged them in.

"I'm not going to ask since I can work it out," said Solomon. "Also, the concierge gave us both highly suspicious looks when she asked if we'd both be staying the night."

"And you said?"

"What she didn't know couldn't bother her."

"This is why you are the boss," I replied. "You are a very smart man."

"You couldn't spring for a better room?" he wondered. Stepping past me, he almost knocked his knee into the desk. With the three of us occupying the room, the space seemed a lot smaller.

"I wasn't planning on actually staying the night."

"Good to know."

"Done," said Lucas. He handed me the key card and returned his equipment to his bag. "Return me to my happy place," he said to Solomon. Solomon looked at him blankly. "The agency will do just fine," Lucas translated.

"Be careful," said Solomon.

"Sure will," I told him, giving him a quick kiss as he followed Lucas out the door. I waited a beat for them to leave, checked my phone, in case Lily called—she hadn't—and left my room, walking along the hallway to Debby's room. Sucking in a hopeful breath, I slipped on gloves and slid the key card into the lock. When the light turned from red to green, I exhaled and pushed the door open, letting myself in.

Debby's room had the same layout as mine. Small bathroom on the left, dressing area on the right. The window overlooked the same patch of landscaped garden. The decor and furniture were all the same too, except this room was clearly lived in. Toiletries were stacked neatly in the bathroom but a quick search revealed inexpensive products. There were no medicines, and nothing with a label I could check on.

I turned away from the bathroom and opened the door to a small closet. Two suitcases were inside, resting against the wall. I opened them but, as I suspected, they were empty save for a couple of shoe bags and a cloth bag with *laundry* embroidered on the front. I zipped up the cases and returned them as I found them before moving to the hanging clothes and rifling through them. I didn't recognize many of the brands; most had what I assumed were foreign labels. Judging by the quality of the stitching and fabric, none were high-end items, which gave more credibility to Debby's claim of a simple life, saying she didn't purchase very much. What she did have was a good sense of style and many of the separates could have been easily coordinated. It was a capsule wardrobe done right and I had to give her kudos for that.

There were a few accessories but nothing that looked particularly special. She had three pairs of shoes: black sneakers, a pair of flat ballet pumps, and the long boots I'd seen her wearing when I first approached her. I stepped back, leaving the clothes exactly as I'd found them and moved into the main bedroom. The closet, like the bathroom, didn't give me anything.

Housekeeping had already made the bed and her pajamas were neatly folded and left near the pillows. I opened the nightstand drawers. Debby didn't bother putting anything inside of either one and the only things on the surface were a matching set of lamps, and a telephone, a pad of hotel paper and a pen on the left nightstand.

I checked my phone again as I walked over to my desk. Nothing from Lily.

The desk seemed to be in regular use but there was no laptop or tablet for snooping. Instead I saw a couple of magazines, one about food and one about travel, and a self-help book for goal setting and ways of achieving them. I wondered what goals Debby had and exactly what she planned to achieve. Was it getting a new job here? Or maybe, the apartment she applied for?

I put the book back on top of the magazines and picked up the next one, a well thumbed romantic novel that had a penciled-in price on the inside cover, as though it came from a second-hand store. There was a newspaper, folded to the classified apartments section, and a couple of the advertisements that were ringed in ink. A travel-sized jewelry box yielded a few inexpensive pairs of earrings and a silver bracelet. I zipped the box shut and put it back before reaching for the notepad next to it. Under the notepad was a passport.

"Jackpot!" I exclaimed as I grabbed the passport and flicked it open to the photo page. The passport was six years old, and the unflattering photo was definitely the Debby I knew as well as all the information listed. I flicked through the pages, noting stamps from numerous countries. I might not have been able to verify the first four years of Debby's ten-year absence but the passport attested to the most recent six. I used my cell phone camera to photograph the pages, holding the passport open by pressing the front and back covers on the desk. I'd just photographed a stamp for Italy when my phone began to ring.

"Hey, Lily. Is she on the move?"

"Yep," said Lily, her voice high and squeaky.

"Did she make you?"

"I don't think so."

"Good. Which way did she go?"

"Umm, I don't know. See, the thing is, it's like... ahh."

I took a deep breath. "What happened?"

"I kind of, sort of, fell asleep a little bit and then I woke up. And Debby's car was gone and I don't know how long and I'm really, really sorry, Lexi!" Lily blurted, the words spilling into my ear in one long rush.

"Shit!" I squealed, clamping a hand over my mouth.

"I know!" she wailed.

"Can you guess how long you were asleep?"

"Maybe thirty minutes. I was so tired. Poppy wakes me up all the time and I got cozy and…"

"I'll call you back," I said before hanging up. I tucked the passport under the notepad and darted toward the door, checking the peephole. No one was in the corridor. Thirty minutes or more were plenty of time for Debby to make it back to the hotel from her parents' house. Without a lookout at the hotel, I couldn't know for sure; and I couldn't risk being caught without finding some reason for being in the room. I might not get another chance. "DNA!" I whispered to myself hurriedly, remembering the other part of my mission. I looked around for something I could grab for Garrett to cross-reference and caught sight of some green plastic by the sink.

Ducking inside the bathroom, I grabbed the toothbrush and dropped it into the plastic baggie I carried in my pocket. With any luck, Debby would assume the maid erroneously disposed of it. I checked the peephole again and saw the coast was clear, so I opened the door. Immediately, the voices drifted towards me, and one, I was sure, belonged to Debby. She and whomever she spoke to seemed very close but they weren't talking in English. I snatched a fleeting look towards my room at the far end of the corridor. There was nowhere to hide along the way and Debby might have been able to recognize me from behind. I couldn't go the other way or I was certain to run into her.

That left me with only one exit. One I hoped I'd never have to use again but I had no choice and no time left to think of anything else. I gently pushed the door to the corridor shut, letting it close with a light click as I jogged over to the floor-to-ceiling sliding doors. I unlocked it and slid it open, stepping out onto a small balcony before easing the door closed behind me. The last time I'd made an escape this way, I was on the same floor and had nothing to aid my climb down. Consequently, I was forced to jump, hurting my ankle in the process. This time, as I peeked over the edge, I could see another balcony almost directly beneath me. I swung one leg over the railing and then the other, perching the toes of my shoes into the gaps.

Inside the room, the door opened and Debby entered, looking into her purse. If she looked up, she would surely have seen me despite the privacy curtains in place. I crouched very low and ran my hands down the railings until I was almost hunched over. Glancing down, I let one leg go, then the other and swung myself down, dropping onto the balcony below, my heart thumping like a bass drum.

I paused, waiting to be discovered, but no one challenged me. Wiping my damp palms onto the legs of my jeans, I repeated the move, only this time, dropping onto the ground. I pressed myself against the cold brick of the building and regained my breath. As I calmed my heart, I decided that I was never, ever leaving a hotel that way again. On the plus side, I was a lot speedier at making a fast exit than I used to be, which was something to be proud of.

CHAPTER ELEVEN

I called a frantic Lily on the way to my car. "I am so sorry!" she cried. "Are you okay?"

I assured her I was fine but was also considering buying an emergency rope ladder. "It was fortunate you called when you did," I told her. "I had just enough time to get out of her hotel room before Debby entered. A couple of minutes later, and she would have caught me."

"I will never sleep again," wailed Lily. She paused and I heard her yawn. "Never," she added, her voice distorted by another yawn.

"Don't worry about it. I got what I came for and I'm fine." I debated over telling her about my swift and vertical exit but eventually decided not to. Lily sounded pretty traumatized already and I didn't want to exacerbate it. If she knew just how close I came to being discovered, she would have been mortified.

"I will make it up to you," Lily promised. "In any way you like. With any cocktail, baby cuddle, or pizza you want. Maybe all three."

"I will take you up on that," I assured her. "Now go home and get some sleep."

"Okay," replied Lily. "Not gonna argue even though I swore I would never sleep again."

"On the job," I reminded her. "You can sleep on a regular schedule otherwise."

"Regular schedule, pfft!"

After we hung up, I got into my car and sat there for a moment, basking in my relief at not being caught. I'd been in far worse situations than that but still couldn't quite get used to it. If dramatic exits were included in the job description, I was definitely not cut out for a career in serial espionage. Not even a serial toothbrush theft. I patted my pocket, checking for the toothbrush and felt relieved to feel the hard plastic through the cloth. It was probably too much to expect my luck to hold out any further and, with the new information, I didn't need to watch Debby any longer today, especially now that Lucas had a bunch of emails for me to browse through. I decided I would drop the toothbrush off at MPD before I went back to the agency and pick up a coffee on the way. I needed nothing more than a relaxing dose of caffeine and some alone time with a highlighter pen. Just as I turned on the ignition, my phone rang and I jumped, feeling startled. Apparently, my nerves were a touch more frazzled than I thought.

"Hi, Maddox."

"You sound out of breath."

"Some impromptu exercise."

"At the gym?" he asked warily.

"No, more like parkour but without the talent."

Maddox hesitated. "Should I ask?"

"Probably not."

"Are you safe?"

"Yes." I was reasonably sure I was. Just to be extra sure, I hit the lock button on my car doors.

"Good. Can you make it over? I have the information you asked for."

"Sure. I can be at your office very soon."

"I'm not there now. Can you come over to my apartment?"

I hadn't been to Maddox's apartment for a while. The last time I went there, he wasn't home, having gone temporarily away on assignment. On one of the more recent occasions, he invited me inside, and I accidentally picked up a booking slip for a romantic weekend. That was how I found out Maddox was dating again. His dating life was none of my business but it stung a little, however irrational that may be, to realize he had moved on. As far as I knew, the romance fizzled out faster than it started but that was none of my business either. I tried not to think about what made the news sting so much, but I had a horrible feeling it involved the green monster, jealousy. If things had been different, Maddox and I might still have been together. I pushed that thought away. "Okay," I agreed. "I'm on my way."

I drove out of the parking lot, noting Debby's car was still parked close to the entrance, and headed for Harbridge. Maddox owned an apartment only a few streets from the Quellers. Instead of driving into the residents' parking lot, I found a place on the street and crossed the sidewalk to press the buzzer. Maddox buzzed me in and was waiting for me when I got to his door on the second floor. "Did you get laid off?" I teased. "Should you be at home at this hour?"

"No, I didn't. My role changed slightly a while back and my hours are more flexible now." He turned and I followed him inside, shutting the door behind us. We went into the living area. His laptop sat on the coffee table with a heavy-looking bag next to it. A couple of pieces of paper were on the table but I wondered if he just cleared all his actual paperwork out of sight from my prying eyes. I was already curious about what exactly he was doing in his new, more flexible, but mysterious role. "I checked the travel details and managed to find a reservation for Debby Patterson on a number of flights, plus a passport renewal while she was overseas."

"How far back did you go?"

"I searched the parameters you gave me and got this list." Maddox handed me a sheet. I scanned over it, feeling certain that the dates matched up with the passport stamps I'd partially photographed.

"There's some big gaps here," I said.

"I noticed that too, but I figured she could have taken the train or ferries. Europe has an excellent train network and she could have easily crossed international borders that way."

"There're no other records of her entering or exiting the US except for when she left ten years ago and of course, when she most recently returned," I observed.

"Her story stand up?" he asked, walking around me and out of the room. I heard him go into the kitchen and when he returned, he had two cups of coffee. He passed one to me and I nearly died from gratitude.

I scanned the list a second time, then opened my phone camera roll and double-checked the dates with the stamps. "So far."

Maddox smiled. "Glad I could help."

"Oh, sorry!" I looked up from the sheet and pulled a face, suddenly aware that I forgot to express my thanks. "I should have said thank you. I didn't mean to be so rude!"

"I wasn't implying you were!"

I gave him an embarrassed smile. "Thank you, anyway. I really appreciate you looking into this. It's a big help." I wasn't quite sure what to make of it. My theory that Debby Patterson never left the country was truly squashed, first by the passport evidence, and second, by Maddox's research. She really had been away traveling.

"No problem at all. So how are things going with you?"

I thought about my lucky escape through the window and settled on, "Good. You?"

"Good, too. I'm not planning a wedding though. Found your dress in your mom's magic book yet?"

I pulled a less-than-pleased face. "I haven't even opened it."

"That sounds like a good start," laughed Maddox. "Set a date yet?"

I paused and sipped my coffee to give my mind time to wonder why Maddox was asking. I was pretty sure he wasn't all that interested in wedding plans, and especially not mine. Was I supposed to invite him, I wondered? He was my ex and that was awkward, and Solomon probably wouldn't like it, so doubly awkward. But he was also my friend and it would have been wrong to exclude him. Plus, there was a time when I had a lovely fantasy about him being the man waiting for me at the altar. Now, however, it just made it unbearably uncomfortable for me. "No," I said, stating the simplest answer and the honest one. "We haven't talked about it."

"How much do you know about Solomon?" Maddox asked. He relaxed on the couch next to me, placing one arm on the edge where he balanced his cup.

"Plenty!"

"No, I mean, how much do you *really* know?"

I opened my mouth to protest that I knew everything before I stopped and thought. I knew a lot of stuff. Like Solomon's parents had died in tragic circumstances, leaving him responsible to raise his younger sister and brother. He flat-out denied ever watching *Glee*, despite owning the boxed set, and was an excellent cook. He could fire any weapon handed to him, ride a motorcycle, and ran a successful business. He made love like I was the only woman on earth and every time might have been his last. However, I was pretty sure Maddox didn't want to know *that*.

"I know all kinds of things."

"Do you know where he was before he came to Montgomery?"

"Um…" I wriggled under Maddox's scrutiny and took another sip.

"Whom he worked for?" Maddox persisted.

"He worked with you!"

"He was under contract. Do you know where he came from?"

I had to search my brain for that answer, then realized Solomon never said. Neither had Maddox. "No."

"Do you know where he lived?"

"He lived in Montgomery a little while. Before that, he, ah, uh…" I trailed off.

"Did he live in an apartment or a house before moving into the Chilton house?" I stared blankly at Maddox, the coffee forgotten. "What about his friends?" Maddox asked. "Do you know who they are? His former colleagues? Have you met anyone who knew Solomon before he came here to help MPD with a case?"

"He has a background in financial crimes," I stuttered. "I know his sister."

"Who were his employers? Girlfriends? Where has he lived? What was his favorite restaurant? Where did he vacation?"

"What is this?" I cut in. "Why are you asking me all these questions about Solomon?"

"Because I don't know any of them and I don't think you do either."

"You've known him for longer than I have!"

"I knew his name. I worked with him. I don't *know* him."

"Well, I do!"

"I hope you do. I've been thinking about it ever since you got engaged. I was worried when you started dating, especially given the circumstances of how we ended, but I've worried more ever since Solomon made it clear he planned on marrying you. I hoped you knew the answers to everything about his past, but I don't think you do. I don't think you know *anything* about the man you're planning to marry and that scares the hell out of me!"

"None of that is your business!"

"I'm your friend. *You're* my business."

"If you are my friend, you should know when to stay out of my affairs!" I set the cup on the coffee table, entirely missing the mat in my annoyance as I jumped to my feet. Who was Maddox to question me like that? Or to infer that I didn't even know the man I shared my life with, and whose ring I wore?

Maddox jumped up. "Lexi, I…"

"I thought you'd gotten over us but you're acting like you're jealous. We split up, Maddox. We *ended*. It hurt me badly at the time but I survived it. Yeah, the circumstances between us weren't great, which was why I decided to stay single for a while and work out what I wanted. Then, I fell in love with Solomon. I know it was hard for us to be friends at first but I thought we were there. I thought you were okay with it and happily dating again and… and…" Tears filled my lower lids. "Now you want me to question Solomon? You want to stir up some kind of idea that he's what… what, Adam? That he's not the person he says he is?"

Maddox met my eyes, his face impassive, but his words shocked me. "He's never said who he truly is."

"Screw this!" I stomped past Maddox. He reached for my arm and caught me at the elbow.

"I'm not trying to hurt you; and I'm not trying to win you back. You made it clear you didn't want me and I respect that. It hurt, but I respect that, and we found a way to remain friends. I *am* your friend. I want to know you'll always be okay because I do care about you. I always will and there will always be a part of me that loves you. Yes, sometimes I'm jealous, but that's not what I am at this moment. I *care*, Lexi. That's why I'm asking you, what do you know about him?"

The first tear broke free. "Do you know what hurt me most about us breaking up? It was knowing that I got it wrong. I saw something that wasn't what I thought it was and you weren't doing anything wrong at all. That hurts. And Solomon was there when I was hurting so badly, and… and… it was too late. I can't change anything that happened after that. Whatever I did, someone was going to get hurt and all I could do was make sure it didn't get any worse. I can't keep going back to that place. It hurts me too much." My jaw trembled and I brushed away the tears.

"Did you ever ask yourself why you were there that night? Solomon sent you, didn't he?" asked Maddox, his voice cool against my rising emotion.

"I was there to do a job and you just happened to be there too. I wish I never saw you!"

"Damn coincidence, wasn't it?"

My jaw stiffened at the implication. Solomon sent me on that job but it was to get photos of another target nearby. I'd just completed that task when I saw Maddox, who was working undercover, which I knew; but I didn't realize he was still in Montgomery. "Let go of me," I said in a low, angry voice. Maddox's fingers loosened and I shook my arm free. "I know what I'm doing," I told him, walking out before he could tell me that I didn't.

~

I stopped by MPD on my way to the agency and met Garrett in the lobby. "Toothbrush," I said, handing the baggie to him.

"I see that."

"Later," I said as I turned to go, walking away, stuffing my hands into my jacket pockets and tucking my chin down. I didn't want to engage in small talk, or any other kind of talk. I just wanted to immerse myself in my work and block out the rest of the world. Especially the part that included Maddox's warnings and my inner voice that apparently only contributed to the harmony. *What did I know about Solomon before the day I met him?*

"What's up with you?" asked Garrett, falling into step beside me.

"Nothing."

"Yeah, right. I've been married long enough to know the words 'nothing' and 'fine' mean entirely different things to women."

"I'm fine."

"Like I said."

"It's nothing, really," I insisted. "Call me when you get the DNA results from the toothbrush?"

"You bet."

I was grateful when Garrett stopped, leaving me to walk to my car by myself without pursuing what was worrying me. I don't know if it was because of worry or anger. Maddox had no place asking me those kind of questions. It was none of his business what I did! Or what kind of discussions I had with my fiancé. *Except*, said a small voice, *we had never had those kind of conversations.* I brought up Solomon's past previously but now that I thought back, he never really gave me an answer that I could fix upon or even recall now. Anything he said was vague, skirting around the topic without ever really answering me. I never felt any cause to worry. Solomon wasn't the chattiest kind of man and neither of us spent a lot of time talking about the past. Mine was a whole catalogue of embarrassments and failures interspersed with plenty of fun. Not only with Lily, but tons of family time with more Graves than I could count, and a lot of shopping. I didn't like talking much about it so that Solomon rarely discussed his past never worried me.

Naturally, I knew some things. For instance, his parents died tragically so I was careful not to bring them up. I met and liked his sister. She and I chatted about her life, but we didn't talk much about Solomon unless it happened to directly involve her. He was a good brother to her, and helped her financially and emotionally. He encouraged her to follow her dream and rewarded her progress. Those things all told me he was a good person, which rarely inspired me to delve any deeper. It didn't occur to me until now that perhaps I made a mistake by not pushing him for more answers. Was I really marrying a man I didn't fully know?

That question replayed in my head all the way to the agency. By the time I sat behind my desk, I had to ignore it entirely so I could focus. Garrett was relying on me to help him verify Debby Patterson's identity, real or not, and whether she was connected in any way to Fiona Queller's murder. That had to be my only priority. Anything else had to wait.

Lucas left the stack of emails on my desk. I checked the date of the top sheet, a month ago. I rifled through all of them to the last document. That date was ten years ago. For ten years, there weren't a lot of emails. I was sure I could have read all of them in less than an hour.

I picked up the desk phone and dialed Lucas's extension. "Is this all you have?" I asked.

"Can you be more specific?" he shot back.

"Sorry," I apologized, knowing my mind was elsewhere. I pushed myself to focus harder. "I just saw the emails you left on my desk and there aren't many for ten years of correspondence."

"There were more. Mostly subscriptions, shopping websites, news blasts, that sort of thing. I figured you didn't want those so I whittled them down to personal correspondence and those became family emails."

"No emails that looked like they were to friends or colleagues?"

"Not in the last ten years. Not much before that either but I didn't look too closely. I have a program that searches for me, based on the parameters I give it."

"Do you still have everything?"

"Sure. I backed it up digitally on a thumb drive."

I paused, thinking. "Can you monitor her account now?"

"Sure, but there hasn't been any activity since you told me she returned home."

"I'm going to take a look at the family emails; then I might want to see the backup."

"I'll bring it down if you have a coffee waiting for me."

When I first started at the agency, I would have been insulted if anyone asked me to make one of my colleagues a coffee, but those days are long gone. "Sure," I agreed. I abandoned my last coffee at Maddox's and I still craved the caffeine. I could get that and be in Lucas's graces in one smooth, coffee-beaned move.

Within a couple of minutes, we exchanged a coffee mug for a thumb drive and I was back at my desk. I turned the email stack upside down and grabbed the new top sheet, starting from the beginning, guessing Lucas had begun his search from the moment Debby was reported missing.

I was right. There were a string of emails from her mother and father asking her to get in touch without any reply for several weeks. Then a short one from Debby in which she apologized for going away without saying anything but, she claimed, she realized her life in Montgomery wasn't what she wanted so she decided to go overseas on a whim. She reassured them she was fine and found a renewed energy for life. Traveling the world opened her eyes in a way she never realized was possible. She assured them she would be in touch soon but she didn't have consistent access to the internet. She signed it "Love, Debby xx."

I could imagine the torrent of words my mother would unleash on me if I gave an explanation like that to my parents. I turned the page, looking for the emailed reply. It came from her mother and was much longer. She wrote how they were a little worried but quite relieved to know that she was fine. They told her someone had reported her missing and admonished her for the trouble she caused. There was another rebuke for leaving her job "when she was an adult now and couldn't behave like a teenager anymore."

The next email from Debby came two months later. She said she moved on from Australia too and was bartending in a pub run by an English-speaking couple in Hong Kong. She was learning a little bit of the language and talked about the food and the scenery. She ended it with how much she was looking forward to the next part of her travels. Her PS was a one-line apology for acting so rashly and how she hoped she hadn't worried anyone. Despite the brevity of it, the words she wrote seemed sincere.

Six more emails passed between Debby and her parents that year, with gaps of several weeks between them. They moved on to light gossip from her parents, and little curiosity about her travels. Debby had an ongoing commentary about the people she met or the strange things she saw. By that time, she was traveling through Europe and made a couple of references to teaching English, which her parents largely ignored in their replies.

I finished the coffee and settled in to read the rest of the family emails. Fiona was mentioned a couple of times, too. Once, for winning the country club amateur tennis competition eight years prior to now; and another, much later one, where Debby's mom mentioned Fiona and Jerry were vacationing in Italy and could Debby recommend any places they should see or go to?

There were several remarks about things her parents were doing, but only one email, five years into her travels, when Debby's dad wanted to know if she planned on returning home. After that question, and a gap of four months in emails, Debby emailed them about teaching English at night and her parents never asked her to come home again. I wondered if they thought she was ignoring them for pressuring her and didn't want to scare her off. Perhaps they weren't really interested in Debby coming home at all. Given Debby's self-absorbed past behavior, I decided her absence might have been somewhat of a relief for them even if she did write very sweet emails about how much she loved them.

CHAPTER TWELVE

Based on a tip from Debby's emails, I parked outside Walnut View Retirement Home so I could watch the elderly residents through the windows. As far as stalking went, this stint definitely required patience. I never saw people move so slowly. They shuffled in short circles, swaying before stepping forwards and backwards in a slow rhythm. A helper in a white healthcare uniform wove her way between them. It looked like they were having fun at whatever they were doing, or attempting to do.

Debby's ailing grandmother lived there and I wanted to speak to her. From what I read in Garrett's file, Grandma Patterson was the matriarch of the family, and the only one I had not yet interviewed. I wondered what she had to say, if anything, about her granddaughter's lengthy trip abroad. Debby said she suffered from dementia and didn't remember who she was anymore. With my suspicious hat on, that sounded rather convenient for a fake Debby. It wouldn't be hard to convince an ailing old lady that her granddaughter had returned.

I hopped out of the car and walked up the curved drive, entering through the main doors. Inside, someone had gone crazy with a plethora of wood paneling and baby blue walls, the expanse only broken up with framed landscapes. I looked closer. Every single picture was screwed into the wall and security alarms were discreetly interspersed amongst the wainscoting. I walked up to the reception desk and plastered a sunny smile on my face. "Hi, I'm here for Mrs. Patterson. How is she doing today?"

The woman in scrubs winced. "It's my first day," she confessed. "I'm Denise. I don't know all the residents' names yet but I can find out for you?" She reached for a phone but I shook my head.

"Oh, don't worry one bit. I'll find her."

"I can't let you go in."

My heart thumped. So much for my luck holding out. "Oh?"

"Not without signing the guest book!" Denise smiled apologetically before standing up and reaching for a big black book. She produced a pen and held it out. "I'm sure you know the drill," she said.

"I do," I assured her as I looked down. It looked simple enough. Sign my name, my check-in time and the identity of the resident whom I was visiting. I paused, wondering if I should sign in my own name, but decided not. I couldn't risk the chance of Debby coming by and signing in and seeing my name. Instead, I swirled a squiggle with loops and flourishes that could have said anything, or, in this case, nothing at all.

"I think everyone is in the rec room," said Denise. "It's work-out time."

So that's what all the shuffling was about. I thanked her and made my way to the corridor, heading in the direction of the room I'd been watching when I arrived. The room's occupants were divided in two. Half of them sat in comfortable wing chairs at the edges, their walkers by their sides, and the other half shuffled aimlessly in the large, cleared space in the center. All were watching the front where a middle-aged woman made slow movements, which they attempted to copy. Several nurses were assisting the less able, more feeble residents.

The smell of roasted meat and cabbage drifted past my nostrils, making my stomach rumble. It had been a long time since I last ate. I was more than ready to go home, kick off my heels, and settle down for a meal in front of the television. But before I did that, I had to find Grandma.

I tapped the nearest healthcare worker on the arm. "Do you know where I can find Gwen Patterson?" I asked.

"By the window," he said, pointing to an old lady parked beside the window, staring out at the street.

"Thanks." I crossed over, skirting around an ancient man's cajoling to get me to join in the shuffle. After slipping away fast enough that he couldn't catch me, I sat in the adjoining chair.

"Hi," I said. When she didn't respond, I tried a little louder, "Hi!"

This time, Gwen Patterson looked at me. "Hello, dear."

"How are you today?" I asked.

"I'm going out today," she told me, a smile lighting her face. "I'm catching a train."

"That's nice. Where are you going?"

"Going to visit my grandpa," she said with a giggle. "We're going to get ice cream."

I wasn't sure how to reply. There was no way Grandma's grandfather was still alive. A nurse stopped and delivered a lidded cup of juice, placing it on the table. "Everything okay?" she asked.

"She was just telling me she's catching a train today," I told her. I wasn't sure what was considered "okay" in the facility.

"Oh." The nurse nodded knowingly as Grandma's attention turned back to the street. Softly, she said to me, "She's not having the most lucid of days today."

"The dementia?"

"That's right. At breakfast, she told us she just became a mom. Then she reverted to being a little girl. You must be Debby?"

"I, uh..." I stammered. Sneaking inside the home to question the old lady was one thing, but impersonating her granddaughter seemed duplicitous. Yet, I did come here to talk. I swallowed the moment of guilt and nodded.

"It's so sweet of you to visit. She talks about you often. I'll leave you two to chat. Just remember to go with whatever she says. We don't want to upset her. Oh, and we can't find her glasses so she's been struggling a little bit to see."

"Debby?" said Grandma, looking at me again. The nurse gave us a pleased smile and left, taking her tray of juice to the next resident. "You were gone such a long time."

"That's right," I said.

"Did you miss me?"

"All the time," I told her. Grandma seemed to like that; she reached out for me with a shaking hand. I took her hand in mine and folded my other hand over the top.

"The postcards were sweet. I liked getting them."

"I'm glad."

"Your writing got a little funny. It must be all them computers. No one writes nicely anymore."

"I'll try harder."

Grandma squeezed my hand. "Did you change your hair?" she asked, squinting at me.

"Just put it up a new way. Grandma, did you think it was strange when I went away?"

"Strange? You're a funny girl, Debby. Always taking off and coming back. Your mom used to worry a bit, but she knows that's just how you are. Must be from your other mom."

"My other mom?"

"Don't act out anymore, okay, Debby?"

"Okay." I paused, wondering what she meant. "Did I act out a lot?"

"You should know! You were always a troublemaker. I told your mom she should pay more attention to you but who listens to their mother-in-law?"

"True."

"I'm glad you came home. It's nice when you come to visit at Christmas every year."

I knew Debby had never visited so I lied, "I'm glad I came too."

"I put your present under the tree," said Grandma.

"Grandma, what did you mean about *my other mom*?" I asked.

"I don't know your mom," said Grandma. "Did you just move here? I'm Gwen."

"Yes," I said, knowing I lost her. "It's lovely here."

"Smells like cabbages," said Grandma, sliding her hand out from mine. "I'm not staying. I'm only visiting."

"I hope you have a lovely day," I told her but her attention was again turned to the street.

"We're getting ice cream," she said, smiling into the distance and I knew she was miles away.

I eased up from the chair and walked quickly from the room, puzzled by Gwen's comment. What did she mean about *another mother*? Was it simply the rambling of an elderly lady who didn't fully live in this world anymore? I couldn't be sure. After I signed out with another squiggle in the guest book, I retreated to my car. Coming there to visit had been a bust. Grandma clearly couldn't keep her memories straight long enough to tell me anything about Debby. And seeing how easily she mistook me for Debby, I knew she could never identify her granddaughter now that the dementia had become so advanced. Had she found her glasses, and had her full eyesight, along with a lucid moment, perhaps she would have known the difference; but today, she was happy enough to think I was Debby although we looked nothing alike.

Reluctantly conceding that there was nothing more I could do for the case this evening, I headed home, wishing I had something to tell Garrett.

As I unlocked the door and stepped into the house, I wondered what more I could do. I interviewed Debby's parents, located her former apartment, questioned her former colleague and boss, visited her grandma, followed her around town, broke into her hotel room, got the FBI to check into her travel history, and had her emails hacked. "What else am I supposed to do?" I asked the empty house. "There is no one else I can talk to in order to verify Debby's identity and every one who is close to her says Debby is really Debby." I paused. No, that wasn't quite right. Only her parents were saying that. Unfortunately, they were also the only people who knew her. Debby didn't contact her colleague or boss, two people who would have recognized her. From what I knew, she seemed to avoid contact with anyone who might have known her before she left. Even if she were introverted, that was strange.

I recalled my meeting with her parents. There were some photos in Debby's room, group shots with friends. Wouldn't she have visited them? If only to renew old friendships? Surely they were worried about her too? Unless, she contacted them while she was still abroad?

Lucas's thumb drive was in my pocket so I pulled it out and headed to the office upstairs. I left my laptop at work but there was a computer I could use. I powered it up and pushed the thumb drive into the USB port. I opened it, finding one file. I clicked on DP-EMAIL and a screen opened up, looking exactly like an email program. My fingers hovered over the keys and I realized I couldn't remember the names of her friends.

I jogged downstairs and opened my purse but the file wasn't inside. I dropped my forehead into my palm. Of course it wasn't. I locked it inside my desk along with my laptop so I didn't have to carry them around. Grabbing my cell phone, I was glad the trip downstairs wasn't for nothing and I called Garrett on my way upstairs. "Hey," he said. "Feeling better?"

"Feeling busy, so as good as," I told him. "Can you help me fill in the blanks on something? I need the names of Debby's friends but I left the file at the agency."

"Give me a minute," said Garrett. I heard the clicking of keys and guessed he was still at the station. "There were two friends. Marley McFadden and Anna Colby. They were both interviewed after Debby disappeared."

"I don't remember the interviews from the file you gave me. Can you email them?"

"I can't, due to the nature of this case," he said cryptically so I figured someone was listening. Since this case wasn't really official, and despite the promise of a tiny check to make it so, Garrett wasn't about to announce it to his superiors.

"Someone there?"

"Gone now. Okay, let's see. Marley McFadden was interviewed by phone. She said Debby was talking about traveling and that's why she wasn't worried about Debby's disappearance. On record, she said, 'looks like she's finally done it, just like she said she would.' She forwarded us an email Debby sent her. There's a copy of it in here somewhere."

I frowned. "Why was she interviewed by phone?"

"Because she was out of town when the investigation started."

"And the other friend?"

"She lived here in town. We interviewed her. Anna Colby was in grad school and she said she'd been so busy she didn't realize how much time had slipped by. At the date of the interview, she said it had already been a couple months since she last saw Debby. She said she tried calling Debby a couple of times but assumed Debby would call back whenever she could. She was pretty upset to find out Debby was missing. Says here: we interviewed her again after the first email from Debby arrived and she was surprised to hear Debby was traveling."

"Why would her two closest friends say such different things?" I wondered, not expecting an answer. "What did Marley say when you went back to interview her?"

"Uh…" Garrett was quiet for a moment but I heard papers turning. "Hmm, looks like we tried to follow up with her but couldn't get in touch. Since the parents were satisfied, and we had a lot of other cases needing more attention, we didn't pursue it after that."

"I'm going to look into the friends again, but I don't expect to find much. If it weren't for Fiona's murder, and based on finding nothing so far, I would say this was a waste of time. She might be a crappy daughter but there isn't a lot that says Debby isn't whom she says she is. The only person who said she wasn't the real Debby is dead."

"Which is why I need you to stay on it."

"Can you get me their addresses? I'd like to speak to Fiona's husband, too."

"That shouldn't be a problem. Jerry Queller returned to their house. I'll tell him I sent you. As for the friends, let me run their names through the system and see what I come up with. Stay on the line."

I said I would and while I waited, I tapped both names into Lucas's email back-up. I added time parameters from now to ten years prior. Two email conversations came back for Marley, the dates roughly three and six months after Debby left. I read the brief emails with Debby enthusiastically raving about her new life and thanking Marley for her encouragement to live out her dreams while also saying how much she missed her. There were a couple of replies from Marley wishing her well, congratulating her on taking a leap into the unknown and hoping she got to see amazing things; then, nothing.

For Anna, there was only one email of any significance. She wrote to Debby saying the police had been to her house and she was worried, asking her to "please get in touch." The reply she received a few days later was very similar to the one Debby sent Marley. She was fine, she was happy, and she was living a new and wonderful life. There were a couple more emails from Anna asking how Debby was but no replies. I guessed Anna eventually gave up.

"I didn't get an address for Marley but I recall she didn't live in Montgomery at the time of the disappearance. I have a local address for Anna. Do you have a pen?" he asked and when I replied I did, he spelled it out. Anna lived in the nicer part of Frederickstown, a low income neighborhood with poor transport links and a bad reputation.

"How many of your friends from ten years ago do you still keep in touch with?" I asked.

"All of them."

"Really?"

"I've lived in Montgomery all my life. It's hard to lose touch with people when you grew up with them and they still live in the same neighborhoods. A couple guys moved away but we still get cards and see each other whenever they're in town or I have the good fortune to escape. Why do you ask?"

"Just wondered if it were unusual not to keep in touch but I suppose not. I'm going to look into the friends." Of my closest friends from ten years ago, my best was Lily and I let my brother marry her. I would never *not* know her, I realized.

"Not tonight," warned Garrett. "Do something nice for yourself. This can wait."

My stomach gave another warning rumble and I decided that doing *something nice* had to involve eating. "Sure thing. Good night."

"Night, sis'.

I made a few notes about our conversation and emailed them to myself so I could add them to my file before I powered down the computer. I turned off the lights and headed downstairs. The refrigerator was sparse, neither Solomon nor I having enough time to shop for groceries. I pulled out the pizza menu and browsed through it. I was trying to decide between a plain margherita and a meat feast special when Solomon walked in. He held a grocery bag in one hand and a pizza box in the other. Even better, it came from Monty's Slices, the best pizza joint in town.

"How did you know?" I cooed, my gratefulness seeping into every syllable.

"Lucky guess," he said as he slid the box onto the counter, turning around to reach for plates.

"Who needs plates?" I flipped open the box and pulled out a slice, biting gingerly around the oozing, hot mozzarella.

"Wine?"

"Now you're talking!"

Solomon returned the plates to the cupboard and extracted a pair of wine glasses. A bottle of white wine came from the grocery bag. He poured both glasses and handed one to me.

"I interrogated a grandma today," I told him. "I pretended to be her granddaughter. It wasn't my finest hour."

"This is why I hired you. You take the toughest nuts and crack them wide open."

I nibbled my way to the end of the crust and took a large swallow of wine, debating whether or not to tell Solomon about climbing down from a third-floor balcony. However, I decided there was no need for that. What he didn't know, he couldn't worry about. "I knew it wasn't just for my gorgeous looks."

Solomon reached over and wiped a stray piece of cheese from my lip. "That's correct."

"How did you hire Fletcher and Flaherty?" I asked, the question spilling out before I could filter it. I remembered the person who planted the thoughts about Solomon's past in my mind. "Or Delgado or Lucas? Did you meet them through work too?"

"I met Fletcher on an op years ago and he showed plenty of interest when I was setting up the agency. I met Flaherty a couple of times and knew he had a solid cop background but didn't want to be completely retired. Delgado was a buddy and Lucas... I *caught* him."

I reached for another slice. "You caught him?"

"When he was hacking. I saw how smart he was, and knew he had a good heart. He didn't belong in prison. I got him turned around."

"What did you do to catch him?"

"His name came up during an investigation while I was monitoring his moves. During the course of his hack, I was watching."

"No, I mean, what was *your job*?"

"Lot of questions tonight, Lexi. What's up?"

"Just curious." I shrugged the question of his job away. Then, I tried to banish the dozen other questions in my mind.

"Your mom called me earlier," said Solomon, switching topics so quickly, I barely had time to notice. "She wants to know what season we plan on getting married."

"She's probably making a new binder. Spring, summer, fall, and winter," I guessed, instantly distracted by wedding plans. There would be plenty of time to ask the more important questions, I decided.

"Lots of options. Should I be afraid?"

"Probably. What else did she want to know?"

"Who my best man was. Needs the names for the guest list."

"Who is your best man?"

"Tony Delgado."

I liked Delgado a lot. My first impression wasn't the greatest; and the idea of running into him in a dark alley without knowing his agenda would certainly fill a lot of people with fear. Now I saw him as the man who chilled my uptight sister out, doted on my adorable niece, and was an all round nice guy. "Aww! That's so nice!" I kissed him before sitting back on my bar stool.

"Glad you're happy about it."

"I can see you two now," I said, holding my hands up to put Solomon in a fantasy picture frame. The wedding talk did distract me rather well from digging into Solomon's past. "Hanging out, poring over my mother's binders for bridegroom inspiration, trying on suits together, crying over your speeches…"

"No," said Solomon.

"Are you going to have a crazy bachelor party?"

Solomon thought about it. "Define crazy."

"*What happens in Vegas, stays in Vegas* crazy."

"You want me to go to Vegas?"

"No, but now I want to go."

"I'm thinking poker, pizza and a lot of beer. What are you thinking for your bachelorette?"

Dancing on tables, brightly-colored cocktails, high heels, sexy dresses, lasting all night long, and doing my best to avoid wearing fluffy boas, princess tiaras, or any accessory with a penis on it. Solomon didn't need to know that either. "Same," I said. "But slightly different."

"How different?"

"No pizza, beer, or poker."

Solomon smiled. "I'm happy to give you any kind of wedding you want," he told me. He reached for a slice and chewed it thoughtfully. "You want a big wedding for two hundred guests? You got it. A small, intimate affair? Not a problem."

"Two hundred guests is considered intimate for the Graves family."

"My point is: whatever you want, tell me and I'll sign the check. I just want you to be happy."

"I am happy. Are you happy?"

"Very," said Solomon.

"I suppose you can have the last slice then." I nodded to the box.

"Now, I'm ecstatic."

CHAPTER THIRTEEN

If anyone knew about Fiona's concerns regarding Debby Patterson, I hoped it would be her husband. With Fiona's suspicions permanently silenced, the only way I could find out what she planned to tell me was if she already shared her thoughts with someone she was close to.

Garrett set up the appointment for late morning. He told me that Jerry Queller decided he couldn't stay in the family home without Fiona and was currently staying with friends. I could understand why he preferred to change his location. I doubted if I could have stayed in a house where my spouse had been murdered only days before. Just the idea of walking past the room where such an event occurred gave me shudders. I had no doubt it was far worse for him.

The man at the door looked gaunt and sad, his eyes rimmed in red, his jaw covered with a week-old stubble that was peppered with gray. He shook my hand politely and invited me inside when I introduced myself, insisting that I called him *Jerry*. "Lieutenant Graves says you have some questions for me," he said, directing me into a spacious living room. "I'm not sure what more I can tell you that I haven't already told the police about my wife's... my..." He trailed off and gulped.

"I really appreciate you seeing me. I know this must be a horrible time," I told him, my heart swelling with sympathy at his distress. "I wanted to talk to you about a few things your wife said to me before she died."

"Will it help with the case?"

"It might, or possibly, a cold case that I'm also looking into."

"Did the fiend who did this to my wife kill someone else?" he asked. He paused mid-step, and I could see the alarm lighting his face up.

"I don't know but I don't think that's the case here. It might be connected, and it might not."

Jerry sat down and placed his palms on his thighs, steeling himself for whatever I was about to shoot at him. I hoped to make it quick and easy without piling on more pain. I took the seat adjacent to him, knowing my time was limited. "Your wife, Fiona, was concerned about a woman she knew. She thought she might not be the person she said she was," I started.

Jerry looked up from where he'd been studying his knees. His pinched eyes stared at me without really looking. "You mean Debby Patterson," he stated.

"I do. Can you tell me what Fiona said about her and her unexpected return?"

"Uh…" He blew out a breath and looked up at the ceiling as he collected his thoughts. "Fiona always said it was the strangest thing when Debby took off and didn't come back. She thought it was damned rude of Debby but Margaret and Rod never seemed to find it odd. I guess they got used to it. Fiona told me she would be pissed if our kids ever acted like that, but it was their family, not ours, so who were we to criticize?"

"Very diplomatic," I said, feeling that way myself.

"They were happy when Debby came home. Right out of the blue, you know? I'm not sure anyone expected it, but they invited us to a dinner to celebrate the event so we went."

"Was that the first time you saw Debby since her long disappearance?"

"First time in a decade or more, but you must have known they cleared up that disappearance thing with the police after a couple of months?"

"The case was officially left open until Debby returned to Montgomery and could be interviewed," I told him even though he probably already knew. Given the trauma undoubtedly on his mind, it wouldn't be amiss if he didn't remember the finer details of the Patterson case.

"That so? Rod never mentioned it, neither did Margaret so I assumed it was over. I didn't speak to Debby much beyond the casual 'hello' or 'great to see you'. She was just a kid when we all met. Besides, I'm not a chatterbox. My wife was the chatterbox."

"Fiona and Debby talked at the welcome home dinner?" I prompted, hoping to spark his memory. Fiona told me they did but she was not prepared to expand on their conversation until we were well beyond Margaret Patterson's hearing distance.

"Yes, not for long, but I remember my wife taking Debby to the side before we left. In the car, on our way home, I could tell something was troubling Fiona so I asked her. She said the darnedest thing: that she didn't think Debby was Debby. So I asked her who did she think she was?"

"What did she say?"

"Fiona said she had no idea but she was sure she wasn't Debby. One hundred percent sure."

"What else did she say?"

"I remember telling her that was crazy and Fiona said she didn't think so. She said people change so much in ten years that it was absolutely possible for someone else to come back instead. She said something must have happened to Debby during those years and someone else just took over her life. I laughed. I said she'd been watching too much TV but now..." He stopped, his fists clenching and unclenching.

"Now you think differently?" I asked.

"I don't know." He shrugged, unclenching his fists and resting his palms on his thighs. "It's so far-fetched. Who takes over someone else's life? It's... it's just crazy."

"What did you think of Debby?"

"I didn't really know Debby back then. She was, what? Twenty-two or something when she left? I was in my forties. We didn't socialize often because we saw her parents at the club or out somewhere. My wife knew Debby a little better because she was friends with her mom."

"Did Fiona and Debby spend a lot of time together?"

"I don't think they socialized, but I'm sure they spoke from time to time. Fiona and Margaret always had some event they were planning, or a dinner to attend, or a meeting. Debby may have dropped in from time to time but I don't think she shared the same interests as her mother. She was a free spirit and her parents were go-getters."

"Do you think Fiona saw Debby often enough to reasonably say that she wasn't convinced the same woman returned?"

"That's what Fiona thought. I asked her the first time she mentioned it why would our friends embrace someone who wasn't their daughter? I said if anyone knows who Debby is, it's Margaret and Rod! They knew her best and that was good enough for me. I'm sure I'd know my kids after any length of time, no matter how long."

"Did Fiona mention her impostor theory again?"

"Yes, a couple of times. She didn't want to say anything to Margaret or Rod but I think she asked around after that dinner."

"What did she find out?"

"Nothing that I'm aware of. She couldn't locate anyone who used to know Debby."

"Didn't you think that was strange?"

"No. Debby left for ten years and didn't keep in touch. It's unfriendly, sure, but not uncommon. I don't think she was very well-versed in social skills. She was always rather awkward, not like Margaret. Fiona always said Margaret must have coined the term, 'social butterfly'."

"Were you aware that Fiona asked me to meet her shortly before she died?" I asked, trying to soften my voice. The words were horribly painful and I didn't want the poor man to suffer anymore than he clearly was. He didn't need me to remind him how dead is wife was; I was sure he thought about that with every breath.

"No, I didn't know." Jerry paused, thinking again, if his zoned-out eyes were any indication. He shook his shoulders, pulling himself back to the present. "Did she want to talk to you about Debby?"

"Yes."

Jerry fixed me with an unwavering stare. "Do you think Debby killed my wife?"

"I don't know."

"Debby didn't even know that Fiona believed she was an impostor. That is, I don't think she did. Not one person mentioned the missing persons case at the welcome home dinner. As far as I know, my wife didn't see her again after that. Rod cleared all that missing persons crap up when Debby came home. You should have seen them when they heard she was coming back. I was playing golf with Rod when he got the email. He was so happy. He could hardly wait to see his daughter again. I can't see any motive to compel someone to impersonate Debby. Even if my wife said something to the Pattersons, it would have been swiftly straightened out."

"Did her father ever say why Debby came home?" I wondered.

"No, I don't think so. He just said they got an email saying Debby had booked a flight and would be home soon. She also said not to worry about putting her up because she booked a hotel."

"Did you think that was odd?"

"That she came home so suddenly?"

"That, and booking a hotel room instead of staying with her parents? Mrs. Patterson showed me Debby's old room. It looked like she never changed a single thing in it."

"Margaret was a little fastidious. I guess I didn't think anything about it. I assumed Debby valued her space. Maybe after her big adventure, she wasn't ready to come home to her high school bedroom." He laughed but there was no joy in it.

The doorbell rang and Jerry looked up. "Are you expecting someone?" I asked.

"There's been a long line of people dropping by with casseroles," he said. "My freezer is full of them and so is the one here. You can take one home with you if you like. There's enough to feed me, my friends and their families for at least two weeks."

"That's very kind of you, but no thank you, I couldn't," I told him, waiting while he got up to answer the door.

When he came back, Mrs. Patterson and Debby were with him. Mrs. Patterson held a large casserole dish. "Look what Debby made for you," she said, blinking in obvious surprise when she saw me. "Detective?"

"I'm not a detective, I'm a consultant for MPD," I corrected her.

"Ms. Graves was asking a few questions about Fiona," Jerry told them.

"Of course, she's been working for you," said Debby. She reached over to squeeze Jerry's hand briefly. It seemed friendly but not overtly affectionate and she moved to lean against the arm of his chair. "We've all tried to help as much as we can," Debby told me.

"She doesn't work for me. You consult for the police department," said Jerry, looking right at me. "That's what you said."

"Thank you so much for your time," I said, rising to leave. I know when my time is up. I didn't want to identify whom I was working for, or have to come up with any explanation as to precisely what I was investigating. Debby thought I was looking into Fiona's murder; Jerry knew I wanted to confirm Debby's true identity and was searching for any connection between his wife and her. If he blew my story, Debby would be on high alert. Trying to get any further information out of her, or anyone close to her, would be almost impossible after that. Even if I deflected Debby now, there was no way I could stop her and Jerry from talking after I left. I had a dilemma: either I overstay my welcome and distract them both; or leave and hope they chose to discuss other things.

Before I could reach a decision, Debby curved her arm around my shoulder and was gently guiding me towards the door. "Thanks so much for coming by," she said, a false smile etched on her face. "I'm sure Mr. Queller has had about all he can handle today."

I glanced back as she propelled me forwards but Jerry's head was bent down, forgetting all about me. Mrs. Patterson placed the casserole on a side table and knelt down next to him, talking softly.

"I'll walk you to your car," said Debby as she steered me outside. With the door closed behind us, she hissed, "What are you really doing here?"

"Just asking a few questions to complete my investigation."

"I don't buy it! You've been sniffing around for days. At my parents' house, the market, my hotel. Are you following me?"

"If I were, wouldn't you have gotten here first?" I asked, redirecting the conversation. That stumped Debby and her eyes narrowed but she regained her composure quickly.

"Are you even working for him?" she inquired. "Did he hire you to follow me?"

"Absolutely not," I told her, letting her pick whichever question she chose for my answer.

"You listen here..." Debby began.

"Why would he hire..." I started to ask at the same time.

"Marley! Marley, is that you?" A woman across the road began to wave frantically. She hopped up and down, trying to catch our attention. Debby glanced at her, then looked away, her face full of annoyance. "It is you!" The woman hurried across the road, looking absolutely delighted as she reached us. She hugged Debby and pulled back. "It's been so long. How have you been?"

"I think you have the wrong person," Debby spluttered. "I don't think I know you."

"Of course you do! We took a cooking class together. Wednesday nights. Remember? Oh, I know, it was years ago but I will never forget you. You made an amazing soufflé while the rest of the class flopped. I'm Amber Yuen. Our stations were right next to each other."

"I never took a cooking class," said Debby.

"Yes, you did… On Wednesday nights. It was designed for beginners."

"No, that was not me."

"You are Marley?"

"No, I'm sorry, you must have me confused with someone else. Excuse me." Debby stepped backwards and turned around before walking away. At the house, she shut the door behind her without looking back.

"I am so embarrassed," said Amber, staring after her. "Obviously, I made a mistake. Sorry to disturb you."

"No trouble at all," I said, grateful for the timely interruption. Scaring Debby off was better than I could have hoped for! Now all I needed was for my good luck to continue inside the house, keeping the topic of conversation on anything but me. If Debby had been a little more insistent, I might have been the one running for my car, scrambling for an explanation to give Garrett the moment someone complained about me to the police.

With my access to Jerry Queller now blocked, I headed for the next name on my interview list. I was determined to find something else to support Garrett's beliefs. I'd exhausted all the other avenues of interviews, except for one: Debby's old friend in Frederickstown. As that lead entered my head, I groaned. Why didn't I pay a little more attention to what the woman outside the house called Debby? *Marley*. Marley McFadden. Marley was the other friend we failed to locate.

I frowned when I thought about Debby's reaction to her intrusion. She pretended like she didn't know that name at all, insisting that the woman was confused, and practically running away when Amber challenged her. Yet Mrs. Patterson said she and Marley were close friends. Why didn't Debby tell Amber that she knew Marley?

I puzzled over that for a few minutes and my thoughts began moving in circles until a new thought appeared in the mix: Maddox. Thinking about him was something I tried very hard to avoid. Every time his name popped into my head, I carefully stuffed it away, refusing to ponder on anything about him. But now, in my empty car with nothing else to distract me, he had my full attention.

He was the reason I poked into Solomon's past the night before. Despite the innocuous questions, Solomon couldn't provide any answers. Was it because of the wedding talk, or just because Solomon wanted to distract me?

Maddox's warning about Solomon's past really got to me. Much more than I ever thought possible and that made me angry. *He* made me angry. I didn't want to question Solomon, much less myself for not knowing more about him; but now, those little questions began to grow bigger in my mind, and the answers grew smaller.

Instead of happily browsing through my mother's wedding binders—which were still on the floorboard of the passenger side—and buying up all the stocks of bridal magazines, I kept wondering what Solomon did and how he lived before we met. What did he do during the time when we did know each other before he set up the agency? Why did he make it clear that he intended to make my town *his* home?

The uncomfortable truth was that I knew very little about the man I was engaged to. Sure, I knew what he liked to eat—everything—and what made him laugh and how deeply he slept. I also knew he worked hard, was an excellent marksman, very athletic, and a superb lover. I knew he ran a successful business, and given the beautiful house we shared, had plenty of money to invest. However, I never saw his yearbook photo, or had any idea about his career trajectory. I didn't even know if he led a wild life in his youth, or a quiet one. Did he go to space camp or basketball camp in the summertime? What was his major at college? Did he even go to a university?

Up until now, what little I knew about him was enough for me.

"Damn you, Maddox," I yelled.

"Dialing Maddox," replied my cell phone. I screamed in fright, jabbing at the screen to make it stop before the call connected. The screen went blank, and I dropped the offending item into my purse, hoping it remained quiet.

Forcing my brain to return to the task at hand, I searched for the address of Anna Colby. She might not have lived in the nicest part of Frederickstown, but it wasn't the worst either. Someone was obviously making an effort to improve the curb appeal of the small house and I took a moment to appreciate the neat fence and pretty, but inexpensive, pots on the porch as I parked outside. I locked the car doors and discreetly surveyed a loitering group of teenage boys, their hoodies up and cigarettes in hand before I opened the chain-link gate and walked up to the door. I knocked and waited, checking to see that the boys hadn't moved any closer to my car.

The woman who answered the door looked tired. The long, black braids were gone, replaced by a chic bob, but her face was still the same, albeit a little older. "I don't buy anything at the door," she told me, preparing to close it.

"I'm not selling anything and I'm not asking for anything but your help," I said. "I'm looking for Anna Colby."

She blinked suspiciously. "Here I am."

"I'm a private investigator," I told her, displaying my license. "Do you have a moment to talk?"

"Is this about my ex-husband?" she asked, heaving out a long sigh. "I already told the last one. I don't know where that no good POS is but if you manage to find him, I want my car back along with seven years of unpaid child support that he owes me so I can move out of this crappy house."

"It's not about your ex. It's about an old friend of yours. Debby Patterson."

"Debby? Oh, wow! I haven't heard her name in a while."

"Mind if I come in?"

"Since you're not trying to repossess anything thanks to my ex, please," she said as she stepped back. I entered a neat but almost bare living room. An old but cared-for couch, covered in a blanket, was adorned with pretty pillows. Books filled the shelves of a half-sized bookcase and a basket of children's toys was on the floor. There was a small TV and some children's DVDs but no child.

"He's at school," Anna explained. "Debby Patterson, huh? What did she do?"

"I was hired to look into Debby Patterson's disappearance," I told her.

"I heard she left town ten years ago and never returned. Isn't it a little late to go looking for her now?"

"We're working on some new leads. Has she contacted you at all in that time?"

"No, I tried to get in touch with her but she never called me back. Then I got caught up in my own life and married a man I now know was a huge jerk who left me with a baby and a stack of debts. I lost my apartment and my job because I couldn't afford childcare, and had to move us here until I get back on my feet."

"That is a lot to deal with."

"Yeah, it is. Every so often, I used to think about Debby, and wonder whatever happened to her, but truthfully, as bad as it sounds, I have so much to deal with in my own life…"

"My sister was a single mom. It's pretty tough work," I told her.

"Yeah? It's funny in a strange way. It's actually easier to be a single mom than to be a married mom with a husband who's hell-bent on screwing up your life."

"I think I know him," I said. "I almost married him!"

"Tell me his name is Olivier Simmons and I will believe you."

"Actually no, but it sounds like he used the same playbook as a man I almost married." We smiled at each other, embarrassed and friendly at the same time. I liked her, I realized. She had a lot of admirable qualities and was rather warm. I hoped she had compassionate people around her who cared about her child and her.

"Almost? Lucky escape for you."

"Yes, it was," I agreed, smiling now that we shared a connection and something to bond over. "So, Debby hasn't contacted you at all in ten years?"

"No."

"Were you close before she disappeared?"

"I thought so. We met at summer camp one year and kept in touch. Neither of us had a great time in high school so we hung out together and later, went to the same college."

"Did you think it was strange that she disappeared so suddenly?"

"Not at first. We were both working, trying to make it as new graduates, until I met jerk-face, and then, we weren't hanging out as much. I didn't realize how long it had been until the police came to see me and told me she was missing."

"Were you worried?"

"Yes and no. Debby sometimes disappeared for a couple of weeks at a time; and she wasn't the best at time-keeping, or even showing up occasionally. She always appeared eventually with some new half-assed apology. I figured this was just like all those other times and, to be honest, I was getting sick and tired of it."

"Did she ever say where she was going, or where she went?"

"No, she was always private like that."

"When did you start to get worried?"

"When the police contacted me, I think. They said she was reported missing and hadn't been seen in weeks, but there wasn't anything I could tell them. I tried calling her but she never called back, and you know, life happened. I used to think about her occasionally but... a little part of me thought that maybe she 'ghosted' me. Maybe she didn't want to be my friend anymore."

"Was that the way she treated people?"

"She didn't have many friends so I can't be sure, but occasionally she did. She was kind of dismissive, like I would call her three times in a row to hang out but she never initiated things or reciprocated. By the time we graduated, I decided I preferred two-way friendships, where both parties make an effort. Debby wasn't like that. That was partly why I didn't see her much in the months before she disappeared. When they told me she was officially missing, I got worried."

"Did she contact you recently?"

"No." Anna paused. "You never said why you are asking me now. It's been so long."

"The case was closed recently."

"You wouldn't be asking me if a body was found," Anna mused. "She's alive?"

"We believe so."

"I doubt I would be at the top of her list of people to contact. Plus, I moved and changed my surname when I got married. I wouldn't have been too easy to find. I only just changed my name back."

"No, but not impossible either. Do you think you would recognize her if you saw her again?"

"Maybe. People can change a lot."

"If I came back with a photo, would you try?"

"Sure, no problem."

"One last thing, do you know where I can find Marley McFadden?"

"Marley? She was another friend of Debby's, right?"

I confirmed she was and Anna continued, "I only met Marley a few times. A couple of times socially and when Debby invited me to her new apartment once to hang out. I thought we were getting take-out since Debby can't even make toast, but Marley cooked us a huge meal. I remember her cooking was really good although I wouldn't call us *friends*. I think she followed Debby around and Debby liked that. I believe they knew each other from high school but she didn't live in Montgomery anymore. I'm not sure where she lived."

I thanked Anna for her time and told her I'd come back soon with a photo. I wasn't sure what to expect when I did, only that she was my best hope for an identification. If she agreed that the Debby I photographed was the Debby she once knew, then I could tell Garrett and call off the investigation before any more time was invested in it. If Anna couldn't identify her, then Garrett would need to know that too. For now though, I planned to keep Anna's name and location exclusively to myself. The last person who questioned Debby's identity wound up dead.

My phone rang as I got into my car and I checked the screen. There was a missed call from Maddox. He was probably wondering why I called him and hung up. Fortunately, it was Garrett calling now. "Hey," I said, "I just visited Anna Colby."

"Anything of interest?"

"Not much. She might be able to identify Debby if I can get her a photo. I think we should keep her name and location secret for now, just in case Fiona's murder is related to Debby."

"I agree to be cautious," Garrett said. "I'm actually calling about Fiona. I rushed the DNA results on the grip from the gun that was used to kill her and we've got a problem. It's male DNA. Our killer could be almost anyone."

CHAPTER FOURTEEN

I perched on the chair opposite Garrett's desk, where Debby's case file lay open between us. The room that housed the homicide division was quiet, something that didn't bode well for the residents of Montgomery. Someone had to have been murdered to keep the squad this busy.

"Don't worry about Jerry Queller," said Garrett after I finished telling him about Debby, along with Margaret Patterson's interruption and the ensuing question about who I was working for. "I'll go talk to him and smooth things over."

"It's probably too late," I pointed out. "Debby has probably already asked Jerry and he'll confirm that I don't work for him. As soon as they start talking about it, Margaret Patterson will remember I said I worked for you."

"You think Debby smells a rat?"

I pulled a face. "She said as much."

"I wish I could tell you to leave her alone but you're all I've got. Stick with her, just be careful."

"No problem." We both paused and took a moment to breathe. Garrett's DNA news wasn't what I wanted to hear. It would have been so much easier if he'd called and told me they managed to link the blood on the gun's grip to *someone*, even if they couldn't match the historical DNA evidence on file from Debby's disappearance. If the Debby we knew was the impostor, then naturally, her DNA wouldn't be on file. When I turned over the stolen toothbrush I had high hopes that it could provide a match. Learning that the DNA belonged to a male and they hadn't turned up even a familial match in AFIS was disappointing. It would have been nice to wrap things up in a neat, little package: Debby wasn't Debby and had to kill Fiona to protect her secret. Of course, that didn't explain why her parents welcomed a stranger into their home although it would have been a pretty good conclusion to the case. It was rare I saw my brother appear so wholly confused and this was definitely one of those times.

"Are you still going to run the toothbrush DNA?" I asked, mostly from curiosity, especially after the lengths I'd gone to in order to retrieve it.

"I planned on it. Back when Debby Patterson's DNA was collected, we didn't have the resources to digitize every record so her DNA never got uploaded to the system. She was officially in a gray area. Still missing because we couldn't reach her for an interview, but according to her parents, she was fine so she dropped to the bottom of our list. I took the sample from the evidence box over to the lab and turned it in but it was too degraded to provide a match."

"The toothbrush is useless?" That was disappointing. I expected climbing out of a third story hotel room should have had a better reason than practicing escape routes under extremely strained conditions.

"Not necessarily. The DNA they extracted is in the system, but no matches. Maybe something else will come up. I did find a couple notebooks in the box that I need to skim through in case there's something I forgot."

"You could ask the Pattersons for their DNA," I suggested. A simple cheek swab would take only seconds and could either prove or disprove Debby's identity. Her DNA couldn't lie.

"On what grounds?"

I hadn't thought of that. Now it was in my mind, I had no doubt the Pattersons had already discussed me and what I might be doing by infiltrating their lives. They were probably pissed. "You could compel them with a warrant?"

"Yeah, like a judge will sign off on that," grunted Garrett.

"Okay, so strike one for the DNA. I'm going to get a photo of Debby," I told Garrett, recanting my conversation with her old friend. "If I can get Anna to pick Debby out of a series of similar-looking photos, would that be enough to arrest her for something?"

"No, that just gives more proof that Debby is who she says she is. Now, if your informant categorically states that none of the photos is Debby, I could pick her up for fraud," said Garrett. He rested his elbows on the desk and steepled his fingers under his chin. "I can find a reason to extract her DNA. Under those circumstances, the Pattersons might even supply a sample, if pressed."

"I hate to ask, but what if she really is Debby? Are we guilty of harassing her?"

"My gut says no."

"There's no one else who can verify her identity and you can't link her to the murder."

"Call it a hunch but she's still my top suspect. There is something way off about that woman. I just wish I could put my finger on it, or anything more definitive than just a feeling in my gut. If we verify she isn't Debby Patterson, that provides a motive for murder and then I can do a lot more. She could have an associate stashed somewhere. Is there anyone else in Debby's life who could possibly identify her?"

"Aside from Anna, the only people I've tracked down are her former boss and her colleague. They both could I assume. There's also the friend Marley who I can't trace."

"I hate to ask but maybe now is a good time to redeem a favor from the FBI to track her down?"

"I don't think I have any favors to redeem."

"That why Maddox called you twice while you've been here?" Garrett asked. My phone had been on his desk, relegated to a small strip of space behind a stack of files, but when the screen flashed a second time, and Maddox's name appeared, I discreetly knocked the phone into my purse. At least, I thought I was being discreet.

"Nope." At least, I didn't think that was the reason. "How do you know he called? You couldn't see my phone from your side."

"It's that look you get on your face when only he calls. He was a damn good detective. Smart, tenacious, with excellent instincts. I wish he'd stuck around instead of suiting up for the Feds. I'd have him back any day."

"Really?" That surprised me. I knew Garrett liked Maddox but I didn't realize he admired him too.

"Yes, really. I know our brothers and I gave him a hard time when he was dating you, and afterwards too, but he sucked it all up."

"I vaguely recall an incident where everyone walked out when he walked into the canteen."

Garrett rolled his eyes. "My point is: Maddox was here long before he was your ex. You don't get dibs on him."

"Dibs?"

"You don't get first option on him."

"I never said I did!"

Garrett rocked back in his chair. "I know I didn't work with him directly, but he could have gone places here too if he wanted to. I don't think any of us realized how ambitious he was. He could have earned a promotion here easily. He had an excellent solve rate, and put in the necessary hours undercover and was well liked. He still is. Don't know what got him thinking about the Feds but maybe I can blame you for that."

"I think he just wanted a change of scenery," I said but my mind flickered to the accusation. I wondered if Garrett were right.

"He happy over at the FBI?"

"Mostly." Maddox and I had engaged in that discussion before. He said he enjoyed the work initially but it wasn't what he expected. Now he was assigned to special projects that remained a mystery to me but he seemed happier doing it. I squirmed in my seat, wishing we could change the subject to anything but the man I was doing my best not to think about.

"He'd be an asset to Solomon if he ever thought about hiring any new investigators."

I thought about that and grimaced. "I don't think either of them would want that."

Garrett raised his eyebrows. "No, I don't suppose they would."

"I can't ask him for a favor," I said. "We're not talking right now."

Garrett gave me a pointed look. "Swallow whatever pride you have and ask, please. I need a break on this case. Officially and unofficially."

"I'll think about it." I grabbed my purse, knowing the best way to end the conversation was to remove myself from it.

"Don't forget babysitting," Garrett added as he showed me to the door.

"On my calendar," I assured him.

"It's officially *Star Wars* night according to the kids. If you can wear a costume…"

"You asked the wrong auntie but I bet Lily has one."

"I won't ask why she has one."

"Probably best if she doesn't tell you."

"It is childsafe, isn't it? I don't think TracI will like slutty Yoda and I don't want to give my kids any bad ideas."

"It's safe and it isn't green. I'll bring the popcorn!"

I waited until I was outside MPD before unlocking my phone and checking the messages. Maddox didn't leave one but he did send a text: *I don't want to argue. Call me*.

I could have ignored it until things got really awkward but since he made the effort to send me a message, I swallowed my pride, crossing my fingers that our prior argument wouldn't restart and called him. I immediately got his answering service. I hesitated before saying, "I'm sorry. I don't want to argue either" and hanging up. Even with my apology expressed I didn't feel much better. It was weak, almost pathetic for me to leave it as a message. *But*, said the little voice in my head, *at least I'd done it!* Then I remembered the favor, and swallowing more pride, I called back. In a small, pleading voice, I asked, "This is entirely unrelated to the apology but please can you trace a name for me? Marley McFadden?"

I was already in my car by the time I remembered something important. I forgot to tell Garrett about Grandma Patterson's rambling on about *another mother*. I was just about to hop out of my car and return to his office when a loud rap sounded on my door window. I scrolled the window down and saw Garrett's face. "What's up?" I asked.

"I had a weird feeling I forget something," he began, "so I took another look into the case file. The DNA thing might not be so conclusive after all."

"What do you mean?"

"Read this," said Garrett, handing me a coffee-stained notebook that was open to a page full of handwritten notes. "Start on this page."

"What is it?"

"My notebook from back then. I didn't add it to the file I gave you because I figured everything you needed was already in there. I was wrong."

"Okay." I took the notebook and squinted at Garrett's cramped handwriting.

Interview with Dr. Patterson, I read, noting the date was only days after Debby was reported missing. *Parents concerned that there might be some influence by biological parents but nothing substantial. Debby found out about adoption accidentally when she was a teen but the issue rarely discussed amongst the family.*

"Debby is adopted?" I said. "Do you think that was a factor?"

"It was mentioned at the time but I don't know. It hasn't been on my mind so I guess I forgot about it."

"The Pattersons never mentioned it."

"From what I remember, they only told me after I interviewed them a couple of times, and even then, they had to be pressed. I got the feeling that it wasn't something they were comfortable discussing. There was no need to collect their DNA because even if we got a corpse somewhere down the line, we wouldn't have had a familial sample to compare it to. So here's the thing, there's no biological connection to Debby that we can work with. That DNA could have come from anyone, even someone close to her. There were no usable prints on the gun so it was the best we had to work with."

"But you already ruled her out as the shooter."

"Not anymore. She had access to guns. That DNA could have come from someone close to her, someone she could have encouraged to kill on her behalf."

"From her dad?" I wondered. "He can shoot."

"That's what I thought."

"Can you get his DNA?"

"No probable cause. Not unless he volunteers it—and why would he?—no judge will sign a warrant without any motive or evidence."

"What if he refuses to give it? Doesn't that make him look guilty?"

"People are funny about handing over their DNA to law enforcement. It's not unusual to refuse even if you have nothing to hide."

"I remembered something too. When I spoke to Grandma Patterson, she mentioned Debby's *other mother* during a lucid moment. Not much, just some ramblings, and before you ask, no, she isn't capable of murder."

"I agree. I'm going to head over to the Pattersons now before I go home. I'd suggest you sit in, but I think it's best that you keep a low profile like we spoke about."

"No problem. I need to get that photo of Debby anyway and see if Anna can identify her as Debby."

"I'll see you later. We can talk then. Don't be late."

"I won't," I promised. "I'm looking forward to it."

I didn't know where Debby was but felt pretty sure I could find her. Plus, the drive gave me plenty of time to ruminate over the newest facts. Adoption was hardly uncommon, nor was the Pattersons' attitude in regard to keeping it quiet. If she'd taken off to see her biological parents, it must have been quite worrisome for them. I could understand why they didn't want to push her any further away, especially if that were the case. It was just strange that no one else ever mentioned it. Surely with a weight like that on her mind, Debby would have told someone? Yet it didn't come up when I spoke to Art and Kara, or even with Anna. I was almost certain I saw no mention of adoption or biological parents in Debby's emails either.

Debby didn't have many places to go so I started at the hotel. Her car wasn't there when I circled the parking lot so I returned to the road, aiming for her parents' house. There, I found her car. I parked and sent a message to Garrett, warning him that she was there, just in case he wanted to speak to her parents alone. While I waited, I took my camera out, hiking it up and getting ready to catch a shot of Debby as she left the house. I had to hope it was soon, lest I be late for my nephews' and niece's *Star Wars*-themed movie night.

Lily called me ten minutes into my stakeout. "Where are you?" she asked, "And do you want a Jabba the Hut costume?"

"Stakeout and no way! Tell me, why do you have a Jabba the Hut costume?"

"I don't want to talk about it. It was a bad night."

"Then I definitely don't want it!" I grimaced.

"But who will you go as?"

"I'm going as me."

Lily exhaled a deep sigh. "I hope I didn't put my hair in Princess Leia buns for nothing. I'm leaving in twenty minutes so if you're late, that's okay. Poppy is dressed as Yoda. It's a Halloween costume for a dog but I figured, what does she care? She's the same size as a Chihuahua and her arms even fit through the front leg holes."

"I can't wait to see her! Is Jord coming?"

"No, he's working late. What about Solomon?"

"Maybe." I hoped he would. He liked my niece and nephews and they liked him. They hadn't started to call him Uncle John yet but I figured that would happen soon enough. Just the idea of it made me melt like ice cream on a hot summer's day. If he cuddled Poppy, I would probably become a puddle on the floor. It was just a good thing we weren't expecting my mom for babysitting duty. She would have had a lot to say about Solomon and fatherhood. "I'll see you soon."

I refocused the telephoto lens and watched Debby walking through the living room. I could just see her pulling on her coat before she slipped out of view. I slumped in my seat behind the wheel, the camera lens perched invisibly on the door frame, and waited for her to exit the house. A moment later, the door opened. I readied my finger on the button, waiting for the moment when she looked my way. She and her mom hugged briefly before Debby walked into the street, her face partially hidden by a large scarf. She got to her car but instead of reaching for the door handle, she stopped and looked up, directly at me.

I snapped a series of photos, realizing the decreasing distance meant she was now walking towards me, and her pace was picking up. Slumping even deeper into the seat, I lowered the camera and hoped she couldn't identify me. The rapping on my window was just too bad.

"That's it!" Debby yelled at me. "Stop following me!"

"I'm not following you," I shouted back while looking up as innocently as I could.

"Open this door right now and tell me who you're working for!" Debby rattled the door handle and I thanked myself for choosing to be less lax about locking my doors. "I'm going to call the police!" she yelled.

"That's fine," I said. "Please do." That reply seemed to flummox Debby and she stopped, although she kept frowning.

"Why are you following me?" she asked, her voice dropping down to a more reasonable tone. "I haven't done anything wrong."

"Okay," I said, opting to lie. My only alternative now that Debby blocked my path of escape was to start my car, mount the sidewalk and drive down it until I could veer back onto the street and fully escape. But that was definitely breaking all the rules. I wouldn't put it past Debby to take her own photo of me and file a complaint. That would beset me with problems that only Garrett could get me out of and I cringed at the idea of begging him. "I am following you," I told her. "I've been hired by a couple who think you're their long-lost daughter."

She pulled a face. "Seriously? What a load of crap!"

"It's true, really. They hired me a week ago after seeing you on the street and they firmly believe you're their long-lost daughter. They wanted me to verify it, if it's true. Are you adopted?" I asked.

"No! You've met my parents. I'm not adopted! Is that why you've been pestering Mr. Queller? To get to me?"

"Absolutely," I continued, smoothly easing into the lie. "I knew someone on the force and used them to get to you."

"That's terrible! How could you harass that poor man just to get to me? You could have simply asked."

"Now I am. I apologize, sincerely. I'll let the family know that you're not adopted so you couldn't possibly be their real daughter. It's a shame too because they are a very wealthy couple with no one else to share their waning years. I think they wanted to make sure all their money, investments, and a very, very large house went directly to a family member, once they passed, which could be very soon," I added. I was watching her closely to see if the lure of vast amounts of cash could sway Debby into temptation but she showed no sign of greed or interest.

"I hope they find their long-lost kid but it's definitely not me," said Debby. "You shouldn't take any more of their money."

"I won't. May I take a photo of you to show them as proof? Once they see that, they'll probably realize the family resemblance is lacking." I raised my camera but Debby put her hand up, covering the portion of window where I rested the lens.

"No, I don't like having my picture taken. Please go away now and stop pestering my family."

"I'm so sorry for any trouble I might have caused you." I put my camera on the seat and made a show of starting the ignition. Debby stepped away from my car and I pulled out. In my rearview mirror, I saw her standing in the street, watching me drive away. She still didn't move when I turned the corner.

The lie I told came to me hastily but the information she provided was useful. I was positive Debby believed she wasn't adopted. Even the chance of being the only heir of wealthy parents didn't spur her to think of the possibility she could be theirs. If she were a liar, and really wasn't Debby, wouldn't she have leapt at the opportunity to get a payday from innocent people who possibly couldn't verify her identity in the limited time frame I suggested? Then, another thought came to me: if she were really Debby, why didn't she admit to being adopted, or maybe even try and wheedle a little more information from me about the fantasy rich parents?

The adamant stance that she wasn't adopted stuck me as strange unless she also shared her parents' view on private family matters. She didn't look surprised at my questions, just a little perplexed.

I circled the block and made my way back to the Pattersons' road. I pulled up on the corner, with only the hood of my car peeking past the corner fence and watched Debby's car move off. I shot a message to Garrett, letting him know that Debby had gone. Before I could pull a U-turn and head for Garrett's house, my phone rang. Naturally, I figured it was Garrett so I grabbed it, answering without checking the screen.

"I asked Debby and she didn't know she was adopted," I said. "Weird or what?"

"I have no idea," said Maddox. "Shall I go with weird?"

"Sorry!" I paused, realizing my mistake. "I thought you were Garrett."

"I got your message."

"And I got yours." I paused before we both started speaking again. "—I'm sorry…"

"—I don't want to hurt you…"

We stopped, then I said, "You first."

"I'm sorry I hurt you."

"I'm sorry I got mad at you."

"Friends again?"

"Yes," I agreed. The worry that I didn't know I'd been holding in dropped swiftly away from me, and the nagging tension I felt before was instantly eased from my shoulders.

"Phew. I was afraid I would have to leave the county."

I laughed. "Garrett asked after you today. He said you were one of MPD's best detectives, amongst other things."

"Nice of him," said Maddox, his voice bubbling with warmth.

"I'd tell you the rest but I don't want your head to swell."

"How's the case going?" Maddox asked, and I was grateful for the change of topic to something safer, something we couldn't hurt each other with.

"Perplexing. Right now, I think I just trapped my target in a lie," I told him, the adoption weighing on my mind. "But I don't know why she's lying. She doesn't have anything to gain."

"Maybe there's something you haven't discovered yet."

"Maybe."

"Do you have all the facts?"

"Probably not," I admitted. "The case is almost a decade old and there wasn't much to go on in the first place."

"I might have something for you. You know that name you asked me to run?"

"Marley McFadden? Yeah, her name came up a couple times. I can't find her and neither can Garrett."

"No one can. Marley McFadden has also been missing almost ten years."

CHAPTER FIFTEEN

Lily's car was already parked outside when I reached Garrett's house and I noticed Poppy's car seat was missing. As I approached the front door, I heard ominous Darth Vader music. I knocked and the door flew open, revealing two small Jedi who were waiting for me with illuminated light-sabers. "Welcome to the cemetery," said Sam, grinning.

"Huh?"

"He means, a lot of Graves are here right now," explained my sister-in-law Traci and Sam laughed at his own joke. "Come on in."

"Where's your costume?" asked Sam, my adorable nephew and occasionally terrifying prankster. He wore a mini Jedi costume and I could only hope he didn't ask me whose it was. I could name a few characters but I didn't have the encyclopedic knowledge Sam seemed to possess.

"Tatooine," I told him, figuring a planet in a galaxy far, far away was a good answer. "I had to leave it in a hurry as the Empire closed in."

"Figures." Sam gave a thoughtful nod. "Mom says I'm not allowed to chop your arm off with my light-saber."

"Please thank her from me."

"She also told Dad she desperately needs a drink. What's a bodyshot?" he asked.

"I did not!" said Traci, coming through the door and ushering me inside while giving Sam a light push towards the den. I glanced over and waved to Lily. Her matching Leia buns shook on either side of her head as she waved back. Addressing me, Traci said, "I do need a drink. Several, possibly, but probably not bodyshots. Thank you for babysitting."

"Anytime. I got popcorn!" I held up the packets I picked up on the way over.

"Yay!" squealed my niece, Chloe. "I can use the microwave!" I handed her one packet and she tore off into the kitchen, Sam right behind her, and both of them with their light-sabers aloft. A moment later and they tore past us.

"Is Garrett here?" I asked Traci, sneaking a look over her shoulder and secretly hoping he had arrived.

"Not yet. He said he had a couple of things to wrap up before he got home. Do you like my dress?" Traci twirled around and smoothed the elegant material over her hips while I made admiring noises.

"Very nice. Is it new? Is this a special occasion?" I wondered what I'd missed and if I should have gotten a card. I glanced around, slightly relieved to see there were no cards displayed across the mantel.

"It's special because we're going out."

"Garrett will love it," I assured her. "And you can stay out as late as you want. I will be here, even after Lily flakes out."

"I am not going to flake," said Lily as she walked over and stifled a yawn.

"These days won't last," Traci assured her, her face full of sympathy.

"I am so relieved to hear that." Lily walked away, dropping onto the couch and yawning again.

Traci grimaced. "I meant, baby two makes it worse."

"There's going to be a baby two?" I gasped.

"No! At least not that I know about!"

"Way to start a rumor!" I held back a laugh. "Let's keep the joys of baby two between us."

Garrett called "hello" from the kitchen and I braced myself against the stampede of small feet. He appeared in the living room doorway and steadied himself before confronting Chloe and Sam who approached him with light-sabers aloft. They pretended to carve him and he dropped to the floor, clutching his arms and gurgling his last words.

"Honey, you need to get changed," chided Traci.

Garrett gazed up from the floor. "You look glamorous," he whistled. Fighting the kids off, he got to his feet and quickly turned them both upside down. He propped them down on their hands, leaning their bodies against the wall. "I didn't forget a gift," he gulped. "It's hidden."

Traci shook her head and rolled her eyes. "It isn't a special occasion. It's just a new dress."

"Phew!" said Garrett.

"I need to talk to you about the case," I told him.

"Can't you two leave work at work? I don't bring work home with me!" sighed Traci.

"Sure you do," said Sam, standing upright. "I'm your work."

"No, you're my kid."

"Same difference." He scooted over to the den and dropped onto the floor next to Poppy, his attention diverted again as he tried to make her giggle and smile.

"He's right," sighed Traci. "He's a labor of love. Fine, you've got five minutes for shop talk then we're out the door. I don't want to lose our reservations."

Garrett steered me into the kitchen. He loosened his tie and wrapped it around his hand, fiddling with the end. "Something happen?"

"Debby caught me outside her house as I was taking her photo. She demanded to know who I was working for so I spun her a line about being hired by some people who thought she was their daughter and wanted to give her a bunch of money. She told me she wasn't adopted."

"Maybe she wasn't interested?"

"That's what I thought. Then I wondered why, if she wasn't Debby, wouldn't she be interested in a big payday? But that didn't fit either because she didn't bite. Then I thought if she was the real Debby, she might still be interested in getting something that was due her, but still nothing. In all, I just thought it was weird that she adamantly insisted she wasn't adopted. The real Debby knew all about her adoption."

"Perhaps she was embarrassed?"

"I wondered if that were the case but even if it was, why lie about it? Why not try and get a little information from me if only to see if I were telling the truth?"

"It's pretty circumstantial. I don't know if I can pull her into the station on that alone."

"I've got something you could use."

"Two minutes," said Traci, ducking her head into the kitchen.

"Be right with you," Garrett assured her. "Go on," he told me.

"I had Maddox run that name." I waited for Garrett to make a smart comment about swallowing my pride and when none came, I continued, "There was one last person from Debby's life we couldn't locate but Maddox found her. Well, not exactly. Debby's friend, Marley McFadden, was reported missing almost ten years ago and hasn't been seen since then. Her name didn't come up because it wasn't under Montgomery jurisdiction; and I'm guessing you didn't search a nationwide database. Mrs. Patterson mentioned that she thought Marley moved out of Montgomery after high school and simply didn't return after college. Anna Colby said Marley didn't live in the area too. We never found out she was missing because no one from here ever went looking for her."

"Two women missing around the same time? That's rather suspicious."

"I think so too. With the two of them so close, I can't help thinking that the same thing happened to them both."

"You think they're both dead?"

"I don't know. Maybe. Let's say someone killed Debby, and Marley found out and they got to her too."

"That doesn't explain who the Debby Patterson we know is."

"Yeah." I thought about it, pushing my mind to reach for something, anything. "What if she's the killer or has an accomplice who did it? What if she killed both women and only came back to stop anyone from uncovering the truth? Fiona could have known both Debby and Marley, and made a connection somehow, which is why she had to die too."

Garrett shook his head, seemingly unconvinced. "I only asked you to look into this because Debby came back. If our Debby killed two women, it would make more sense to stay absent, never coming back or needing to assume another identity. I have another idea. What if they ran away together?"

"That makes sense, especially if they were both under some kind of pressure and wanted to start a new life. Debby goes first. Then Marley follows her a couple months later. Or Debby sends for her."

"They were close friends, and perhaps both were under pressure. Debby had a new job, her parents were disappointed in her, and maybe something about her adoption was getting to her. Maybe this Marley girl had pressures we don't even know about. They could have decided to take off and start a new life somewhere. Maybe they were even lovers."

"Lovers?" I asked.

"I never saw any reason to believe Debby had a boyfriend or was dating. Perhaps she was in the closet. Okay, say the two of them ran off together. Who came back? Just Debby? Where's Marley? She can't be the shooter either, given the DNA evidence."

"If the real Debby came back, it supports her parents' belief that she's their true daughter. If she's not Debby, that means Fiona was right, which almost certainly got her killed. I don't know what happened to Marley. Maybe they got into a fight and Debby ran away again, only this time, coming home," I said, my words and ideas tumbling out of my mouth. "Maybe something happened to Marley."

"What if something happened to both girls during these past ten years?"

"Are you thinking stolen identity?"

"I'm thinking both girls ran away, and somewhere along the line, they told the wrong person about Debby's family having some money. Perhaps this person thinks they can tap them for it in a big con."

"That's nasty."

"Very. Maybe both girls are already dead. Or maybe they're still out there traveling and having a big adventure."

"There haven't been anymore emails from Debby's account since she got home."

"I'll put in some calls tomorrow. Maybe we have some Jane Does on file that fit their general descriptions. If not, I'll widen my search to Interpol; but if I have to do that, we may never find them."

"Did I just make things worse?" I wondered.

"No, you contributed a bunch of new pieces into the puzzle. I think I should get Debby Patterson, or whoever the hell she is, into the station tomorrow and ask her a few questions about Marley. Send me the details of anyone who can identify her. I won't be able to put her in a line-up but we can probably get someone to sit in the corridor when I escort her in."

"That could work," I agreed. "Did you speak with the Pattersons?"

"I tried but Mrs. P. said she was busy and Dr. P. wasn't at home. She all but shut the door in my face."

"I guess they're not too happy that we appear to still be butting in."

"We are still butting in," Garrett pointed out.

"Time," said Traci, appearing in the doorway again. I didn't fail to notice she had her coat on, and a pleading expression on her face.

"Give me two minutes to change," said Garrett. "Good work, Lexi. I appreciate it. I know it hasn't been an easy case."

"Where's the fun if it were easy?" I asked and he laughed.

~

"Let's start the movie," I said when the door was closed behind Garrett and Traci. "Original, or prequel?"

"'The Phantom Menace'," said Sam.

The doorbell rang. "Prequel it is. Find the DVD and set it up," I told him as I went to answer the door. My mom and sister were standing in the doorway and Serena was holding her daughter, Victoria.

"Did you read the binders?" asked my mom, kissing my cheek and hurrying past me to squeeze each of her grandchildren before I could even ask her why she was here.

"Not yet," I told her.

"You need to be more organized," Serena told me. She handed me Victoria while she took off her coat and hung it on the rack. Victoria squirmed and wriggled so I put her on the floor and she toddled over to see her cousins.

"Serena has almost finished planning her wedding," said Mom. "She's very organized."

"She's had a lot more practice," I shot back.

"One has to be diligent about these sorts of things. There's venues to book and caterers and a band. Plus, a bridal gown can take months to find and have properly fitted. You can't leave it to the last minute."

"I'm not."

"Have you even set a date yet?" asked Serena.

"Um…"

"I am not telling you my date," snipped Serena. "You can't have it."

"How can I have it if I don't know when it is?" I wondered, sticking my tongue out at her as she turned her back.

"I made you appointments to try on wedding dresses," said Mom, barely looking at me as she tickled Chloe. "We can go together."

I squeaked out a noise that I hoped was both positive and non-committal. Lily held back a laugh as she walked over.

"Serena's bridesmaids are wearing pink so you mustn't choose pinks for yours," continued Mom. "Have you considered yellow?"

"Bridesmaid," corrected Serena.

"No, I hadn't," I told Mom. Addressing Serena, I asked, "Who are your bridesmaids?"

"Bridesmaid. We're doing low key so we're only having Victoria."

"What about Chloe and Rachel?" I asked.

"They can be your bridesmaids," said Serena. "I think that will be fine."

"Thanks for letting me know," I said but I wasn't annoyed. It hadn't occurred to me. Why not have all my nieces as bridesmaids? I was definitely not choosing yellow though.

"Where is Rachel?" asked Mom, instantly aware of the absence of her other grandchildren. "Where is Ben? Why aren't they here?"

"Daniel and Alice have bad colds and Rachel and Ben had small coughs too so they stayed home. Why are you here?" I wondered. Neither Garrett nor Traci had mentioned either one of them coming over for movie night.

"Traci told us you and Lily were babysitting and we thought you might need some help."

"We can manage fine."

"Sam obviously hasn't pranked you yet."

"That's because I'm staying on full alert," I told her.

"It's a good thing I came because we can discuss your wedding plans. Where are the folders? You should be looking through them. This is serious planning, Lexi, not a tea party."

Mom, we want to watch 'A Phantom Menace,' not talk about weddings."

"But…"

"It's for the kids, Mom," I cut in. "I promise we'll talk weddings soon. We can have lunch together."

"That sounds terrific." My mom beamed at me then directed her happy face toward Serena while reaching for Lily's hand. "We'll all have lunch together. All my girls."

"Great. Movie time!" I dimmed the lights and settled in next to Lily with Chloe wedged between us, and Sam and Poppy on the floor as the credits came on.

My mother and Serena moved into the kitchen to talk, probably about my wedding and my inability to make any steps towards organizing it, but I didn't mind so long as they were occupied with each other and not me.

I tried to lose myself in the film, getting warm and cozy, popcorn in one hand, but my mind kept turning to the strange case. I couldn't shake the thoughts that plagued me so when Sam started to speak, I almost missed paying attention but something prodded at me. Something he'd said was important and I missed it. "Say that again," I told him.

"Who is that on screen?" asked Sam, pointing to a woman in an elaborate costume.

"Natalie Portman?" I asked, certain she was portraying Padme.

"Nope!"

"It is."

"No, that's Queen Amidala there," he said pointing to another character. He shuffled forward to touch the TV screen. "That's her handmaiden and she's Queen Amidala's decoy too. She's Keira Knightly."

I peered at the two women. "Are you sure?" I asked. "She looks like the queen."

"Yep. Mom told me that even their mothers couldn't tell them apart on set when they had their makeup and costumes on. They could play tricks on each other like Amy and Megan in my class do. They're twins."

"No one could tell them apart?" I mused.

"Not even you," said Sam, "and you're smart."

"Aww, thanks." I beamed at him and ruffled his hair. So far, this was a good evening.

"Everyone says you're smart."

I brightened. "Really?"

"Yeah, a regular smartass."

"Sam!" said my mom. "Where did you hear that?"

"I heard Serena say it in the kitchen when I was getting a drink!"

My mother sighed but I ignored her, too focused on what Sam had just told me. "So, you're saying with the right conditions, one girl that looks a little bit similar to the other can fool everyone into thinking she's someone else?"

"I don't know what you mean by 'right conditions' but yes, that's what they're doing. They're fooling everyone so the queen doesn't get killed by her enemies."

"Sam, you are wonderful!"

"I know," said Sam, looking more than pleased.

"I know how they did it," I said to myself. We'd run by so many different scenarios but only one stuck out. I knew now how Debby had returned. I just didn't know why. However, I figured I could work that out now that the pieces were becoming clearer. All I had to do was prove it.

"Me too," said Lily. "Sam just explained it."

"No, not that! I got it all wrong. I know what happened to Debby Patterson."

CHAPTER SIXTEEN

"It was one hell of a night," said Garrett, "and I don't mean in a way that thrilled my wife."

"Sorry!"

"Don't be. You hit on something and I know I can crack her." Garrett and I both turned our attention to the woman on the other side of the two-way mirror. Debby Patterson sat upright, her hands folded on the table. Every so often, her eyes flickered, glancing at different portions of the gray wall. Garrett had left her alone for fifteen minutes and she showed no signs of cracking under the strain yet. "Why don't you sit in on the interview?"

"Can I?"

"You are an official consultant. You want in, you're in."

"I really want in," I told him. My phone beeped and I glanced down, seeing the information I expected to see. Just like Garrett and I had planned, Anna was sitting in the lobby when he brought Debby in. As far as I knew, Debby hadn't seen Anna but Anna managed to get a good, long look at Debby. I held the phone up to Garrett, showing him what Anna had just sent in a text. If I needed more proof, it wouldn't take me long to track down Amber Yuen, who clearly recognized Marley from their cooking class.

He nodded. "Let's go."

Garrett walked in first, holding the door open for me. We were silent as we took the chairs opposite Debby and sat down. Garrett placed a file on the table between us and leaned back in his chair, waiting another whole minute for the tension to rise before he spoke. "Do you want to do this the easy way or the hard way?" he asked.

Debby stared. "I want to know why I'm here. You came to my hotel and hauled me in here, barely awake. What's going on?"

"I think you know why you're here."

"No, I really don't."

Garrett crossed his arms and fixed Debby with a hard stare. "I'll tell you a story. You jump in whenever you're ready. Ten years ago, there were two women. One was a hardworking graduate who disappointed her parents by not following their advice. She was their only daughter, very precious, and very much wanted, but she couldn't please them. She was a dreamer. She didn't really think too much about other people. Sometimes, she even took off without telling anyone so when she took off for the final time, no one close to her got worried."

"You're talking about me," said Debby.

Garrett raised his eyebrows, just barely. "Am I?" he asked.

"I didn't take off. I was traveling."

"Let me tell you about the other girl. She was a hard worker too but things went south for her. Her parents decided to move away when she finished high school and took her with them. She attended college but had a hard time keeping up and it only got worse when her parents died. First, she had to care for her dying mom. Then she had to become a full-time nurse to her dad. She struggled with her studies and barely passed the courses. When her parents passed on, she didn't know what to do with herself anymore. She had trouble finding a job and her closest friend hardly bothered to care because she was so wrapped up in her own world."

Garrett and I had worked up the profile over a couple of hours, finding all the information easily once we knew where to look. I could play out in my head exactly what he intended to say, even before he said it but I tried not to. My job was to watch Debby closely. I had to monitor her for any flicker of recognition, any chink in her well-constructed facade.

"This is fascinating," yawned Debby.

"We're just getting to the fascinating bit," said Garrett, dismissing her. "You see, both these women went missing at the same time, and ten years later, only one of them came back. You want to know what happened to the one that came back?"

"This is the interesting bit," I said. Debby looked at me but didn't say anything. "You might want to pay attention now."

"She killed someone," said Garrett simply as he watched her. Debby didn't flinch. "Someone who knew she was living a lie as an impostor."

I reached for the folder and opened it, pulling out two photos, which I lay flat on the table. "This is Debby Patterson and this is Marley McFadden." I pushed them towards her and tapped one of them with my forefinger. "They were old friends. See how much alike they seem? Same height, similar facial features and comparable figures. It wouldn't take too much of a stretch to tip the scales. After ten years, it could be hard to tell them apart, almost impossible to determine if you hadn't seen either woman in all that time. See how Debby has this little bump on her nose? You, Marley, don't have one at all but that was easy enough for you to explain. If anyone mentioned it, you replied that you got it surgically corrected during your time away. No one could ever confirm you didn't. No one saw you recovering from it. Everyone assumed you got a nose job but it never happened, did it? It was just a story to explain how that little feature disappeared."

"I'm Debby!"

"No, you're not. We know you're Marley McFadden and we can prove it."

"But that's not the bit we're most excited about proving, is it, Lexi?" said Garrett.

"No, Lieutenant Graves, it is not," I replied, playing right along.

"We're really excited about the next bit where we arrest you for the murder of Fiona Queller."

This time, Debby's head shot up, her eyes widening in alarm. "I didn't kill Fiona!"

"Fiona discovered your secret," I told her. "Maybe you said something, or did something, but she was on to you almost right away. She confronted you at your welcome home dinner, and told you she knew you weren't the real Debby Patterson and said she was going to announce it. She told me about her suspicions and you knew you had to kill her before we could meet because once someone knew, your gig was up. If Fiona told me everything she knew, it was only a matter of time before your happy, new life disappeared and you couldn't let that occur."

"No, that's not what happened! I mean, yes, Fiona said she didn't believe I was Debby but I didn't kill her. You have to believe me!"

"How long do you think she'll get?" I asked Garrett.

"Murder one?" he asked and I nodded. "Twenty-five years minimum. If she's lucky, she might even make parole early, but that's improbable if she doesn't show any remorse."

"Juries don't like to see any lack of remorse, do they?"

"No, they don't. Do you see any remorse here?"

"None. We have quite the story for the jury," I finished, just as we planned. Debby, or Marley, didn't know we were bluffing her. We'd already decided the best thing to do was stick to the facts we knew and hope the impostor caved and filled in the rest. Fear played a good part in that strategy. We needed Marley to confess her crime and tell us what happened because so far, we had nothing to tie her to the murder, only the appropriation of the real Debby's life. Plus, there was the enormous question we hadn't even begun to answer: where was the real Debby Patterson? We had a theory, sure, but no evidence.

"We have DNA," added Garrett. "We have everything we need to prove you killed Fiona. You went to her house with a gun and confronted her. You shot her and ransacked her house to make it look like a robbery. Taking a weapon to the scene is premeditation; and that's a murder charge you can't get out of. After you killed Fiona Queller, you just carried on like nothing happened. You thought you'd stick it out in Montgomery, milking the real Debby's parents for whatever you could get while you probably planned on taking off again. Tell me, Marley, did I get all of that correct?"

"This is crazy! You're both crazy. She's been stalking me," said Debby, waving a finger at me. "She's been trying to pin Fiona's murder on me from the start and now she's got you believing it too. You badgered my parents and Mr. Queller."

"I was never investigating Fiona's murder," I told her. "I was investigating you! You were right, I was following you but I've also done a lot of checking into your background. Or should I say, Debby's? I even have your DNA to compare to the real Debby." It was a lie but Marley didn't know that. The one hole in her plan was not knowing how much information MPD held on Debby. DNA had been extracted, sure, but she didn't need to know it was now unusable.

"You can't!"

"I do. It's being tested right now. I already have one witness who will attest that you aren't Debby Patterson and I can get plenty more to join her. You don't have a lot of time to admit the truth."

"I'm not admitting to something I didn't do. I did not kill Fiona!"

"You killed her, just as surely as you killed Debby. You took over her life entirely. You became her." Garrett and I discussed the whole thing over a breakfast of coffee and donuts in his office. Both of us came to the conclusion that Debby couldn't still be alive. Whether she died right away, or sometime during the past ten years, we weren't sure. However, we felt certain Marley couldn't have become Debby without the real Debby being gone entirely. The only thing standing between our theories and the actual truth was time. "I'll make sure we get you for her murder too. If you want any chance of getting out of jail while you're still alive, you need to start talking," finished Garrett.

Debby crossed her arms, her lips pinched together. "I want a lawyer," she said.

"You want to ask the Pattersons to retain one?" shot back Garrett but Debby had already clammed up.

Garrett looked at her for a long minute, then he scooped up the photos and closed the file. He stood, indicating I should follow him from the room.

"Well, crap," said Garrett, closing the door and stepping away. "Now we have to wait for her lawyer to turn up."

"How long is that going to take?" I wondered.

"The public defender's office will send over whomever gets freed up next. It could be in an hour, or it could be tomorrow. We just have to wait." We walked over to the coffee machine in the homicide squad room and Garrett pulled two cups from the shelf. He filled them, passing me a coffee which I took gratefully, wrapping my hands around the mug.

"She's cool as a cucumber under pressure," I said.

"She is."

"I really thought she would admit to everything once we told her we had her."

"It's rarely that easy. My guess is she will keep trying to wriggle out of it until we stick irrefutable evidence in front of her. By that time, her lawyer will try and cut us a deal. It will be interesting to hear what she has to offer in return for a plea bargain."

"Would you really consider giving her a deal?"

"Depends on what it is. We've got Jerry Queller grieving and he deserves to know why his wife died and her kids sure as hell deserve to know. Plus, the Pattersons should know what happened to their real kid. That woman in there is the only one who can help."

"If she doesn't tell us anything, she's in a really strong position to deny everything."

Garrett grimaced. "Let's hope she gets so worked up over wondering about what we know that it doesn't occur to her."

My phone buzzed and I plucked it from my pocket. "Solomon," I said to Garrett before excusing myself.

"What's happening?" asked Solomon.

"She lawyered up right after Garrett told her she killed Debby and he would get her for Fiona's murder too."

"Sounds like she's panicking. What's your read on her?"

"When it comes to Debby, she isn't protesting much about the fraud, but mention murder and she's adamant she didn't kill anyone. In Fiona's case, I hate to say it, but I think I believe her."

"Evidence backs that up."

"I know," I said, recalling the blood on the gun. "She seems genuinely upset that anyone could suspect her as a killer. We might have a long wait for the lawyer. She's getting a public defender."

"She didn't ask for the Pattersons' lawyer?"

"No, I think she's cracking. She knows she can't keep up the ruse much longer."

"Hang in there. You'll get her."

I smiled. "How are things going at the office?"

"Busy. Two new clients walked in with two big security breaches in their software. I'm thinking there's a connection but they don't know it yet. It might keep me busy."

"That's why they pay you the big bucks," I pointed out. "Garrett's waving to me so I have to go. See you later?"

"Absolutely."

I stuck my phone in my pocket and hurried over. "Something happen?" I asked.

"Debby, Marley, whoever the hell she is, struck lucky. A lawyer was already in the lobby and he went in just now. He's not the best attorney but he's here. We might get this over with a lot faster than I thought."

"That's great news."

"I've got to admit, I'm looking forward to hearing the story even if we already have it all figured out."

I nodded. I'd thought a lot about the case in the past few days and once it all started clicking together, I was almost certain what the woman currently speaking to her lawyer would say. There was only one thing I couldn't be sure about. "Do you think she'll confess to the murders?"

"You read my mind. Depends on what kind of offer I put on the table and that depends on what she says."

"Two murder charges and a fraud doesn't sound too tempting to me," I said.

"It might be if it reduces her sentence and gives her the chance of seeing daylight before she dies, or if Debby's death were truly an accident. Even so, the DA will say she covered up the death for who knows how long rather than calling it in. As for Fiona, I'm stumped. Did you check into the fake Debby's alibi?"

"Rod Patterson told us he spoke to her at six-forty-five which fits with what fake Debby told us. I spoke to the place where she got her food and they confirmed a sighting; and the concierge at her hotel also gave me a positive. Unless she's hiding a pair of wings, I don't see how she could have gotten to the Queller house and murdered Fiona or staged a robbery."

"Shit." Garrett ran a hand over his hair. "I still like her for killing Debby."

"What if Debby's alive?" I asked, even though I didn't believe it.

Garrett raised his eyebrows. "If she were, she would be here."

"Perhaps she's living a whole new life and willingly sold her identity?"

"It's been done before but I'm not buying it. My gut says Debby's dead and she did it," he said, thumbing his hand in the direction of the interview room where fake Debby was holed up with the public defender. "Even if she didn't kill Fiona, I think she might know who did so I'm going to press her hard."

The door to the interview room opened and a short, balding man stepped out. With his gray pallor and even grayer suit, he had all the warmth and presence of a vending machine. He beckoned us over. "I'm Stanley Chalke," he said, shaking Garrett's hand then mine with a toasty palm. "My client is ready to talk to you." Stanley turned and shuffled back into the room, taking the chair next to Debby. Garrett and I resumed our positions opposite them.

"I'm listening," said Garrett.

"My name is Marley McFadden and I've been using the identity of Debby Patterson," she said, keeping her eyes firmly fastened on the table.

"Can you prove it?" asked Garrett.

The woman we know knew as Marley looked up and frowned. "You said you could?"

"I mean, do you have anyone who can attest to whom you say you are?" Garrett asked, recovering quickly from his slip.

"There're a few people from my old life but I have hospital records too. I broke my arm in three places when I was twelve. You can get the records and X-ray my arm to confirm that."

Garrett made a note. "That will help. Any family who could vouch for you?"

"My parents both passed away and I don't have any other close relatives so there's no one left who can help. The girl you mentioned earlier is me. I did nurse my mom and then my dad. They didn't leave anything behind for me. We lost our house to the medical bills. Fortunately, I'd already finished college on scholarship but there was nothing left from them. I didn't have many friends. I used to be shy and since I was caring for my parents, I didn't have time for many people or social outings. One day, I realized I had almost no one left."

"What about Debby Patterson? You two were friends," I said.

Marley lifted one shoulder in a half-hearted shrug. "We met in high school. I enrolled sophomore year when my parents relocated here but we left a week after graduation when my dad got a new job. I wasn't one of the popular kids, not athletic or even musical, but I was smart. Lonely, too. Debby took me under her wing."

"That was nice of her."

"I thought so too but looking back now, I'm not so sure. Debby had a lot of friends but they never lasted very long. She often joined groups and dropped out only to join another group. I thought we were best friends but during college, I realized we weren't. I think she liked me at first because I was new and lonely and shy. I didn't have a lot of confidence so Debby called all the shots in our friendship. She decided where we went and what we did. If I didn't please her, she'd freeze me out and later, warm up to me again. I wanted her to like me. I wanted her to be my friend."

"You kept in touch during college?" I asked.

"Yeah, but I called her more often than she called me. We would visit each other and hang out but she was always so critical. Everything had to be how she liked it. I was studying a lot and doing well and my parents were getting sick. She wasn't very supportive."

"How so?"

"She couldn't understand why I wasn't available for her all the time. She wanted my attention and I couldn't give it and that's when I started to realize how self-centered she really was. I needed her support and she froze me out. I graduated college, then my mom died. Debby was wonderful. She called me every day and patiently listened to me talk and cry. Then she took off one day and I didn't hear from her for two weeks. She went back to being the old Debby and when we did speak, all she wanted to do was tell me all the fun she was having and her great new job. My dad died and she didn't even call me. Not even a card."

"Is that why you killed her?" asked Garrett. "Did she screw you around one too many times?"

"No!"

"Then tell us where she is?"

"Tell them," said Stanley. He waved a hand from Marley to us. "Make this easier on yourself."

"If you tell us where we can find the body, I'll put in a good word to the DA. We can give the body to her family so they can plan a decent funeral. It's still a charge of murder one but we can work something out. Maybe make your time inside a little easier."

"It's a good deal," said Stanley, nodding as he rubbed his chin pensively. "What about the other charge? The Queller case?"

"We're looking at premeditation. Taking a gun to a crime scene proves there was intent to cause harm," said Garrett. "We have the weapon. We don't think you committed the murder but it's my belief now that you must have an accomplice. I want a name."

"I can't give you a name!" Marley looked at her lawyer, desperation filling her eyes with tears as she turned to me. "I told you where I was. You can check!"

"I have checked it out already and your alibi stands up," I told the room. "Maybe it stands up a little too well."

"Do you think I paid someone to hurt Fiona?"

"You tell me."

"She was a nice lady. I didn't kill her. I don't even have the money to hire someone. I'm living strictly on my savings."

"If you give us the name of the person who killed Fiona Queller, I'll drop the charge to second-degree murder for your role in inciting the crime."

"But I didn't kill her!"

"I want it on record that I'm advising my client to take a deal," said Stanley.

"I'm not taking any deal! I'm not," she said, breathing hard as she stared down her lawyer. "I am not admitting to a murder I didn't commit. I am Marley McFadden. That's all I can confess to."

"Tell us something we don't know," said Garrett. "We already know who you are whether you admit it or not and I will have a warrant for your DNA in the next hour to prove it. Unless you can tell us something good, something useful, you're still on the hook for two murders."

"I swear I didn't do it! I didn't even see Fiona on the day she died but I know what happened to Debby. I can tell you that. Will that help?"

"Did you kill her?" asked Garrett.

"No!"

"Is she dead?" I asked.

Marley stopped, a tear slipped from her eye. Finally, she nodded.

"When?" I asked. "Did she die abroad?

"Anything my client says from here on is purely hypothetical," butted in the lawyer.

"I want to tell them," said Marley.

"Tell them hypothetically. I'm trying to help you here. Please allow me to do that," he said, sounding exasperated.

Marley nodded. "No, I didn't kill Debby. She died ten years ago, before she was even reported missing. She never even left Montgomery."

"Start talking," said Garrett."It was one hell of a night," said Garrett, "and I don't mean in a way that thrilled my wife."

"Sorry!"

"Don't be. You hit on something and I know I can crack her." Garrett and I both turned our attention to the woman on the other side of the two-way mirror. Debby Patterson sat upright, her hands folded on the table. Every so often, her eyes flickered, glancing at different portions of the gray wall. Garrett had left her alone for fifteen minutes and she showed no signs of cracking under the strain yet. "Why don't you sit in on the interview?"

"Can I?"

"You are an official consultant. You want in, you're in."

"I really want in," I told him. My phone beeped and I glanced down, seeing the information I expected to see. Just like Garrett and I had planned, Anna was sitting in the lobby when he brought Debby in. As far as I knew, Debby hadn't seen Anna but Anna managed to get a good, long look at Debby. I held the phone up to Garrett, showing him what Anna had just sent in a text. If I needed more proof, it wouldn't take me long to track down Amber Yuen, who clearly recognized Marley from their cooking class.

He nodded. "Let's go."

Garrett walked in first, holding the door open for me. We were silent as we took the chairs opposite Debby and sat down. Garrett placed a file on the table between us and leaned back in his chair, waiting another whole minute for the tension to rise before he spoke. "Do you want to do this the easy way or the hard way?" he asked.

Debby stared. "I want to know why I'm here. You came to my hotel and hauled me in here, barely awake. What's going on?"

"I think you know why you're here."

"No, I really don't."

Garrett crossed his arms and fixed Debby with a hard stare. "I'll tell you a story. You jump in whenever you're ready. Ten years ago, there were two women. One was a hardworking graduate who disappointed her parents by not following their advice. She was their only daughter, very precious, and very much wanted, but she couldn't please them. She was a dreamer. She didn't really think too much about other people. Sometimes, she even took off without telling anyone so when she took off for the final time, no one close to her got worried."

"You're talking about me," said Debby.

Garrett raised his eyebrows, just barely. "Am I?" he asked.

"I didn't take off. I was traveling."

"Let me tell you about the other girl. She was a hard worker too but things went south for her. Her parents decided to move away when she finished high school and took her with them. She attended college but had a hard time keeping up and it only got worse when her parents died. First, she had to care for her dying mom. Then she had to become a full-time nurse to her dad. She struggled with her studies and barely passed the courses. When her parents passed on, she didn't know what to do with herself anymore. She had trouble finding a job and her closest friend hardly bothered to care because she was so wrapped up in her own world."

Garrett and I had worked up the profile over a couple of hours, finding all the information easily once we knew where to look. I could play out in my head exactly what he intended to say, even before he said it but I tried not to. My job was to watch Debby closely. I had to monitor her for any flicker of recognition, any chink in her well-constructed facade.

"This is fascinating," yawned Debby.

"We're just getting to the fascinating bit," said Garrett, dismissing her. "You see, both these women went missing at the same time, and ten years later, only one of them came back. You want to know what happened to the one that came back?"

"This is the interesting bit," I said. Debby looked at me but didn't say anything. "You might want to pay attention now."

"She killed someone," said Garrett simply as he watched her. Debby didn't flinch. "Someone who knew she was living a lie as an impostor."

I reached for the folder and opened it, pulling out two photos, which I lay flat on the table. "This is Debby Patterson and this is Marley McFadden." I pushed them towards her and tapped one of them with my forefinger. "They were old friends. See how much alike they seem? Same height, similar facial features and comparable figures. It wouldn't take too much of a stretch to tip the scales. After ten years, it could be hard to tell them apart, almost impossible to determine if you hadn't seen either woman in all that time. See how Debby has this little bump on her nose? You, Marley, don't have one at all but that was easy enough for you to explain. If anyone mentioned it, you replied that you got it surgically corrected during your time away. No one could ever confirm you didn't. No one saw you recovering from it. Everyone assumed you got a nose job but it never happened, did it? It was just a story to explain how that little feature disappeared."

"I'm Debby!"

"No, you're not. We know you're Marley McFadden and we can prove it."

"But that's not the bit we're most excited about proving, is it, Lexi?" said Garrett.

"No, Lieutenant Graves, it is not," I replied, playing right along.

"We're really excited about the next bit where we arrest you for the murder of Fiona Queller."

This time, Debby's head shot up, her eyes widening in alarm. "I didn't kill Fiona!"

"Fiona discovered your secret," I told her. "Maybe you said something, or did something, but she was on to you almost right away. She confronted you at your welcome home dinner, and told you she knew you weren't the real Debby Patterson and said she was going to announce it. She told me about her suspicions and you knew you had to kill her before we could meet because once someone knew, your gig was up. If Fiona told me everything she knew, it was only a matter of time before your happy, new life disappeared and you couldn't let that occur."

"No, that's not what happened! I mean, yes, Fiona said she didn't believe I was Debby but I didn't kill her. You have to believe me!"

"How long do you think she'll get?" I asked Garrett.

"Murder one?" he asked and I nodded. "Twenty-five years minimum. If she's lucky, she might even make parole early, but that's improbable if she doesn't show any remorse."

"Juries don't like to see any lack of remorse, do they?"

"No, they don't. Do you see any remorse here?"

"None. We have quite the story for the jury," I finished, just as we planned. Debby, or Marley, didn't know we were bluffing her. We'd already decided the best thing to do was stick to the facts we knew and hope the impostor caved and filled in the rest. Fear played a good part in that strategy. We needed Marley to confess her crime and tell us what happened because so far, we had nothing to tie her to the murder, only the appropriation of the real Debby's life. Plus, there was the enormous question we hadn't even begun to answer: where was the real Debby Patterson? We had a theory, sure, but no evidence.

"We have DNA," added Garrett. "We have everything we need to prove you killed Fiona. You went to her house with a gun and confronted her. You shot her and ransacked her house to make it look like a robbery. Taking a weapon to the scene is premeditation; and that's a murder charge you can't get out of. After you killed Fiona Queller, you just carried on like nothing happened. You thought you'd stick it out in Montgomery, milking the real Debby's parents for whatever you could get while you probably planned on taking off again. Tell me, Marley, did I get all of that correct?"

"This is crazy! You're both crazy. She's been stalking me," said Debby, waving a finger at me. "She's been trying to pin Fiona's murder on me from the start and now she's got you believing it too. You badgered my parents and Mr. Queller."

"I was never investigating Fiona's murder," I told her. "I was investigating you! You were right, I was following you but I've also done a lot of checking into your background. Or should I say, Debby's? I even have your DNA to compare to the real Debby." It was a lie but Marley didn't know that. The one hole in her plan was not knowing how much information MPD held on Debby. DNA had been extracted, sure, but she didn't need to know it was now unusable.

"You can't!"

"I do. It's being tested right now. I already have one witness who will attest that you aren't Debby Patterson and I can get plenty more to join her. You don't have a lot of time to admit the truth."

"I'm not admitting to something I didn't do. I did not kill Fiona!"

"You killed her, just as surely as you killed Debby. You took over her life entirely. You became her." Garrett and I discussed the whole thing over a breakfast of coffee and donuts in his office. Both of us came to the conclusion that Debby couldn't still be alive. Whether she died right away, or sometime during the past ten years, we weren't sure. However, we felt certain Marley couldn't have become Debby without the real Debby being gone entirely. The only thing standing between our theories and the actual truth was time. "I'll make sure we get you for her murder too. If you want any chance of getting out of jail while you're still alive, you need to start talking," finished Garrett.

Debby crossed her arms, her lips pinched together. "I want a lawyer," she said.

"You want to ask the Pattersons to retain one?" shot back Garrett but Debby had already clammed up.

Garrett looked at her for a long minute, then he scooped up the photos and closed the file. He stood, indicating I should follow him from the room.

"Well, crap," said Garrett, closing the door and stepping away. "Now we have to wait for her lawyer to turn up."

"How long is that going to take?" I wondered.

"The public defender's office will send over whomever gets freed up next. It could be in an hour, or it could be tomorrow. We just have to wait." We walked over to the coffee machine in the homicide squad room and Garrett pulled two cups from the shelf. He filled them, passing me a coffee which I took gratefully, wrapping my hands around the mug.

"She's cool as a cucumber under pressure," I said.

"She is."

"I really thought she would admit to everything once we told her we had her."

"It's rarely that easy. My guess is she will keep trying to wriggle out of it until we stick irrefutable evidence in front of her. By that time, her lawyer will try and cut us a deal. It will be interesting to hear what she has to offer in return for a plea bargain."

"Would you really consider giving her a deal?"

"Depends on what it is. We've got Jerry Queller grieving and he deserves to know why his wife died and her kids sure as hell deserve to know. Plus, the Pattersons should know what happened to their real kid. That woman in there is the only one who can help."

"If she doesn't tell us anything, she's in a really strong position to deny everything."

Garrett grimaced. "Let's hope she gets so worked up over wondering about what we know that it doesn't occur to her."

My phone buzzed and I plucked it from my pocket. "Solomon," I said to Garrett before excusing myself.

"What's happening?" asked Solomon.

"She lawyered up right after Garrett told her she killed Debby and he would get her for Fiona's murder too."

"Sounds like she's panicking. What's your read on her?"

"When it comes to Debby, she isn't protesting much about the fraud, but mention murder and she's adamant she didn't kill anyone. In Fiona's case, I hate to say it, but I think I believe her."

"Evidence backs that up."

"I know," I said, recalling the blood on the gun. "She seems genuinely upset that anyone could suspect her as a killer. We might have a long wait for the lawyer. She's getting a public defender."

"She didn't ask for the Pattersons' lawyer?"

"No, I think she's cracking. She knows she can't keep up the ruse much longer."

"Hang in there. You'll get her."

I smiled. "How are things going at the office?"

"Busy. Two new clients walked in with two big security breaches in their software. I'm thinking there's a connection but they don't know it yet. It might keep me busy."

"That's why they pay you the big bucks," I pointed out. "Garrett's waving to me so I have to go. See you later?"

"Absolutely."

I stuck my phone in my pocket and hurried over. "Something happen?" I asked.

"Debby, Marley, whoever the hell she is, struck lucky. A lawyer was already in the lobby and he went in just now. He's not the best attorney but he's here. We might get this over with a lot faster than I thought."

"That's great news."

"I've got to admit, I'm looking forward to hearing the story even if we already have it all figured out."

I nodded. I'd thought a lot about the case in the past few days and once it all started clicking together, I was almost certain what the woman currently speaking to her lawyer would say. There was only one thing I couldn't be sure about. "Do you think she'll confess to the murders?"

"You read my mind. Depends on what kind of offer I put on the table and that depends on what she says."

"Two murder charges and a fraud doesn't sound too tempting to me," I said.

"It might be if it reduces her sentence and gives her the chance of seeing daylight before she dies, or if Debby's death were truly an accident. Even so, the DA will say she covered up the death for who knows how long rather than calling it in. As for Fiona, I'm stumped. Did you check into the fake Debby's alibi?"

"Rod Patterson told us he spoke to her at six-forty-five which fits with what fake Debby told us. I spoke to the place where she got her food and they confirmed a sighting; and the concierge at her hotel also gave me a positive. Unless she's hiding a pair of wings, I don't see how she could have gotten to the Queller house and murdered Fiona or staged a robbery."

"Shit." Garrett ran a hand over his hair. "I still like her for killing Debby."

"What if Debby's alive?" I asked, even though I didn't believe it.

Garrett raised his eyebrows. "If she were, she would be here."

"Perhaps she's living a whole new life and willingly sold her identity?"

"It's been done before but I'm not buying it. My gut says Debby's dead and she did it," he said, thumbing his hand in the direction of the interview room where fake Debby was holed up with the public defender. "Even if she didn't kill Fiona, I think she might know who did so I'm going to press her hard."

The door to the interview room opened and a short, balding man stepped out. With his gray pallor and even grayer suit, he had all the warmth and presence of a vending machine. He beckoned us over. "I'm Stanley Chalke," he said, shaking Garrett's hand then mine with a toasty palm. "My client is ready to talk to you." Stanley turned and shuffled back into the room, taking the chair next to Debby. Garrett and I resumed our positions opposite them.

"I'm listening," said Garrett.

"My name is Marley McFadden and I've been using the identity of Debby Patterson," she said, keeping her eyes firmly fastened on the table.

"Can you prove it?" asked Garrett.

The woman we know knew as Marley looked up and frowned. "You said you could?"

"I mean, do you have anyone who can attest to whom you say you are?" Garrett asked, recovering quickly from his slip.

"There're a few people from my old life but I have hospital records too. I broke my arm in three places when I was twelve. You can get the records and X-ray my arm to confirm that."

Garrett made a note. "That will help. Any family who could vouch for you?"

"My parents both passed away and I don't have any other close relatives so there's no one left who can help. The girl you mentioned earlier is me. I did nurse my mom and then my dad. They didn't leave anything behind for me. We lost our house to the medical bills. Fortunately, I'd already finished college on scholarship but there was nothing left from them. I didn't have many friends. I used to be shy and since I was caring for my parents, I didn't have time for many people or social outings. One day, I realized I had almost no one left."

"What about Debby Patterson? You two were friends," I said.

Marley lifted one shoulder in a half-hearted shrug. "We met in high school. I enrolled sophomore year when my parents relocated here but we left a week after graduation when my dad got a new job. I wasn't one of the popular kids, not athletic or even musical, but I was smart. Lonely, too. Debby took me under her wing."

"That was nice of her."

"I thought so too but looking back now, I'm not so sure. Debby had a lot of friends but they never lasted very long. She often joined groups and dropped out only to join another group. I thought we were best friends but during college, I realized we weren't. I think she liked me at first because I was new and lonely and shy. I didn't have a lot of confidence so Debby called all the shots in our friendship. She decided where we went and what we did. If I didn't please her, she'd freeze me out and later, warm up to me again. I wanted her to like me. I wanted her to be my friend."

"You kept in touch during college?" I asked.

"Yeah, but I called her more often than she called me. We would visit each other and hang out but she was always so critical. Everything had to be how she liked it. I was studying a lot and doing well and my parents were getting sick. She wasn't very supportive."

"How so?"

"She couldn't understand why I wasn't available for her all the time. She wanted my attention and I couldn't give it and that's when I started to realize how self-centered she really was. I needed her support and she froze me out. I graduated college, then my mom died. Debby was wonderful. She called me every day and patiently listened to me talk and cry. Then she took off one day and I didn't hear from her for two weeks. She went back to being the old Debby and when we did speak, all she wanted to do was tell me all the fun she was having and her great new job. My dad died and she didn't even call me. Not even a card."

"Is that why you killed her?" asked Garrett. "Did she screw you around one too many times?"

"No!"

"Then tell us where she is?"

"Tell them," said Stanley. He waved a hand from Marley to us. "Make this easier on yourself."

"If you tell us where we can find the body, I'll put in a good word to the DA. We can give the body to her family so they can plan a decent funeral. It's still a charge of murder one but we can work something out. Maybe make your time inside a little easier."

"It's a good deal," said Stanley, nodding as he rubbed his chin pensively. "What about the other charge? The Queller case?"

"We're looking at premeditation. Taking a gun to a crime scene proves there was intent to cause harm," said Garrett. "We have the weapon. We don't think we committed the murder but it's my belief now that you must have an accomplice. I want a name."

"I can't give you a name!" Marley looked at her lawyer, desperation filling her eyes with tears as she turned to me. "I told you where I was. You can check!"

"I have checked it out already and your alibi stands up," I told the room. "Maybe it stands up a little too well."

"Do you think I paid someone to hurt Fiona?"

"You tell me."

"She was a nice lady. I didn't kill her. I don't even have the money to hire someone. I'm living strictly on my savings."

"If you give us the name of the person who killed Fiona Queller, I'll drop the charge to second-degree murder for your role in inciting the crime."

"But I didn't kill her!"

"I want it on record that I'm advising my client to take a deal," said Stanley.

"I'm not taking any deal! I'm not," she said, breathing hard as she stared down her lawyer. "I am not admitting to a murder I didn't commit. I am Marley McFadden. That's all I can confess to."

"Tell us something we don't know," said Garrett. "We already know who you are whether you admit it or not and I will have a warrant for your DNA in the next hour to prove it. Unless you can tell us something good, something useful, you're still on the hook for two murders."

"I swear I didn't do it! I didn't even see Fiona on the day she died but I know what happened to Debby. I can tell you that. Will that help?"

"Did you kill her?" asked Garrett.

"No!"

"Is she dead?" I asked.

Marley stopped, a tear slipped from her eye. Finally, she nodded.

"When?" I asked. "Did she die abroad?

"Anything my client says from here on is purely hypothetical," butted in the lawyer.

"I want to tell them," said Marley.

"Tell them *hypothetically*. I'm trying to help you here. Please allow me to do that," he said, sounding exasperated.

Marley nodded. "No, I didn't kill Debby. She died ten years ago, before she was even reported missing. She never even left Montgomery."

"Start talking," said Garrett.

CHAPTER SEVENTEEN

"I hadn't seen Debby in two months," Marley began, "and I missed her. Then she called out of the blue and said she'd been really busy and we should hang out. I wasn't doing anything so I said sure, I'll come over now. I got into my car and drove over there. I remember it was a really beautiful day and we decided to take a walk near my old house. We used to hang out there when we were teenagers. It was kind of nerdy but we once made a fort and wanted to see if it was still there."

"That your idea or Debby's?" asked Garrett.

"I don't know. I can't remember."

"Go on."

"We were walking for about half an hour when we realized we lost our sense of direction and Debby started to get mad. She said she had other things to do and was calling it a waste of time to be coming out there. She said it was stupid kids' stuff looking for the fort and she was a grown-up now. I laughed and told her it was just some fun and we'd find our way back but it began to get dark. Debby only got madder and madder. She started yelling at me. Kept saying she was going places and I was holding her back and that's why she never returned my phone calls. She said I was a loser."

"That must have hurt," I said.

Marley nodded. "It did. It was like being in high school all over again, only this time, my best friend was calling me names. I told her she was self-centered and horrible and she would never get far in life because she didn't care about anyone except herself. She told me to shut up. We started yelling at each other until I saw the road and realized in all our stumbling around we had actually found our way back! I tried to tell her that but she wouldn't listen." Marley stopped, straining to compose herself. Her eyes seemed out of focus, like she'd physically returned to that day. Where I saw gray walls, she probably saw trees and leaves. I smelled fresh coffee, while she was reliving the rich scent of damp earth. "I told her to stop whining," continued Marley, "and she turned on me. She started yelling again and then she just stopped. She was gurgling gibberish and her eyes were rolling around. She slumped to the ground. I tried to wake her up. I even tried CPR but I couldn't find a pulse. She died. She just died!"

"You could see the road. You knew houses were nearby. Why didn't you call for help?" asked Garrett.

"I panicked. Who would believe that Debby just dropped dead? There was no one I could turn to, and no one I could call. I thought about phoning the police but worried I'd be arrested and go to jail. Who would defend me? Who would stand up for me and say I wouldn't hurt anyone? Debby was right. I was doing nothing with my life. I didn't have a good job like she did, or even a family anymore. All I wanted to do was pretend it never happened, so I did."

"What did you do with Debby's body?" asked Garrett.

Marley stared at the table. "Nothing," she said in a quiet voice. "It had been raining the day before so the ground was still soft. I dug it out with my bare hands and scraped and scooped until I had a hole and then I… I just pushed her in it." Marley broke off, her breath coming in harsh sobs. "I covered her up with leaves and stones and branches on top before I left. I just walked away. I returned to my car and I drove home. When I got back, I realized what I'd done. I buried her in the woods where no one could ever find her. There was nothing I could do now. It was bad enough when I realized she was dead, but now I had buried her. I couldn't tell the police. I couldn't tell anyone. I buried her!"

"That's not exactly nothing," I pointed out. "That's really something."

"But I didn't kill her." Marley stopped and rested back in her chair, looking defeated as she heaved a long breath. Garrett, meanwhile, just looked confused. I guessed he was probably trying to work out what to charge her with. I figured his number one suggestion was still murder.

"Why did you take over Debby's life?" I asked.

"I didn't mean to. I went home and cried and cried. I didn't know what to do. I kept thinking I had to tell someone but I didn't know whom to tell. I thought about sending an anonymous note to the police, then I thought

I shouldn't tell anyone anything. When I started thinking about her family, I knew if I didn't tell them, no one else ever would. Debby's disappearance would have hurt them so much. They were nice people and Debby was their only child. I knew how bad the pain of losing someone you loved felt after I lost my parents. I figured it would be so hard for her parents to lose a child so…"

"So you took over her life," I finished for her.

She nodded. "Yeah, I did. I'm not proud of it but it was easy. We looked like each other. People used to think we were sisters! I went to Debby's apartment. I knew where she kept her spare key so I picked up her passport and a few other things and walked out. I booked a ticket in her name and I started traveling and I didn't stop. I knew no one would miss me here. My lease was due to end on my apartment and I hadn't gotten a job yet. Everything of my parents was gone. It was easy to let Marley slip away. No one cared about Marley. I was the one to send Marley emails from Debby after we were both gone. Except, Debby got to live a second life."

"Did you send the emails to the Pattersons?" asked Garrett.

"All of them. I guessed Debby's password and I read a lot of her emails so I could get her writing style and when I was gone a good while, and far enough away, I wrote to them. I wanted to tell them Debby was okay, and that she was happy."

"But Debby wasn't," I pointed out. "Didn't they deserve to know their daughter was dead?"

"They didn't deserve to endure that kind of pain. They got to live out their lives without suffering from unparalleled grief and they were happy. They were happy for me. They told me so!"

"They never got to grieve when they should have," said Garrett. "Don't you feel at all bad about that?"

"No, you see, they never *had* to grieve! They never had to know she died. They liked thinking I... Debby... was traveling, and seeing all kinds of new places and wonderful things, and learning about and experiencing life. Mom said she loved getting my emails and Dad wanted to know all about the things I saw. They liked everything about me."

"But they weren't your parents."

"I know. Mine were gone and so was their daughter. It seemed too perfect for a while. I know we couldn't be a real family, but we could still be a family."

"But they loved Debby and you took her life," I pressed.

"I did everything I could to make them happy. I sent them postcards and gifts and I never forgot their birthdays or Christmas, not like Debby did. I tried to be a really good daughter. I wasn't selfish or self-absorbed. I never said anything nasty and I never asked them for anything in return. I made them both happy."

"Did you envy Debby?" I wondered.

Marley paused and glanced toward her lawyer. He inclined his head, indicating she should reply. "Why do you ask that?"

"You seemed to enjoy living her life."

"I just enjoyed being free and Debby gave me the freedom to do that. Being her changed my life."

"What about before you became Debby? Did you envy her then?"

"A little bit maybe. She had parents and a lovely house and college was so easy for her. Plus, she walked straight into a job after graduating. She had so much but she was never grateful for any of it. She took it all for granted. She had no idea what it was like to have all those things ripped away."

"If your life was so great while traveling, why did you bother to come back?" asked Garrett. "Why not stay away forever? What's here for you to come back to?"

"There's never been anything here for me…" Marley started.

"New life, travel, adventure, freedom." I counted "what was here" out on my fingers, leaving the most important one for last. If Marley had called the police, Debby's body could have been examined; and if she had simply dropped dead, they might have detected why. I wasn't sure if that were possible after ten years. The ME could have verified any bone injuries or trauma but the kind of incident Marley described would have been even rarer. If Debby had a heart condition or an aneurysm, I wasn't sure it could be proven after a whole decade. It was possible it also couldn't be disproven. I glanced at Garrett and saw the heaviness of his eyes, which made me realize he was coming to the same conclusion. Debby's death was going to be a messy one to decipher.

"That's not what I meant! I mean, I'm not after anything. I don't want to take anything from my mom… or from the Pattersons."

"What about an inheritance?" I asked, a new thought occurring to me. The Pattersons weren't Debby's only living relatives, she had an ailing grandmother too. Walnut View didn't look like a cheap sort of establishment. It was the kind of place relatives chose only if there was a lot of money available for support. I thought back to the interview Garrett and I had with Debby, and recalled that she said her grandparents were well off. That meant the elderly Grandma Patterson must have paid for her own care. If she were doing that, then she must have made sure her legal affairs were in order before her health began to decline.

"No, I…"

"Debby's grandma isn't looking too good," I told Garrett. "Debby could be named in her will. She's the only grandchild, you know."

"Maybe you came back to help her along?" suggested Garrett.

"No, no, I would never do that! I keep telling you, I'm not a killer."

"Maybe you needed more money to sustain your fantasy life and thought Grandma could fund that."

"I wouldn't, plus, I only saw her once since I came back when I was with my mom. I was never alone with her. There's no way I could have hurt her even if I wanted to."

"Let's stop right there," said Stanley, apparently coming back to life. "There's nothing to suggest that my client harbored any ill will towards the old lady. Let's keep this on track."

"We'll verify everything you told us," said Garrett. "Let's say you're right, tell me why you came back."

"My mom, Debby's mom, emailed me and said she was sick and—" Marley sighed. "Also, something happened overseas and I knew I couldn't be Debby anymore. I came back to see Mrs. P. one last time. She said she couldn't die without seeing me so I prepared to come home."

"Do you know anything about this?" Garrett asked me.

I shook my head. If I'd known about an illness, I would have mentioned it before now but I couldn't since I'd never heard of it until now. "No."

Garrett turned to Marley. "Prove it."

"Ask Dr. P." she said. "We spoke by phone a couple months ago. Debby and I sounded alike too and we hadn't spoken in so long that he never suspected I wasn't Debby. He told me how sick Mrs. P. was. He said he didn't know how much longer she had."

"We'll need to verify that too."

"I am not lying, I swear."

Garrett made a displeased noise but something in Marley's voice made me think she was telling the truth. "What about the other thing?" I asked. "You said there was something else that meant you couldn't be Debby anymore."

For the first time since Garrett brought her into the station, she smiled. "I met someone."

"A man?" I asked.

"Yes. I met him in Athens. I just walked around the corner and smack! I plowed right into him. Then he called me by my name. My *real name*. I hadn't heard my name in so long, I almost didn't know what to say to him. He had no idea I had gone away or was missing. He moved to Maine in our junior year of high school and didn't keep touch with anyone but he remembered me. We got coffee and talked for so long. He told me he had a crush on me. He was staying in the city too and we started hanging out. After we kissed, I knew I couldn't be Debby anymore."

"You find any sign of a guy?" Garrett asked me.

"No, none. No phone calls, texts, or emails."

"So, you have some mystery guy that you've known five minutes and you decide to unravel a ten-year lie?" asked Garrett, his tone of disbelief lacing his words.

"It wasn't just five minutes! It's much more. It's not a fling. We're in regular contact. I call him every day and right now he's waiting for me to come back. We're getting married."

"You got any way of proving this right now?" asked Garrett.

"If you were poking around in Debby's emails, there's a reason you wouldn't find any messages to him."

I clicked, realizing just as she said it, why there wasn't any proof. "You wouldn't email him as Debby since he knows you as Marley. You must have another account," I deduced aloud.

Marley nodded. "It's a free one with an online email provider and it isn't registered in my name so it's completely untraceable. I have a disposable cell phone too. It's in my purse and I can give you the PIN. You can access my email from my phone and read everything. I'm not lying about him." She reached into her purse and pulled out a phone, placing it on the table between us. The screen was black and I suspected she switched it off until she needed it so she didn't have to explain what the phone was for. Once it was turned on, I was pretty sure we'd find everything we needed and a way to contact the mystery man. Hearing the way she spoke about her man made me believe her. Another thought occurred to me. "Were you on the phone to him the night Fiona died?"

"Yes. I got a call after I hung up with my dad. We talked for twenty minutes."

"What did you talk about?"

"When I was coming back. The future. I'm not lying, I swear."

"We'll need to verify everything you told us," said Garrett. "It might take some time."

"I don't care how long it takes so long as you know I didn't kill Fiona. You can do that thing where you triangle my phone and it tells you where I was, right?" she said, looking from Garrett to me. "I told you I couldn't have done it."

"You'll need to show us where Debby's body is too," said Garrett.

"I think I can do that."

"Write down everything that you just told me," said Garrett. He pushed a pad of paper and a pen across to her and took the phone. "Don't leave anything out."

"Do you believe me?" she asked as Garrett and I got to our feet.

"I'm going to verify everything," he said, skirting around the question.

"I want murder on both counts taken off the table. There's no way my client could have killed Fiona Queller and she told you Debby Patterson died of natural causes," said Stanley.

"Thanks for catching us up," said Garrett. "I'll get back to you on the charges."

"That was some story," I said as we left the room, shutting the door firmly behind us. We moved into the adjoining room where we could watch Marley through the two-way mirror. She bent over the paper, writing quickly as Stanley spoke to her. Every few minutes, she would shake her head or stop and look at him, then say something before she continued writing.

"What do you make of all that?" asked Garrett.

"I think Stanley is one badass lawyer," I deadpanned.

"Ha-ha. He's lazy and my guess is Marley already figured that out."

"I think she's telling the truth."

"Yeah, me too. It shouldn't be hard to confirm she didn't kill Fiona now that we have new cell phone evidence to look at, which provides her with an alibi. Hard to kill someone when there's a bunch of people who can verify she didn't. Doesn't mean she's off the hook though."

"How so?"

"Even if she didn't kill the real Debby Patterson, she also didn't report the death. She used a passport that wasn't hers. The moment she first contacted the Pattersons, she opened up a world of trouble. She was taking over someone else's life. The list goes on."

I pondered that, wondering if Marley would ever get to live happily as herself. "I hope her lawyer does a good job defending her," I said.

"I might drop a hint to the boyfriend to get her a better one. This case is going to be complicated to straighten out and Stanley will cop to anything just to get out of court. She needs good representation."

"That's generous of you."

"You don't have to stick around. I can wrap up the case from here. If you can get me the paperwork from your investigation into Debby, I'd appreciate it."

"No problem. Garrett?"

"Yeah?"

"If Marley didn't kill Fiona, who the hell did?"

CHAPTER EIGHTEEN

"I love paperwork," I said, glaring down at the tall pile amassed on my desk. I was making good progress towards finishing the file I promised Garrett but there was still a long way to go before I could close it. The biggest problem hampering my process was my mind, which kept drifting back to Fiona Queller.

With Debby-slash-Marley now possessing an airtight alibi, our number one suspect for Fiona's murder was gone. Not only that, but given that she was our *only* suspect, the entire list was now empty. Garrett was sure Marley must have incited an accomplice but the more Marley talked, the less it seemed likely that she instigated any murder. She simply had no motive. Marley didn't want anything from the Pattersons and planned to abandon her life as Debby. There was no need to protect a secret that was almost over, especially if Mrs. Patterson was as sick as Marley seemed to think she was.

So much for providing some relief to Fiona's husband! Now, not only would the Pattersons be devastated that their real daughter was dead—and had been for ten years—but Fiona's husband was still no closer to getting the answers he deserved.

I tried to force my attention on the emails Lucas retrieved for me, inserting them into the file, and added the surveillance photos I'd taken, along with Anna Colby's statement that she recognized Marley, but I couldn't concentrate on anything.

Knowing it was no use to force my mind to stick with the file, I got up and walked over to the boardroom. I picked a pen from the the windowsill and moved to stand in front of the whiteboard. In large letters, I wrote WHO KILLED FIONA?

Stepping back, I tapped the end of the pen against my chin, searching my mind for a motive. After spending days thinking Marley had killed Fiona to hide her secret, that theory had evaporated entirely. Someone else must have wanted Fiona dead, but who? Who would have benefited from Fiona being out of the way? Underneath, I added *husband*? Jerry Queller might have been in line to receive an inheritance or maybe he had a secret lover stashed somewhere. Perhaps he wanted to get rid of Fiona so he could live out a fantasy life, one where she wouldn't be in the way. His grief seemed so real, but I had been duped before.

Unfortunately, my list of names ended there. I didn't know nearly enough about Fiona because my focus remained on Marley as Debby. Where the fake Debby went, whom she spoke to, all the possible motives for taking on a false identity. Marley had given us an alibi very early on but until she confessed to having a secret phone, it was possible that she could have carried out the murder. She had the most obvious motive, since her alibi was a big secret. I added Marley's name in its own column and drew an arrow from Fiona's name to Marley, while adding *framed*? Could someone else have realized who Debby really was and used that knowledge to set her up? Were they hoping that the police would zero in on Marley once her identity was uncovered? Yet, no one tipped Garrett or me off about her true identity. If they wanted to frame Marley, someone should have actively pointed us in her direction and yet, no one had.

Where did that leave me? I added revenge, jealousy, and secret to the list of motives. After a moment, I added *burglary*. The police might have ignored the idea of burglary but perhaps that was a premature conclusion. Could something have been stolen that no one realized yet?

"What are you doing?" asked Solomon.

I jumped, surprised, and whirled around, seeing him in the doorway. "Solving a murder," I said, turning back.

"Why isn't Debby's name on the list?"

"Long story, but Debby isn't Debby and she didn't do it."

"That was very long," teased Solomon. "I wish you just told me the short version. I don't think I can stay awake any longer to process all that information."

I laughed at his good-natured teasing. "Sorry, but that is pretty much it. The real Debby died in a freak incident involving natural causes and her friend, Marley, simply took over her life. I think it spiraled out of control. She intended to give up her fake life after visiting one last time," I told him before turning back to the whiteboard. "With Debby out of the picture, I want to know who killed Fiona."

"Is it possible the two cases aren't even related?"

"Yes, but that doesn't help me at all." Having considered that idea more times than I could count, there was something about the timing, along with the violence of the crime that made me certain we were missing an obvious clue.

Solomon stepped into the room, reaching me in a few long strides. I felt his warmth against my back and was tempted to rest against him. "Okay," he said, "What makes you so certain they're connected?"

"Fiona was living a perfectly normal life until the fake Debby Patterson showed up. Fiona didn't trust her from the start and didn't hesitate to tell other people that, including me."

"I think you're looking at this backwards."

"What do you mean?"

"I mean, you've been thinking since Fiona's murder that Debby, sorry, *fake* Debby, killed Fiona to protect herself as well as her identity. Now, you're considering someone wanted to frame Debby and out her true identity but there's another motive you haven't taken into account."

"I considered burglary again, even though violent burglary isn't normal here. And I added the husband. See?" I pointed to the board.

"No, I mean, what if someone killed Fiona to protect Debby? To ensure Debby's identity wasn't discovered?"

I frowned. "Why would anyone but Debby do that? Everyone wanted the real Debby to come home." Even as I said it, I knew that wasn't quite true. Debby had annoyed a lot of people and it seemed the only ones who had any continued interest in her were her parents. I was sure her grandma would have wanted her home too, if she stayed lucid long enough to recall who Debby was.

"You tell me. Maybe someone had something to gain from keeping Debby alive."

"Like what? Fake Debby didn't have the money to be blackmailed or provide anything big. The only thing she was useful for was as someone's patsy."

"Could that be the same person who wanted her to come home?"

"No, her mom asked her to come home. Plus, Marley said she met a guy she wanted a future with and he motivated her to stop living the lie permanently."

"Who's Marley?"

"Marley is the fake Debby."

"I think I'll need the long version. Over dinner?"

"I would love to but I still need to work on this. I know I'm missing something."

"Work with what you know. Assuming this guy isn't in Montgomery and doesn't know anything about anything, her mom asked her to come home. Go talk to her mom."

"You mean the *real* Debby's mom?"

"Tell me everything very soon," said Solomon. "I don't know who's real or who's fake."

"I'm real," I told him as I stood on my tiptoes to kiss him.

"Mmm, yes, you are," he mumbled over my lips before deepening the kiss. He pulled me against him, wrapping his arms around me. For a few pure minutes, I forgot about the case. A cough from the doorway barely registered until someone cleared their throat loudly. We broke away, Solomon looking over his shoulder.

"That had better be your fiancé, boss," said Delgado.

"How many other women in this office wear pink pants?" asked Solomon, moving slightly so I could wave to Delgado.

"You want to complain to HR about harassment?" Delgado asked me.

"Yes, and I want it known that I protested a lot."

"I let her harass me," said Solomon. "I like it."

"I don't know who to believe," said Delgado. "We got a client meeting. I'll wait in the car for you to finish ruining the work environment."

"One day," said Solomon when Delgado had retreated, "I will really ruin the work environment by doing things to you that have never been done in this office before."

"Disconnect the security cameras first," I told him, since that seemed both sensible and exciting.

"Done." He kissed me once more, breaking it off before my heart could pound again. "Don't spend too much time on this. I have another case for you."

"Looking forward to it." I waved to him as he left, my spirits buoyed by the kisses more than the promise of another case. Solomon had been good enough to let me take on this case, largely as a pro bono favor even if it were one that would support our good reputation with MPD and the wider law enforcement community. But he was also running a business. Paid work came first and that meant my time was almost up. I knew I had to find Fiona's murderer. I couldn't turn in the case file knowing that something connected to Debby was left unsolved.

I turned to the sparsely filled whiteboard, and Solomon's words rattled in my head. He was right, I had to talk to Margaret Patterson. Marley might have wanted to start her life again, but it was Debby's mom who asked her to come home. Another thought occurred to me, something I hadn't considered until now. Marley said Debby's mom *needed* her home. For such a sudden and urgent request, it must have been a serious illness, maybe even life-threatening. Yet, Mrs. Patterson didn't look ill when I spoke to her and I didn't recall seeing anything in the emails I examined.

Walking over to my desk, I opened my laptop and found the file Lucas gave me. I clicked on the email program and typed "sick" into the search box. Seconds later, the search engine didn't return anything. I tried "illness" and nothing came back. I tried several other variations of ill health but nothing came back.

"That's weird," I told the computer. There should have been some evidence of Debby's mom asking her to come home. I cleared the search box and scrolled down the page, finding Mrs. Patterson's last email quickly. It wasn't long. She asked about Debby, said she was interested to know what made her stay in Athens so long and was the weather good? Then she moved onto some gossip about the neighbors, mentioning she was planning on redecorating the living room before she signed off, but not without saying her father was working too hard as always. Not a single word about Debby coming home.

I reached for the file I'd prepared for Garrett, opening it to the phone records before I immediately realized my mistake. These were Debby's decade-old phone calls, not her new ones. She had purposefully avoided calling, ensuring the only method of communication was email or snail mail until very recently. The email had to be in here somewhere.

The trash icon caught my eye and I clicked on it. There were plenty of emails Marley shot directly into the trash. I scrolled past store mailshots and subscriptions, finding a recent one from Mrs. Patterson. I clicked on it and began to read.

In a short email, Mrs. Patterson implored Debby to come home. She said she'd received a terrible diagnosis and needed to see Debby again, maybe for the last time. She said she would die unbearably unhappy if she couldn't see her daughter, and if Debby loved her, she would come home. Finally, she said, there was no need to talk about it when she returned. She'd just be happy to see her again and would she please delete such a sad message.

"That is so, so odd," I said as I hit the print button, sending the email to the printer. As it whirred out, I folded it into my purse. I flipped the file closed and shut my laptop, locking them both into my desk drawer and grabbing my purse before taking the stairs down to the parking lot.

During the drive to the Pattersons' house, I wracked my brain for any mention of illness and still nothing came to mind. Surely either of the parents would have mentioned it when questioned? Or maybe they thought it was none of my business since, as far as they knew, I was merely conducting a few formalities to close the case on their daughter.

I was certain that if I wanted to know what happened to Fiona, I had to find out everything I could about Debby coming home. As I arrived outside the house, it occurred to me that Garrett might have already told the Pattersons the truth. That could make me very unwelcome, not to mention, intrusive on their privacy and most recent source of grief. I parked, and called Garrett.

"Hey, are you coming over with the file?" he asked.

"Tomorrow," I told him. "I'm just wrapping up a couple things. Have you told the Pattersons about their daughter yet?"

"No. We decided to wait until we have a body. There's no point in dragging out their sorrow."

"Has Marley's story checked out?"

"For the most part, yes. We're on the way to get the body now, assuming it's where she says it is."

"Now? It's going to be dark soon."

"She said it's in a shallow grave and she thinks she remembers where. Plus, I called in a favor with Boston PD and borrowed their cadaver dogs."

"Are they what I think they are?"

"Mutts that sniff out corpses," Garrett said, not sugar-coating his words to save my ears.

"That's… useful," was the best thing I could come up with.

"If there's a body out there, they'll find it. I just hope wild animals haven't scavenged it too much over the years. I'd like to bring her in whole."

I gulped. "Please don't tell me anymore."

"I was going to say, that way, the medical examiner has a better chance of finding the cause of death. I don't want to tell the Pattersons until I can give them all the answers because they, no doubt, will have a lot of questions."

"Actually, that's a good thing. I want to ask them a couple more—"

"Hey, Lexi, I gotta go. We are at the location and I can see one of the detectives is already there with Marley. I'll speak to you soon."

"Gar—"

"Thanks for everything. I really appreciate your help on this case but I've got it from here," he said and hung up.

Since I was already at the Pattersons, it would have been a waste of my time to turn around and go home. Plus, I really wanted to know more information about the mystery illness. I wondered if it were something Fiona had known about, perhaps making her all the more determined to uncover the truth about the impostor Debby Patterson before Mrs. P.'s health worsened. As soon as the thought came into my head, I was confused. Killing Fiona to hide her identity still gave Marley the most compelling motive but her interview had all about eradicated any motive to kill Fiona.

I was still considering the motive as I knocked on the Pattersons' door. If Mrs. P. were surprised to see me, she didn't appear to be, however, she did look awfully gaunt. Her cheeks were a little more sunken than the last time I'd seen her and her hair had lost most of its bounce. Was it from sadness at losing her friend? Or illness? I was sure I was about to find out.

"I'm sorry to bother you again," I told her, feeling guilty because I knew she had much worse to come and very soon. "I'm just tying up a couple of loose ends."

"My daughter said we shouldn't talk to you anymore," she replied. Her fingers curled around the door handle, probably preparing to slam it in my face.

"I know recent events have been very upsetting but I only need to ask a couple more things," I told her, hoping I sounded reassuring. "Then I promise I won't bother you with anymore questions."

Mrs. Patterson hesitated. "I'm not sure."

"I absolutely promise and if you have any complaints, you can contact Lieutenant Graves and let him deal with me," I told her.

"Five minutes," she said. "We can talk here at the door."

"That's great, thank you. I wanted to ask you why Debby came home?"

"I think I told you before that she was homesick. She decided to come home."

"Did you question why it took her ten years to get homesick?"

"It crossed my mind but I didn't want to seem ungrateful. She came home. That was all I wanted."

"Could there have been any other reason?" I pressed.

Mrs. Patterson frowned, then shook her head, looking confused. "I don't think so."

"Did you ask her to come home?"

"I mentioned it indirectly a few times but I didn't want to push. If you push Debby, she pushes back and I didn't want her to never return."

"What about your illness?"

"My illness?" Mrs. Patterson blinked with surprise. "I'm not ill!"

I reached for the email printout, unfolded it and showed it to her. "Did you send this to your daughter?"

Mrs. Patterson took the sheet and slipped on a pair of glasses from her pocket, skimming over it before handing it back. "I didn't send this."

"Could you look again? It's from your email address to your daughter."

"I don't need to. I can tell you now I'm not sick. I had a full medical only last month and I'm in excellent health. Where did you get this?"

"From your daughter's trash in her email program. Do you see here?" I said, pointing to the sentence I wanted her to pay attention to. "It says not to mention it to you and to trash the message. Don't you think that strange?"

"Of course I do. If I were sick, I wouldn't hide it and I wouldn't insist no one talk to me about it."

"Does anyone else have access to your email?" I asked. "Do you ever use a public computer? Maybe at the library? Or an internet cafe?"

"No, we have a computer at home. My husband and I share it."

"Just you and your husband?"

"Yes."

"Has your husband ever used your email?"

"Of course he does. We share this email address and we both contact Debby on it. Is that all? I really must go."

"Yes, thank you for your time."

"Before you go, do you know anything about Fiona's case? Is there any news?"

"No, I'm sorry, there isn't."

Mrs. Patterson closed the door and I turned away, returning my car. In the driver's seat, I sat patiently for a moment, collecting my thoughts. One thing I had to do was tell Garrett about the email. I called him, and just as I was about to hang up, he answered.

"What's up?" he asked.

"I found something out…" I started.

"Yeah? Me too. We got a body."

"Debby's?"

"Looks that way. Not quite where Marley thought she buried her but close enough. Wearing the same clothes, or what was left of them. The ME is preparing to transport the corpse."

"Any idea of what killed her?"

"A little too early to say but the ME says there's no obvious sign of cause of death. No gunshot wound or head trauma so Marley's story is holding up so far. Looks like we won't be charging her with murder."

"That's great!" I stopped, wincing. "Obviously, it isn't. It's sad. It's horri—"

"Listen, I gotta go," Garrett cut in. "I'm on my way to inform the family."

"Are you absolutely certain it's her?"

"We don't have a formal ID yet and there's no delicate way to say this, but we'll be looking at the dental records, and not asking the family for identification. I expect they'll come back with a positive match to Debby. We did find something on her, a necklace that her parents might be able to identify. I want to notify them as soon as possible. They shouldn't have to wait for word to get out that we have Marley in custody."

"I just spoke to her mom. She didn't know anything about any illness," I told him.

"Hardly matters now," said Garrett. "I'll make sure you get credit for all your work on this, okay? Bye."

"Wait! What…?" I started but Garrett had hung up on me again. I drove back to the agency, stationing myself in front of the whiteboard, Debby's case file once again next to me. I looked through it at least a dozen times, focusing on her alibi.

Marley, as Debby, had ordered some food and was seen by the serving staff. She walked to the park and called her dad. They spoke briefly and then she enjoyed a long phone call on her burner cell to her boyfriend abroad.

But who did Fiona speak to in that time?

I picked up my phone and called Lucas. "Can you get me Fiona Queller's phone records?" I asked him.

"Does a duck quack?" replied Lucas. "Sure I can."

"Right now?"

"Sounds serious."

"I have a feeling."

"Whoa!" Lucas teased.

"Yeah, I know."

"Give me the number?"

I reeled it off and Lucas assured me he would bring the phone records as soon as he had them. Ten minutes of hard staring at the whiteboard later and he entered the room, a thin sheaf of paper in hand. "Here's the last month of calls," he told me.

I took the sheet, searching the most recent and comparing them to a data sheet I already had. Fiona called her husband and her kids on their cell phones. The last number was one I didn't recognize. I reached for the phone on the boardroom table and dialed it.

"Patterson and Bryce Fertility Clinic," said the voice that answered. I dropped the phone into the cradle, almost breathless. Fiona had called Rod Patterson an hour before she died.

The answer flashed into my brain. I suddenly knew how Debby's return indirectly caused Fiona's death. It was horribly clear now who had killed her.

CHAPTER NINETEEN

"Pick up. Pick up!" I yelled into the phone and, for the third time, my call clicked through to voicemail. "Garrett, call me back! It's Rod Patterson," I said simply before hanging up. Hastily tapping a few keys on my laptop keyboard, I forwarded the email luring Debby home, the one that I retrieved from Debby's trash can. I sent it to Garrett's email address, adding a short message. I told him that Fiona was killed to protect Debby, to protect his daughter who was coming home, whoever he thought she was.

"What's going on?" asked Lucas, watching me.

I grabbed him by the shoulders, my body full of a panicked excitement that I felt sure shone on my face. I could only hope in my excitement, I didn't have crazy eyes but I wouldn't place any wagers on it. "I just figured it out!" I told him.

"The meaning of the universe?" he replied nonchalantly.

"No! The case!"

"You're either a little behind or stuck in some weird time loop. You already solved the case of the impostor."

"No, not that one. The *other* one. The one no one asked me to solve."

"Is it buy-one get-one free week at the agency?"

"I have to go," I said, ignoring his snappy retort. "Garrett is about to walk straight into a trap."

"That sounds bad."

"Very bad. I'm going to get my gun."

Lucas grimaced. "Oh, boy!"

I barely had a chance to formulate my plan as I raced from the building, taking the stairs two at a time, hearing Lucas calling after me. In just a few short moments, it all became clear in my mind. Debby had already confided that she wanted a new life, to leave all her Debby lies behind, and do it in a way that wouldn't devastate her parents. The only obstacle she encountered on her return was Fiona, the one person who knew Marley wasn't Debby, which was exactly why he killed her. The murder might not have been committed by Debby but it was still on her behalf. I knew Debby couldn't have committed the murder because she had a rock-solid alibi. She wasn't anywhere near Fiona at the time of her death.

But Fiona did call someone, someone she thought she could trust: her friend, Rod Patterson. I could imagine how that conversation went. She phoned him with some evidence, something irrefutable that could prove Debby couldn't possibly be Debby, or maybe even a gut feeling that just wouldn't go away. Perhaps it was like what Garrett felt and could not shake off, that something was wrong. Dr. Patterson probably told her he was on his way over to speak to her, and find out why she was so adamant his daughter wasn't whom she said she was. Maybe he even told her not to tell anyone else until he got there.

When he arrived, Fiona probably showed him her evidence or explained what she knew. She could have told him how sorry she was to ruin the wonderful homecoming of their only daughter, or maybe implored him to go to the police to protect himself and his wife from whatever scam she suspected Marley was trying to pull.

In the car, I buckled up before tearing out of the lot, aiming for home. I couldn't stop thinking about what the conversation might have been. Fiona probably theorized that fake Debby was up to no good. She was undoubtedly afraid for her dear friends. Why not? It wasn't an unreasonable assumption. Few people took over another person's life simply for altruistic reasons. Marley might try to insist that she was doing that, but it didn't excuse her for concealing a dead body to do it.

What Fiona never accounted for was Mr. Patterson's unfailing desire to protect his family. I wanted to believe that he didn't swallow Fiona's theory—and thought she was wrong—but a small part of me wondered if he already knew the Debby who came home wasn't his real daughter. Then I could only imagine what *he* got out of playing along.

It made sense to me that Dr. Patterson had written the email that enticed Debby to come home. He told her not to mention the fake illness to his wife since it wasn't true. Perhaps he expected the real Debby to return. It was too awful for me to contemplate the idea that he might've known all along that his daughter was dead. That meant he'd known about it for ten years without telling another soul, not even his wife. Only someone complicit in her death would have known that, I decided; however, there was nothing in Marley's testimony to suggest Rod was there when his daughter died.

Did he realize at some point over the last ten years that Debby was actually dead? Or that someone was posing as her? That would provide another reason for him to lure Debby home; if only to put an end to the farce.

"So, why wait?" I wondered out loud. "Why welcome Debby home and say nothing? Why pretend to be a father to someone you know isn't your daughter?"

Hard as I tried, I couldn't wrap my head around accepting an impostor as a family member. It was hard enough when an actor replaced another in the same character on TV, but in real life? There had to be something to gain. I just wished I knew what it could possibly be.

I screeched to a halt outside my home and ran inside. "Solomon?" Are you home?" I called into the silence. No answer.

Since moving there, I kept my gun stored in his gun safe, hidden behind a false panel that looked like any of the other kitchen cabinets. I pressed the door and it popped open, then slid to the side. I punched the numbers into the keypad and the lock clicked. My gun was safely inside, neatly stowed in its case along with my holster. I opened it, loaded the bullets and pushed the safe door and false cabinet closed before holstering my gun and making sure my jacket obscured it.

One thing I'd learned since becoming a PI was to always be very careful about walking into an unknown situation unarmed. Unfortunately, it happened to me more than once. Now, I refused to face a killer with no weapons but my manicured nails, a fabulous sense of style, and the pocketknife my wise mother gave to me some time ago.

All I had to do now was find Dr. Patterson. If he were in his office, surrounded by employees and maybe even a few patients, I assumed there was less chance of him becoming dangerous. Certainly not with so many witnesses around. A glance at the clock told me he was still in surgery, although it was close to ending. If I hurried, I could catch him before he locked up for the day. Calling ahead wasn't an option. I didn't want to spook him into hiding.

I dived back into my car and tore up the tarmac, recklessly close to breaking traffic rules as I raced towards his office. One thing puzzled me. I had often seen the surgery hours displayed at the office. For Dr. Patterson to have killed Fiona, he must have left his office during his open hours. How could he manage that without being seen? If he didn't confess outright, I predicted he would argue that he'd been in the office the whole time. Especially since he'd already told both Garrett and me that. There would be no reason for him to deviate from his original statement. If he tried to argue that in court, I wondered if one or more of his employees would back him up.

The surgery had a small parking lot of its own. I pulled into one of the spaces and hopped out. Inside the building, I took the elevator up and stepped out into the lobby. The receptionist behind the desk wore a pristine, white wrap tunic that I was sure had never seen a day of surgical service. "Is Dr. Patterson here?" I asked.

"Do you have an appointment?" She tapped her keyboard and looked at the screen hidden from my view behind the chest-height partition.

"No, I need to ask him a question regarding a case," I told her, showing her my license and hoping she didn't inquire too closely.

"I'm sorry. Dr. Patterson has left for the day."

"You sure about that?" I asked, and she ducked her head down. The moment she did, I jogged around the desk and aimed for his office at the far end of the corridor.

"Hey! You can't go back there!" called out the startled receptionist. "Come back!" I quickened my pace as I heard her running after me. Grabbing the handle of Dr. Patterson's office door, I turned and pushed it open. The lights were off but daylight seeped through the broad windows. His computer was switched off, the screen blank, and his chair was pushed under the desk.

"He really isn't here," I said, surprised and a little disappointed that I didn't catch him.

"I told you he left fifteen minutes ago. Come out of here right now or I'll call security!"

I stepped out of the room, allowing the receptionist to pull the door shut, and blinked at the exit door in front of me. "Where does this lead to?" I asked.

"The stairwell."

"Does Dr. Patterson make a habit of leaving early?"

"No, hardly ever."

"Can you tell me if he left early any other evening this week?"

"No, he hasn't. I would have known."

"Would you have seen Dr. Patterson if he left via this stairwell?"

"No, but he wouldn't do that. He uses the elevator like everyone else. It's six stories down!"

"Did he say where he was going when he left today?"

"Home, I guess. He got a phone call that sounded urgent and he said he was leaving early. Before you ask, no, I'm not telling you where that is!"

"Very responsible. Thanks for your time," I told her, hurrying to the elevator. Like she said, it was six stories down, and I didn't need to prove my theory that Dr. Patterson must have snuck out early via the stairwell and returned just as easily without anyone knowing. I didn't have to walk the six stories down to know that. It was enough to know that *he* could.

I stepped into the open elevator and gave the receptionist a cheery wave as I hit the first floor button. I was pretty sure she would be on the phone to Dr. Patterson as soon as the doors closed but I couldn't help that. So I hoped with all my heart he was driving and couldn't pick up the phone. I wanted to get to him before he had time to seriously wonder why I was still investigating a case that was supposed to be closed. I definitely wanted to be there before Garrett turned up to tell the Pattersons that Debby was not only dead but also on her way to the morgue.

My heart pounded at the thought of Garrett being on his own with Dr. Patterson. If Dr. Patterson could murder a close family friend to protect Debby's secret, I was sure he would have no problem dispatching my brother.

The very thought of it tore me up inside.

Garrett had always played a huge part in my life. Already a teen by the time I was born, he was so much more than just a brother. We never had the sibling rivalry so common in children that are close in age. We never fought over toys or activities, and we never shared friends growing up. He was away at college by the time I started kindergarten and joined the police academy while I was still in elementary school. He's always been a loving, guiding force in my life and there was no way anyone could snuff him out.

I had to get to the Pattersons' house first.

I struggled to drive at a reasonable speed, my palms sweating, my heart pounding, as I navigated the streets I'd always known. In my head, I played out various scenarios. Would I arrive early and subdue Dr. Patterson before calling the police for backup? Or would I arrive too late and find my brother on the floor, with a lethal gunshot wound all too similar to Fiona's?

Reaching for my phone, I triggered voice activation and instructed it to call Garrett. "Calling Maddox," said the phone.

"No!" I yelled.

"Are you okay?" said a voice through the speakers.

"Sorry, misdialed," I yelled.

"What's going on?"

"I can't explain. I have to go!"

"Explain. Do not hang up!" Maddox yelled back.

"I know who killed Fiona and I need to get to him before my brother does."

"Which bro... Never mind. Do you have any backup?"

"No. Garrett isn't picking up."

"Give me the address." I started to protest but Maddox yelled, "Give it to me now!"

I reeled off the address.

"On my way. Do not engage," said Maddox before he hung up.

"Call Garrett," I yelled again.

"Calling Garrett," said my phone. I thought I detected a hint of smugness in the voice.

Without ringing, the call went directly to the answering service. "Garrett, I'm on my way to the Pattersons' house. If you hear this before you get there, please don't go inside. It's Dr. Patterson. He killed Fiona and I can prove it."

I turned the corner, putting my foot on the gas and flooring it. When I screeched to a halt outside the Pattersons' house, my stomach lurched. Garrett's car was already parked outside. I looked around for the Pattersons' cars but couldn't see them. With Garrett's car empty, I had to assume he was already inside the house. One or both of the Pattersons must have parked their cars in the double garage.

Instead of aiming for the front door, I jogged to the garage, trying to find a crack to look inside. The garage adjoined the house, although recessed slightly backwards, leaving only a small, circular window for light above the electric doors. There was no way I could see inside. I sorely needed a ladder but couldn't see any available to use.

With no other options, I stooped and scurried in front of the house, peeking in all the windows as I moved stealthily, hoping I could catch a glimpse of Garrett and the Pattersons. There was no sign of them in the first window so I moved on, peeking through the tall window panes on either side of the door, and then onto the next window. I rose slowly, my arms brushing against the brittle leaves, my eyes rising past the sill.

Garrett was facing me, talking. Mrs. Patterson had her back to the window. A wave of relief flooded over me. I made it before Dr. Patterson arrived. Mrs. Patterson looked fine. There might even have been enough time to explain to them both what happened. I dropped to the floor again, shuffling backwards towards the door so they wouldn't see me snooping. I was just preparing to turn around when behind me, I heard the unmistakable sound of a gun being cocked.

"Don't move," said Dr. Patterson. "Get up very slowly."

"Which is it? I can't do both."

"Get up," said Dr. Patterson with audible exasperation etched into his voice. "Put your hands in the air. Don't make any sudden moves."

I wasn't sure what kind of sudden moves he didn't want me to make so I shelved the idea of any cartwheels, flying kicks, or Miss Universe promenading. Instead, I got up very slowly and raised my hands in the air, turning around when he instructed me. "Go inside," he said, stepping back to let me pass. "Scream and I'll shoot."

"In front of all your neighbors?" I asked.

"Do you see anyone?"

That was a good point, I didn't see any but I didn't tell him that. Plus, it was in my best interests to get inside and alert Garrett. My brother almost certainly had a gun.

"Someone will hear the gunshot."

"My neighbor's son's motorcycle has been backfiring for the past three weeks. No one will notice a thing. Open the door," said Dr. Patterson when we stopped in front of it.

I reached for the handle. "I know it was you," I told him. "I know you killed Fiona."

"You don't know anything!"

"I know everything."

"Inside," he said, nudging the gun into the small of my back. I pushed the door open and Dr. Patterson stepped in after me. "Go into the living room."

"Okay." I moved forwards slowly, my hands still in the air. As I entered the room, two sets of eyes turned on me. Garrett's mouth dropped open in alarm as Dr. Patterson stepped out from behind me.

"I found this one outside," said Dr. Patterson.

"Do something," I hissed to Garrett. "Shoot him and I'll explain everything later."

"Lieutenant Graves won't be shooting anyone," said Mrs. Patterson to my surprise. That was right about the moment I saw the gun she had fixed on Garrett.

CHAPTER TWENTY

"What are you doing here?" asked Garrett, an unmistakable edge to his voice. His strained eyes glanced behind me, assessing the situation. Blood drained from his face and I knew he must have seen the gun pointed at my back.

"Didn't you get my messages?" I asked.

Garrett nodded towards Mrs. Patterson's gun. "No," he said, his eyes rolling upwards slightly.

"I came to rescue you."

"Gee, thanks. Doing a great job."

"I didn't say I was finished," I shot back just as Dr. Patterson nudged me again with his gun.

"Take a seat," he told me with another small prod.

I took the seat adjacent to Garrett, both of us facing the Pattersons. A gold necklace lay on the coffee table. Garrett's gun was beside it, but sadly, out of snatching distance. At least Dr. Patterson hadn't frisked me. However, there was no way I could get my gun out without being shot first. "This sucks," I said to Garrett.

"Tell me about it."

"What are we going to do with them?" asked Mrs. Patterson. For the first time, I noted a trace of alarm on her face. I suspected my own face probably reflected a lot of confusion.

"I don't know. Shoot them?" suggested Dr. Patterson.

"Two bodies? That's a lot of work!"

"We can't leave them. They worked it all out. We have no choice."

"What exactly have you worked out?" asked Mrs. Patterson, looking from me to Garrett.

"One of you killed Fiona," started Garrett. "I thought it could have been you but now I'm not so sure."

I added, "My money was on Dr. Patterson but seeing both of you with guns really throws me. Was it a team effort?" I asked, my jaw trembling despite my glib words.

"Do you think this is funny?" asked Dr. Patterson. "Tell us what you know. You first, Lieutenant."

"We know your daughter, Debby, is dead," Garrett said bluntly. "She died ten years ago and her body has been concealed in Montgomery all this time. As I was explaining to your wife when she drew her gun on me, the woman who came back is not your daughter. Her name is Marley McFadden. We believe she was your daughter's friend and took over her life. To paraphrase her words, she didn't want you to experience the pain of knowing your daughter died."

"We know all that," said Dr. Patterson. "We worked that out already."

"So did your friend, Fiona," continued Garrett. "She warned you, Mrs. Patterson, about the woman we now know as Marley posing as Debby but you were both so adamant she was your daughter. She came to you with her concerns and that's why you shot her. You probably learned how to shoot from your husband, an accomplished marksman."

"Actually," I chipped in, "Fiona called Dr. Patterson at his office shortly before she died. He had already spoken to Marley on the phone, which gave him an alibi, but then Fiona called. I think Fiona told you she could prove Marley wasn't Debby and you decided you had to silence her. You snuck out of your office and made your way down the stairwell, ensuring no one would see you leave. You went to Fiona's house under the pretense of listening to what she had to say and you shot her. In a panic, you tossed the gun and returned to the office, like you never left. You knew your colleagues and employees would blindly vouch for you. Plus, you had already spoken to the fake Debby by phone, so you had the perfect alibi. I think when we run the DNA we found on the grip, it'll be an identical match to yours."

Dr. Patterson nodded thoughtfully. "You're right, of course, Ms. Graves. All I had to do was say I was busy with paperwork and everyone knew not to disturb me. It was so easy. I didn't want to kill Fiona but she wouldn't stop prying. She was going to ruin everything!"

"Did you know Marley was Debby?" I asked.

"We knew someone was pretending to be her," he replied simply, as if it were a stranger he were talking about and not his daughter.

"To know that, you would have to…" I stopped, squeezing my eyes shut, thinking hard as the grim realization swam into my brain. "You already knew Debby was dead," I finished.

"We knew she died ten years ago," said Mrs. Patterson. "Debby called us that night. She was full of anger. She said she'd been on a walk in the woods and something happened. She got a terrible pain in her head and thought she collapsed. When she woke up, she was covered in dirt and it was dark and her head hurt terribly. She wanted us to come find her."

"It's not the first time we had to pick her up from somewhere," said Dr. Patterson. "We've lost count of the times she took off or ran out of money. She begged us. I told her this is a last time we get her out of a jam. We got to the woods where she said she was and walked around in the dark, calling for her. Then I tripped over something. I thought it was a log but it was Debby. She was just lying there on the ground, barely warm, half inside a hole, like she was in a shallow grave. I felt for her pulse but she didn't have one. She was already dead."

"So you just left her there?" asked Garrett.

"I didn't know what else to do! I panicked. How could I explain why my daughter was dead in the woods in the dark? Everyone knew Debby had problems and had given us a hard time over the years. We had to bail her out so often. School, college, boys. She always blamed the adoption for an excuse but she was never really interested in her biological family. She just had a habit of pissing people off. I knew someone would probably think I killed her! Someone did!"

"If you told the police that, they could have investigated. You could have proved that she called you," I told him. "You were just a concerned dad who intended to help his daughter."

"Plus, the ME thinks your daughter might have suffered an aneurysm. No one killed her," Garrett told them.

Dr. Patterson sat down heavily on the sofa, breathing hard. I couldn't work out if it was from the trauma of reliving the events, or knowing that his daughter hadn't been murdered after all. Perhaps he was still planning on whether or not to kill us and add two more bodies to his murder spree. If I were asked which reason I felt most comfortable with, I would probably have chosen one of the first two options.

"Why keep up the pretense?" I wondered.

"I told Margaret about our daughter right away. We spent all night talking and most of the next day and then more days passed. How could I ever tell anyone? The longer we left it, the worse it looked. Then her landlord reported her missing and we had to go along with it. At least, we didn't have to pretend things were okay anymore. We expected someone to find her but no one ever did and then the emails started."

"It was surreal," said Mrs. Patterson. "My husband assured me that he saw Debby dead, but then we got the emails and it was almost like she was alive again. I said to him, he must have gotten it wrong. She wasn't dead after all. She probably woke up in the woods, alone and cold and absolutely furious. I said she, no doubt, intends to make us pay for leaving her there."

"At first, we had no idea what to think. I couldn't go back into the woods. I wasn't even sure where I found her and those emails… they sounded just like Debby. Whoever was writing them knew all kinds of things about her life, and about us. We agreed it must be her, and assumed she must have wanted something from us. We waited for the demands," added Dr. Patterson.

"They never came. It seemed to be enough that Debby would never come home. We didn't push her. We thought she must hate us."

"You never questioned if it was your real daughter?" asked Garrett.

"Of course we did! There were little things. Debby started talking about taking a cooking class and she always hated cooking. Then she was so sweet and nice to us and almost encouraging. Again, not like Debby at all. We wondered but she knew too much about Debby's life to be a stranger, so we guessed perhaps she changed, if anyone could change so much. We wondered if by having a near death experience she had finally woken up." Mrs. Patterson stopped and took a deep breath. "Truthfully, we were relieved she appeared to be alive. We didn't want to think of our daughter's body lying out there in the woods. Even if she hated us, we wanted her to be okay."

"And that's why you never pushed the investigation any further?" I asked.

Mrs. Patterson nodded. "We didn't want to believe anything else. Plus, an investigation would have been horrible. It would have shamed the whole family."

"Why did you ask her to come home?" asked Garrett.

"I didn't. That really wasn't me," said Mrs. Patterson, looking at her husband. "I didn't know anything about it until Rod told me after you asked me."

"I wrote the email," admitted Dr. Patterson. "After ten years of wondering if she was our daughter, I figured, she had to be over it by now. We wanted to see Debby again and I saw how hard it was on my wife. We spent all those years without pushing our daughter in case she lashed out, just going along with her travels. Just like always with Debby and I thought we deserved more. I knew she wouldn't come home just because we asked her so I made up a story about my wife being sick and said she *needed* to come home. I had to make her feel guilty."

"Did you know the woman who returned wasn't Debby?"

"Not right away," said Dr. Patterson. "She was so similar but I spotted little differences."

"The nose job?" I asked.

He nodded. "Debby had a little bump here," he said, touching his nose, "but this woman didn't have one. It was easy to call it a nose job. And as for looking differently, well, everyone changes after ten years. Debby didn't have many friends or even a boyfriend who'd remember her. Our only other family nearby is my mother and she doesn't remember anything too well anymore. She's dying."

"I couldn't stop looking at her at first," added Mrs. Patterson. "It took a couple of days to be sure but we accepted it eventually. We knew she wasn't Debby. Then we knew Debby had to be dead."

"Fiona suspected that too," I said.

"She never knew Debby that well and it had been ten years. We figured if we accepted the new Debby into our lives, then so would everyone else, but Fiona knew right away. She just knew," said Mrs. Patterson.

"I still don't get why you would accept a total stranger as your daughter," said Garrett.

"We didn't. We accepted *our daughter*. We told everyone our daughter was coming back and she did. We threw a welcome home dinner for her. How could we tell everyone that she wasn't Debby? She was so charming, so lovely. She was actually a much nicer person than our own daughter."

"And she never asked us for anything. Not once in ten years and she had plenty of opportunities. We offered to send her money or plane tickets or to put her up in a nicer hotel but she always refused. Even when she came back, she graciously refused to take anything at all from us. She insisted on paying for her own hotel, her rental car. She even sent flowers. She cooked for us too, using recipes from all the places she traveled to. Debby never did that. She was never so thoughtful."

"So you thought you would... what? Keep her around?" asked Garrett.

"Debby told us she wanted to return abroad because she met a nice man. We knew she was leaving soon so it wasn't like we would keep her here forever. We knew it was unlikely we'd ever see her again," said Dr.

Patterson. "But Fiona kept butting her head in. She was well aware of the investigation into Debby's disappearance so we knew it was only a matter of time before she spoke to someone else about our daughter; and then what would have happened? We couldn't admit she wasn't ours without saying where the real Debby was, could we? And then it would have been our arrests and court cases and I couldn't fathom spending my life in prison for something I didn't do!"

"So you killed Fiona," I said.

"Yes," said Dr. Patterson. "I killed her."

"All we needed was a little more time, but Fiona refused to listen," said Mrs. Patterson. "She kept bringing it up, and had a couple of times already that day."

"Why did you need more time?" I asked, wondering.

"My mother is dying," said Dr. Patterson. "She wanted to see Debby before she passed."

"Your mother is a wealthy woman," I started, thinking harder. The Pattersons had to know all about the legal affairs of Rod's mother. "Debby, I mean Marley, said you took care of her finances when she moved into a nursing home for her care. What happens to her estate when she passes?"

"It all goes to Debby," said Mrs. Patterson. "She doted on her."

"And if Debby preceded her in death, as she did, what happens to the estate then?"

"It's bequeathed to charity."

"So, if Debby stuck around until your mom passed, you could all pick up the check?" asked Garrett. I saw the tension increasing in his body, although it was barely noticeable. He could understand a parent's need to have a living daughter again, I realized, but not when money became a motive to the crime. That changed things.

"We decided we'd sell our house and move away," said Mrs. Patterson. "We've worked hard all our lives and had a few bad investments, meaning we can't retire anytime soon. With that money, we could start a new life, far away from here. It belongs to my husband anyway."

"Did Debby's stand-in know about the money?" I asked, hoping that she didn't.

"Of course not! We planned to give her some, of course, and help her start a new life and disappear. We were grateful to her in a way. We've spent ten years not worrying that my husband will be arrested for murder because we thought she was mad at us and took off."

"If Fiona told someone else about the impostor, that money would've disappeared," I stated, finally fully understanding how complicated the Pattersons' lies had become.

"So you see why neither of you can tell anyone," said Dr. Patterson.

"Not particularly," I said, my attention momentarily distracted by the black-clothed figures running across the lawn. "Would it help if I promised not to say anything?"

"I'm so sorry. I don't want to kill you both, but I have to," he said, his shoulders slumping as the gun dangled in one hand. He aimed it slowly, a flash of disappointment crossing his face. I didn't think he really wanted to be a killer but he still chose to become one. He was going to kill us both now.

"Here's the thing. See that little red dot on your shirt? Yeah, that one," I confirmed as Dr. Patterson looked down. "It's coming from a sniper's rifle. Shoot either one of us and you'll be dead in nanoseconds."

"If my husband dies, I'll shoot you both," said Mrs. Patterson, raising her gun.

"Why not just blame him for everything and walk away free?" asked Garrett.

"It's not his fault!" wailed Mrs. Patterson.

I opened my mouth to argue whose fault it was, then shut it again. I had no idea whom to blame. Marley for panicking when Debby seemed to die? Or for committing fraud by taking over her life? Dr. Patterson for panicking that night and leaving Debby in the woods? Or Mrs. Patterson for not reporting everything ten years ago, or even now? It seemed they were all at fault, in one way or another. I did not envy the attorney who had to plead any one of their cases.

Fortunately, I had more pressing things to think about. Namely, grabbing my gun and hitting the floor.

"Duck," I whispered to Garrett.

"Huh?"

Raising my eyebrows, I darted a glance to the windows, encouraging him to follow my line of sight.

"Duck?" he repeated.

"Get down," I yelled, abandoning all subtlety as I grabbed his arm and pulled him to the floor.

A huge crack sounded through the house as the front door was breached and several figures raced inside. Dr. Patterson swung around and fired a shot that splintered the door frame. He shot again and someone grunted before a figure slumped to the floor. Then Dr. Patterson yelled out and crumpled, his knees hitting the rug as he clasped a hand over his chest. I grabbed my weapon from the holster and pointed it at him before he keeled over, face down.

"I'll shoot!" yelled Mrs. Patterson, pointing her gun at me. "Don't come any closer!"

"It's over," I told her. "There's nowhere you can go."

"Check my husband! Is he okay?" She glanced down and I aimed my gun, this time straight at her. When she looked back, she saw the gun and flinched. The two of us stood there, each aiming our weapons at the other.

"He's fine," said Garrett. "Took one to the chest but he'll survive."

"Lower your weapon," said Solomon, his voice low and threatening as he aimed the laser beam between Mrs. Patterson's eyes.

"Do as he says," said Maddox, barely a step behind him. "In case you're not sure, there're seven guns trained on you right now, including a sniper's. Don't be stupid."

"I can't," said Mrs. Patterson, tears welling in her eyes. "What about Debby?"

"Marley," I corrected her, "is already in police custody. She confessed already."

"No, I mean *my* Debby."

"She's at the morgue."

"At least she isn't alone," said Mrs. Patterson, turning the gun on herself.

"No!" I launched myself at her, knocking her to the floor. The gun went off, and the sound was blisteringly close to my ear. Mrs. Patterson closed her eyes and slumped against me.

"Lexi!" I couldn't tell who yelled first or whose hands grabbed me, but someone was pulling me off, and more hands were reaching for Mrs. Patterson. I felt heavy, dizzy, and the room spun in circles.

"I think I've been shot," I told them breathlessly, surprised I was still standing when I felt a trickle descending to my clavicle. I touched my fingers to it and they came away sticky and red. "Or is it hers?"

"She fainted when the gun went off," said Solomon, pulling me against him and peeling back my jacket. "You definitely got shot. But it's just a nick on the shoulder." He kissed me on the forehead and held me tightly against him. "I wasn't worried," he said, although he sounded horribly worried. "I knew you had this."

"Our mother is never going to let me forget this," sighed Garrett.

"You're welcome!" I told him. "I saved your ass."

"I think *we* saved both your asses," interjected Maddox, pointing to himself and the cavalry.

"Potato, po-tah-toh," I mumbled.

Maddox inspected the wound, nodded, and stepped back after being apparently assured that I wasn't going to bleed out imminently. "I got here as soon as I could and called everyone on the way. Isn't it fun when the gang all gets together?"

"Lily is going to be so pissed that she was left out," I said.

"Where did you all come from?" asked Garrett when the figures moved around the room. He did not fail to notice all the Kevlar vests on the men or the guns strapped to their hips and thighs. The man on the floor eased upright and patted his Kevlar vest before grinning.

"Look, we almost got our soon-to-be brother-in-law killed too!" I giggled, giddy with life as Solomon gripped Delgado's hand and pulled him onto his feet.

Garrett held out a hand to Delgado. "Welcome to the family," he said. "You're not one of us until someone shoots you. Now if you'll excuse me, I have to arrest these idiots."

CHAPTER TWENTY-ONE

"I think she's coming around."

"Nuh-uh. She isn't moving."

"Her eyes are twitching."

"Do you think she'll mind if we balance some things on her? It'll be fun to watch everything go flying when she finally moves."

The voices got louder and I knew I had to stir before they seriously pranked me. "I'm not dead," I told them, opening my eyes and yawning simultaneously. I was comfortable, partially swaddled in a blanket, still enjoying the remnants of a terrific dream about being a top runway model with a closet to die for. My feet were on Solomon's lap, his warm hands wrapped around them, and my head was on a pillow. Only the aching throb in my shoulder marred the moment. I looked away from Solomon, finding Lily and Jord hovering over me.

Jord had the baby cuddled up to his chest, her tiny legs tucked up under her. "I was taking a nap," I groaned. "The best nap."

"Solomon told me you were shot. I got here as fast as I could." Lily dropped to her knees and parked her face directly in front of mine. I had to lean backwards into the couch to get her face in focus. "You don't look shot," she said. "What was it? A potato gun?"

"It was just a nick and I didn't even get stitches. Plus, it happened a couple of days ago. How could that be as fast as you could get here?" I complained. "Also, what about flowers? Chocolate? No?"

"Everything takes more planning with a baby but I think I've got the routine down now. Next time you get shot, I'll be here faster, okay? I did bring you chocolate though," she added, producing a prettily wrapped box. "I wasn't sure what to get you for your umpteenth injury but I'm thinking your next Christmas present might be a medical kit."

"I'm not getting shot again." I looked at Lily's disbelieving face. "I'm not!"

Jord laughed and Solomon sighed.

"Just in case, Poppy's bag is packed. Do you want me to move in and nurse you back to health?" asked Lily.

"You're desperate for something to do, aren't you?"

"So desperate. Mostly for sleep. You say it, I'll do it."

"I could take a coffee."

"On it." Lily pushed back on her heels and got up. She kissed Poppy on the head, then Jord on the lips. Both gazed after her as she headed for the kitchen.

"How long were you all staring at me?" I asked.

"Not long," said Solomon. "How are you feeling?"

"My shoulder is a little sore but it's okay."

"Do you need a painkiller?"

"No, thanks."

"Don't be brave," yelled Lily from the kitchen.

"I don't need one, really," I told them all. I could feel from the itch under the dressing that my wound was already healing. As I suspected, it was just a hot scrape across the shoulder. It didn't even need one stitch. The bruising would fade in a couple of weeks and it was unlikely to leave a scar. I was very lucky that Mrs. Patterson was such a lousy shot. She was lucky that she didn't blow her own head off. I could sew up the hole on my jacket, and maybe even add some kind of embroidery, but I had to draw the line at cleaning off brain matter.

"You could have been killed," said Jord.

"But I wasn't. I was ready," I told them. "I had a gun. It was loaded too."

"Not that you even used it," pointed out Solomon.

"Garrett and I had guns aimed at us," I told him again. "I was lucky that Dr. Patterson didn't frisk me. I just couldn't get to mine without being shot first."

"Sure, you were ready," said Lily as she returned to the living room. She brought a tray containing a French press, four cups, and she even found the little milk and sugar bowls I brought with me on my official move-in day. She poured a cup and handed it to me before getting one for herself. "Ready, aim, under fire. That's you."

"Garrett said he'd come by when you were awake," said Solomon. "I think he wants to check up on you."

"Just him? Or anyone else?" I asked.

"Just him. Everyone else is taking turns keeping your mom busy. She only called three times today."

"Oh, no," I groaned.

"It's cool," Solomon assured me. "The first time, she yelled again. The second time, she thanked me for saving you, and the third time, she wanted to know if you opened the wedding binders while you were convalescing. I assured her you were enjoying them."

I looked around. There were no wedding binders in sight. "Where are they?"

"I have no idea. I'm going into the kitchen to check on dinner. Jord, do you want to help?"

Lily gazed after Solomon and Jord as they left the room, the baby still cuddled up to his chest. "So manly and can cook. Jackpot!" she grinned.

"Which one?" I asked.

"Both of them." Turning back to me, she said, "I feel very left out. Everyone else was there. Solomon, Maddox, Delgado. It was almost like a family outing and no one invited me! I failed when you asked me to do surveillance and I couldn't help you when you really needed it. You might need to get a new best friend."

I reached for Lily's hand. "You have a baby. I understand. Don't beat yourself up about it."

"I didn't think things would change so much when Poppy was born. I thought I would still be me. Now, I'm no more than a shell, a very tired shell. I'm not even Lily anymore. I'm a two-legged milk machine."

"That's why I'm here to help you. We all are. You're not alone in this."

"You were alone. I am so sorry."

"I was never alone and you have nothing to be sorry for." I shuffled upright and pushed back the blanket, swinging my legs around. Lily took the blanket and folded it, replacing it on the couch.

"I promise I'll be more helpful next time you need me."

"And I promise I'll help you more with Poppy. How does that sound?"

"Sounds good. I even got Poppy some costumes so she can blend in on our stakeouts. I have French baby, Italian baby, redneck baby, ghetto baby, and pumpkin."

"You absolutely never ever—*ever!*—will need any of those costumes."

"Are you sure? The pumpkin would work for Halloween."

"Maybe the pumpkin," I conceded.

"Oh, good!" Lily clapped her hands, her face looking thrilled. "Wait until you see thief baby. It's a striped romper with its own swag bag."

I blinked, my jaw going slack. "You have got to be kidding."

"I am," she laughed as she dropped onto the couch beside me. "I've heard so much about your case from everyone else and it sounds crazy. How did you work it all out?"

"The more information I got, the more it all clicked together. Once I was reasonably sure armed burglary was out of the equation, I figured someone close to Fiona had to be the murderer. There weren't that many suspects and certainly no one with an obvious motive. Every time I thought about it, all I could come back to was Debby Patterson's sudden reappearance. I knew from my brief conversation with Fiona that she was suspicious of her; plus, Garrett was suspicious too. The two incidents seemed to be connected but I struggled with how."

"I wonder what Fiona knew."

I asked Garrett the same question. "Garrett dug around but couldn't find anything to suggest Fiona had any evidence so I think it was just a gut feeling. Same as his. At first, I thought Debby killed Fiona to protect herself but her alibi nearly stood up. She didn't have time to get to Fiona and shoot her, and there were just too many witnesses in her alibis, plus, it wasn't her DNA on the gun."

"Whose was it?"

"Her dad's. Garrett confirmed it yesterday. Dr. Patterson wasn't in the system. Debby was supposed to be, from when she was officially a missing person, but the DNA was too degraded. Even though I stole the toothbrush, there was nothing left of the real Debby to match it to, so it didn't turn up anything in the system either. We couldn't even match it to the blood on the gun because Debby wasn't the real Debby and even if she were, she was adopted. Fake Debby confessed everything about her part in the fraud to Garrett and me. She knew Debby was dead and decided to take over her life."

"Wow. Imagine just walking away from your name and everything you know to become someone else. I don't think I could do that."

"Me neither. I don't think Marley ever intended to be malicious in her impersonation. In a strange sort of way, she thought she was helping Debby's parents, sparing them from the pain of losing their daughter. It doesn't matter how awful the real Debby was, they still loved her. When Dr. Patterson emailed her and told her that her mother was sick, she felt she had to come home even though by that time, she wanted to become Marley again. After pretending to be Debby for ten years, she felt too guilty not to return for one last time and say goodbye. She thought enough years had elapsed that she could pass herself off as Debby. After all, they really did look alike when they were younger."

"Still pretty weird," said Lily.

"I didn't know if the Pattersons were even sure if Debby had run off or was dead. I think they were probably both in denial. They sounded very confused and sad. They hoped the real Debby was coming home and when she didn't, they used it as an opportunity to claim the inheritance they felt was due them."

"How is Grandma Patterson?"

"Blissfully unaware of anything."

"Good. What happens to fake Debby now?"

"I don't know. She committed identity theft, fraud, countless other crimes. Plus, trying to spare a family from pain is no reason to cover up a death."

"But she didn't kill anyone," Lily pointed out.

"Garrett thinks she can negotiate a deal. She never used Debby's identity to defraud anyone and the Pattersons are a better target for the prosecution. She might even get away with no jail time at all since it's unlikely that the Pattersons will agree to prosecute her."

"What about them?"

"They don't have to worry about their retirement fund any longer. They'll be guests at the nation's expense for a long time. Dr. Patterson killed a woman, Mrs. Patterson conspired with him and knew all about it. Both of them planned to fraudulently claim an inheritance. I just hope they didn't plan on helping Grandma Patterson pass on a bit sooner."

"I felt sorry for them up until the bit where Dr. Patterson killed Fiona. That was mean. They could have just told her."

"Told her what? That their real daughter was lying in a shallow grave in the woods and they were happy to claim an impostor as their own? Any good friend would have freaked out."

"I would. I know we're BFFs but I'm not covering for you if you murder any family members."

I pondered that. "How about anyone else?"

"Hypothetically... yeah, I'd probably cover for you, so long as it was justified."

"Dinner's ready," said Jord. He held up Poppy and she wiggled her arms and legs like a toy baby. "Look who just woke up for her dinner."

"Like clockwork. She doesn't want me to eat hot food ever again," said Lily, reaching for Poppy as she stood up. I followed the three of them into the kitchen and they made funny noises at the baby while trying to make her giggle.

Solomon set the table for the four of us with nice napkins and crystal drinking glasses. A small flowering cactus in the middle provided a little extra adornment. "This is like a celebration," said Lily. "We should make a toast."

"What to?" I asked. "Surviving another case?"

"Something better," said Solomon. He uncorked the wine and poured. "How about a wedding date?"

"Do you have one in mind?"

"I thought we could discuss it with a wedding planner tomorrow while you still have a few days off work. How do you feel about that?"

"Is the wedding planner my mother?"

"No."

"Then I feel very happy."

Lexi Graves returns in *Rules of Engagement…*

When her fiancé is shot in an apparent assassination attempt, private investigator Lexi Graves' world is thrown into chaos and turmoil. With the list of suspects growing by the minute, and the hit man still on the loose, there's no way Lexi can sit idly by Solomon's bedside and hope he survives when she could be out hunting for the person or persons responsible.

After taking charge of Solomon's private detective agency, Lexi enlists the help of her friends and family in her effort to bring the perpetrator to justice. Investigating, however, will lead Lexi into some areas of Solomon's life that he purposefully left behind and unveil some startling revelations about the man she loves. With the situation becoming increasingly dangerous, Lexi has no choice but to unravel his past and ask a surprising source for help in her quest to discover why Solomon was targeted. Yet with her successive questions come some shocking answers and a conspiracy far bigger than Lexi could have ever anticipated.

When Lexi knows everything, and the mysterious details of Solomon's past become clear, she can only wonder if anything in her life will ever be the same again.

Out now!

If you enjoyed *Ready, Aim, Under Fire*, you'll love *Deadlines*, a spin-off from the bestselling Lexi Graves Mysteries...

Shayne Winter thinks she has everything she ever wanted: a job as chief reporter at the LA Chronicle, a swish new apartment in a fabulous neighborhood, and a Californian-cool lifestyle just waiting to reveal itself. But on the first day of her new life, it all goes horribly wrong. The apartment is less 'young professional' and more 'young offender', the only furnishing a handsome squatter with roving eyes. Even worse, Ben, her predecessor at the Chronicle, has returned to claim his old job, leaving Shayne nothing but the obituary column and a simple choice: take it or leave it.

Her first assignment should be easy: write up the accidental death of washed-up former child-star Chucky Barnard and file her column. Yet when Shayne interviews the people close to Chucky, his sister claims Chucky had everything to live for and his untimely death could only be murder.

Convinced this could be the perfect headline to put her life back on track, Shayne vows to find the truth, convince a reticent homicide detective to investigate, and bring a killer to justice, all before Ben grabs her story and the killer makes Shayne his or her personal deadline.

Out now!

Made in the USA
San Bernardino, CA
05 July 2019